MY RIDE IS A BITCH

MY RIDE IS A BITCH

THE KURTHERIAN GAMBIT™ BOOK 13

MICHAEL ANDERLE

L M B P N

DISRUPTIVE IMAGINATION

MY RIDE IS A BITCH TEAM

Beta Editor / Readers
Bree Buras (Aussie Awesomeness)
Tom Dickerson (The man)
Sf Forbes (oh yeah!)
Dorene Johnson (US Navy (Ret) & DD)
Dorothy Lloyd (Teach you to ask...Teacher!)
T S (Scott) Paul (Author)
Diane Velasquez (Chinchilla lady & DD)

Thanks to our JIT Readers for this Version
Brent Bakken
Timothy Cox
Heath Felps
Andrew Haynes
Kelli Orr
Gage Ostrander
Leo Roars
Hari Rothsteni
Björn Schmidt

**Thank you to the following Special Consultants
for MY RIDE IS A BITCH**

**Jeff Morris - US Army - Asst Professor Cyber-Warfare,
Nuclear Munitions (Active)
Heath Felps - US Navy CPO (Active)
Toru Sekkiguchi - Björn Schmidt - Japanese Translation
Support**

Editor
Lynne Stiegler

To Family, Friends and
Those Who Love
To Read.
May We All Enjoy Grace
To Live The Life We Are
Called.

PROLOGUE

Berlin, Germany

Seven locations were tossed out to the group of men and women invited to Germany's Federal Intelligence Operations Center.

"We have," Dr. Schäuble, a professor borrowed for this project from Humboldt Universität, told those gathered around the long, hand-carved rosewood table, "seven locations, but we only have resources to check three at this time." He was leaning over the table, looking at the different cards that had been laid out. "As you can see, one of these is in Antarctica. It's based on the rumors of people from the Nazi party. Somebody, possibly the Thule group, built and left a base in the severe cold. Americans," he tipped his head to three men sitting at the table, "went there in 1947 and had, I've heard, a bad time."

"I thought the Americans' situation was just bad weather?" a young woman asked from the end of the table.

"You would think so, but one of the ships was supposedly cut in two," Dr. Schäuble replied. "Right now, the Americans are claiming it was weather that forced the fleet exercise to turn around. However," he looked down the table, "my contacts say

1

the American government is setting up their own expedition to this area on the off-chance it might reveal any secrets the Nazis took with them."

He sat down and opened the manila folder in front of him. "If you would all open your folders to the first location for our common vote, we will discuss whether the Nazi base has enough interest from those represented here to be on our short list. As you are aware, the German government has the authority to check into these seven locations, and with a significant monetary buy-in, your companies will be able to benefit from technologies we find."

Dr. Schäuble looked up from his papers. "We have someone to speak to us regarding additional Nazi records not shared with the American government. That person…" there was a knock on the door, and the doctor turned around while finishing his comment, "has arrived to update you, it sounds like."

CHAPTER ONE

QBS _ArchAngel_ Over Japan, Seventeen Hours before Meeting in Japan

John walked toward Bethany Anne's suite, the hairs on the back of his neck standing up.

Gabrielle had said she hadn't seen or spoken with Bethany Anne for a few hours. She thought Bethany Anne was with him or one of the other guys, but John had confirmed she wasn't with any of them. The last time anyone had seen her, she was walking into her suite with Ashur, an apple, and a pile of mail that had come up on the last transport.

Curious, but only a little concerned, John asked ArchAngel if Bethany Anne was asleep, but he was informed she wasn't. Arch-Angel said she didn't know where Bethany Anne was at the moment.

That could only mean one of two things. Bethany Anne wasn't on the ship, or she had explicitly told ArchAngel not to let anyone know where she was.

Or both.

John entered, walked through the outer suite, and knocked on Bethany Anne's bedroom door.

Nothing.

John grimaced and knocked harder. He got nothing a second time. John called, "ArchAngel. This is John Grimes."

ArchAngel replied, "Yes, I recognize you, John. There is no need to tell me who you are."

"There is this time," John snapped. "ArchAngel, by my right as a Queen's Bitch, I am implementing Queen's Permission to enter her suite."

"Approved, John," the voice replied, and the suite locks disengaged. All seven of them.

He opened the door a few inches. "Bethany Anne?" He heard nothing and opened it wider. "BA? Boss?"

The suite was empty.

John noticed her bed was made and stepped around to her personal closet. It was closed and locked.

Fuck, he thought.

John looked up, his eyes closed. Thank God a migraine wasn't possible. "ArchAngel, Please unlock this door. I promise not to step foot into the room."

"You know she isn't in there, John," ArchAngel responded.

"Yes, I know that. I need to see what she took with her," John answered, and the door unlocked. This was much better than the rooms in the Florida house, where no one could open the door from the outside. Here, ArchAngel could open and close, lock and unlock, all doors. He pulled the door open, the lights came on, and he peered into her closet.

Her pistols, leather pants, and her protective chest piece were missing. Her *katana* was on its stand. John turned, stopped, and then looked back. Her shorter sword, the *wakizashi*, was missing.

So it was probably humans, not Forsaken.

John closed the door. "Thank you, ArchAngel." He heard the doors lock behind him and turned to her master suite's bath. It, like all of her rooms, was huge. He looked in and saw an envelope and a piece of notebook paper.

John stepped over to her vanity, which was triple-wide, with two sinks and a large area between for makeup and other stuff. John thought it was a bit much. Bethany Anne rarely wore more than a little blush and maybe some lipstick.

He read the note, which was written in blue crayon in a young person's handwriting.

Ms. Anne,

I'm not sure you can help, but my father is in trouble. My mother was taken by evil people who hurt her and then hurt my dad.

They want him to help them because he works on science and they want something. They made him promise not to tell the police.

Since he can't tell anyone, and I can't tell the police either, I thought maybe someone powerful like you could help my mom and my dad.

If not, I understand. I know you are pretty busy with your ships and stuff.

Thank you for listening,

Anne

p.s. I love your last name. It is the same as my first name.

John could see the smearing where Bethany Anne's tears must have soaked into the page. He shook his head, grabbed the envelope with the address, and started walking out of her suite.

John now knew the approximate where and the why. He just had to figure out what to do about it.

He held down the small call button on his collar. "This is John. Our Queen is AWOL."

QBS *ArchAngel* Over Japan, Eighteen Hours before Meeting

Bethany Anne reached out to grab the offered mail. "Thanks, Kevin." She nodded her thanks as well and grabbed an apple from the fruit bowl on the sideboard. "Ashur!" she called over her shoulder. She heard Ashur get up from under the table where Team BMW was eating. They were such wusses about feeding him. One sad face, and all three men caved and tossed him food.

Then they blamed each other for being the one who fed him.

Ashur caught up with Bethany Anne on her way to the suite, and she ruffled his head. She would swear he had grown a couple of inches.

TOM.

Yes?

Could Ashur grow in size after coming out of the Pod?

Yes, that's possible. The nanites might have decided he needed to change for some reason, possibly due to his continued physical exercise during your training. We can always put him back in the Pod and have a look.

No, it's not that important. At least, not yet.

Bethany Anne nodded to the guards near the doors leading to the Bitches' and Elites' areas and finally reached her suite. She could have just walked Etherically to her suite, but it was good for everyone to see her.

She entered her room, the door having been already opened by ArchAngel, and mumbled "Thanks" as the door shut behind her. Biting into her apple, she walked into her bathroom. Ashur jumped up on her bed.

"Hey!" She turned toward her door. "Don't shed all over my bed. I had to get the last bedspread cleaned. What the hell were you pissed about, anyway?"

Ashur chuffed from her bedroom.

"That's not my fault! Your lazy ass didn't go to the cafeteria in time to catch them." Another chuff. "Bullshit, they aren't required to eat at the same time every day because you have a preference. Besides, you always have dogfood available." Bethany Anne grinned when she heard Ashur's whined response.

She tossed the apple core into the trash can and started going through the mail.

She picked up the first letter.

I've won an island...

File thirteen." Then the next.

I've been asked to join a symposium on technology next month.

Another file thirteen.

Apparently, she had unpaid speeding tickets in Florida. "Huh, wonder if I should frame this one?" She shrugged and tossed the envelope into the trash.

She saw an envelope in nice block handwriting done in a crayon. Weird. She opened it and read the letter inside.

Then she read it again, slowly.

ADAM, track this address. Is this legitimate?

>>Yes, there is a family of three living at that address in Las Vegas.<<

Who does the dad work for?

>>Security blocked, unknown at this time.<<

Seriously? Fuck. Bethany Anne tapped the letter on her palm a couple of times. *Can you figure out if there's a problem?*

>>The daughter, Anne, is twelve. She has been absent from school for two days. Previously, she had not missed the last one hundred and eighty-two days of school.<<

"Trap or real, trap or real?" Bethany Anne mused aloud.

Are they mutually exclusive? TOM interrupted.

No, they are not, Bethany Anne agreed.

Are you going to send someone to check it out?

No, I'm going to do this. It needs a deft touch and a woman's hand.

What about Gabrielle?

I don't want to mess up her time with Eric.

What about...huh, right.

What do you mean, "right?"

You're bored.

I've always heard the problem with royalty is that they don't stay connected with the people. I'm not going to let that happen to me.

You're bored.

That, too.

Just the three of us?

No, it will be the four of us.

Well, thank God. For a second, I thought you would go and not take any support. TOM sighed mentally.

"Ashur." Bethany Anne started toward her closet. "Let's go rescue a little girl." His return chuff was excited. "I know, right? Silly of my Guards to leave me alone and allow me to get into mischief all by my little lonesome." This time, Ashur sounded like he was laughing, not chuffing.

"Oh, shut up," Bethany Anne snapped. "Be happy your lazy ass is going, or you'd be stuck in here."

She changed clothes and loaded her weapons. Spying the *wakizashi*, she smiled and grabbed the shorter blade. "Come here, you. We haven't partied in a while." She looked down at her boots on the floor. "Ugh, no boots this time. Pumas, it is."

She grabbed a jacket and hid her weapons. "ArchAngel, lock this door."

Why did I think you were going to be mature about this? TOM asked.

Beats the fuck out of me, she replied. "Let's go, my furry white Guard." Bethany Anne grabbed Ashur's neck and took a step forward, disappearing.

A minute later, the lights went off in the closet.

TQB Base Denver, Colorado

Bethany Anne and Ashur stepped into one of her arrival rooms at the Colorado headquarters. It took her a little while to sneak outside.

Unfortunately, the modified F12berlinetta that had been upgraded for her was locked up in the garage and had an on-duty guard. It had required her to order him to not speak about her taking the car for twenty-four hours.

Leaving the base forced her to order personnel at two additional security checkpoints to not mention her presence, at least for twenty-four hours.

Bethany Anne enjoyed the crisp air for a couple of hours as she and Ashur drove through the mountains heading toward Las Vegas. She looked in her rearview mirror to confirm no one was behind her and then told TOM to punch it.

Their car lifted off the road and started flying through the night sky.

Within fifteen minutes, they set down on a small road outside North Las Vegas. She entered the address into the onboard navigation and drove into town as the barest hint of dawn was cracking the sky.

"Hey, no shedding on my leather." She reached over and brushed a few of Ashur's white hairs off the seat. "We should look for a girlfriend for you. Maybe she could teach you to not shed on the seats." Ashur glanced at Bethany Anne, cocked his head to the side, and chuffed. "I don't know how to tell if she's smart. Probably the best test will be if she bites you in the ass the first chance she gets."

He chuffed again and looked out the window as Bethany Anne laughed.

>> I could have easily given you the directions to the location.<<

I know that, ADAM, but sometimes the little computers need attention too.

You just wanted to play with your new toy.

You say that as if it's a bad thing, TOM.

The directions took her to the west side of Las Vegas, and she pulled up at a neighborhood security gate.

Bethany Anne could see the Red Rock Casino a couple of miles away, and Red Rock Canyon just beyond it.

Casper was reading the latest Vegas news when a car pulled off Spanish Trail and the headlights flashed through their window. He looked up in time to see a Ferrari when his partner Jocelyn offered, "Ten bucks says it's an old man with gray hair wearing a toupee."

While he couldn't see inside too well, he did notice what looked like a large white dog in the front seat. "You got a bet," he replied and stepped out of the air-conditioned guardhouse, closing the door behind him.

The Ferrari pulled up smoothly beside him, and the tinted window started dropping.

So did Casper's jaw. "Hello," he managed to croak. Jocelyn owed him ten bucks. No mistaking this lady for an old, fat, balding white guy using a car to market himself. She didn't look like she needed the car to sell herself, either, but this was Vegas. Casper supposed she could be an elite "companion." If she was, Casper couldn't afford her.

"Hello, Casper, is it?" She smiled and nodded at his name badge. "I'm here to surprise my brother." Her voice, velvet-smooth over steel, warmed his soul. "Would you mind letting me do that without putting me down on your notepad?"

Moments later, Casper stepped back inside and put his clipboard in the slot. He barely noticed when Jocelyn slid the ten dollars in front of him. "You win the ten bucks. She wasn't an old fat guy." Then Jocelyn pulled the money back toward herself. "But you lose the money for not putting her name down on the clipboard. It's now hush money."

Casper nodded his agreement to the deal.

Bethany Anne drove up in front of the four-thousand-square-foot two-story. It had a Spanish brick roof and a nicely kept lawn. All the homes in this gated community were well kept.

She slid out of her car and walked around to open Ashur's door. He jumped out and looked around, sniffing the air.

A few cars were leaving for work already, but her car showed everyone living in this neighborhood that she belonged.

The two of them walked up to the door.

"He has visitors," Dieter reported as he looked out the window through his binoculars. "Attractive woman, and…a dog."

"Not exactly your standard military rescue team," Gunter commented as he drank his coffee. He walked up beside his partner. "Maybe his family?"

"Can't tell." Dieter lowered the glasses. "Here, take a look, I'm going to wake up Klaus in case we have a snag in the plans. Today he's supposed to pull the data in exchange for his wife."

Gunter put his coffee down and accepted the binoculars. "Yes, attractive. Weird that she's wearing a jacket in Las Vegas." Gunter looked back at the car. "Dealer plates, I can't see what state. Perhaps she is not from around here?"

Dieter called back from the room across the hall, "I don't know." He knocked. "Klaus, wake up. We have an unexpected visitor."

"Here?" the tired man asked.

"No," Dieter replied. "Across the street. We might need to intercept, so get ready." He stepped back into the front room. "What now?"

"She's knocking on the door," Gunter continued. "Is the volume up?" Seconds later, they heard the door across the street open, and Mason's voice came in loud and clear.

"Hello?"

The woman's voice answered, "I'm sorry, Mr. Jayden, but the Clark County School District is concerned about your daughter, Anne. She's missed two days of school already."

"Anne? Yes, she's sick."

"May I see her?" the lady responded.

"What? No. I'm sorry, who did you say you were again?"

"My name is Bethany Anne…"

───────

If anyone had looked straight up, they would have seen a tiny black dot in the sky.

Well, actually…would they be able to see it? No.

John was listening to the conversation below. "ArchAngel, are you capturing the audio from wireless signals?"

"Yes, John. Wireless signals that are coming from the house Bethany Anne is at, sending in the direction of a couple of houses across the street."

"You can't tell which one?"

"No, only direction. It is either the house directly across, or the one to the south of it."

John continued listening to the conversation as Bethany Anne spoke.

"My name is Bethany Anne, and I help the Clark County School District maximize their income by confirming all able-bodied children are attending school. It reduces truancy."

"In a Ferrari?"

John chuckled, wondering how his boss was going to answer this question. He could hear the pause, almost seeing her turn around to confirm that yes, she had driven a Ferrari.

"Well, yes. It's my new car. You see, I'm a helper for the school district in the mornings. The rest of the day, I play a trophy wife."

Up in the sky, John was slapping the side of the Pod, trying to control his laughter. "Oh, God!" he screamed. "ArchAngel, please tell me you're recording this?"

"I am, John."

He wiped a tear from his face as he tried to stifle his laughter.

"Sweet blessed mother of Saint Payback-is-a-Bitch, I'm going to use this." John had put his hand over his mouth as the two beneath him continued talking.

"She is a school helper?" Gunter asked, puzzled.

"American schools get paid by how many children are in the classroom each day. It is very expensive for the local school district when a child is out sick," Klaus explained as he walked into the room, adjusting his holster and slipping in his pistol.

"This could be a problem," Dieter explained. "We only need him to go to work one last time. Do we snatch her, or what?"

Gunter shrugged. "We only do something if she won't leave."

The voice of the lady in front of Mason changed, sweeter somehow, and yet more commanding. "Let me in, Mason."

Mason opened the door wider and stepped back. "Why don't you come in, Ms. Anne?"

Bethany Anne stepped into the home behind Ashur, who had jumped in ahead of her, and she looked around. "My name is just...you know, never mind." She looked down at Ashur. "Find out if we have a problem." Ashur took off and ran up the steps.

"NO!" Mason scrambled behind Bethany Anne, pushing her out of the way as both of them heard a chuff from the room up the stairs. Mason grabbed the railing, swinging to jump to the third step. He started running up the stairs and was surprised when he stumbled off-balance, feeling as though he had been pushed aside. He righted himself and continued racing to his daughter's room.

She absolutely, positively couldn't leave that bed.

"*Gott Verdammt!*" Klaus bolted out of the room and ran down the hall to the front door. "If that bitch pulls the child off the bed, the operation is a bust," he yelled, frantically trying to unlock the door.

Gunther and Dieter were hot on his heels as he yanked the front door open, all three men racing down the front walkway.

"ArchAngel, get me down there!" John ordered as he started unbuckling. The Pod came screaming down out of the sky.

The three men hadn't made it to the street when the top of the house exploded. They all covered their heads and flattened themselves on the lawn as debris pelted them. A large piece impaled the grass just a foot from Gunter's face.

Standing up and pulling their pistols, they turned back toward the home. There was fire pouring out of the top windows.

"Shit!" Klaus stomped his foot. "We were so close!" They jogged over to the front door.

Dieter was the first to notice the object descending to their left. Thinking a large part of the house was landing, he jerked his head. "Look out!"

The men ducked, but nothing hit the ground. When they looked up once again, a large white man, vitriolic hatred that promised a painful death painted on his face, stood to their left. He stared at them and aimed the two unique-looking guns in his hands at their heads.

The three men pointed their guns back. "Who are you?" Klaus asked.

"I am," he responded with barely-restrained emotions, "the man who is going to kill you for who you just blew up."

They eyed each other for a few seconds.

A woman's voice came from behind them. It started low and slow, but raised in both pitch and volume as it continued, "You cock-biting ass-backward fuck-faced sodding tea-bagging wrinkled old dickless twin-headed alien tramp-whackers!" she screamed. "That fucking hurt!"

One of the three men turned around. The two facing John didn't like the smile that graced his face or his next statement. "Boys, *I* was just going to kill you. Now, you've gone and fucked up real good. You will wish for death by the time she gets done with you."

The one on the left looked back and exclaimed, "The trophy wife?"

John snorted as the lady spoke in a clipped fashion. "You, I kill first."

The white dog beside her barked. "No. You may not bite his nuts off. I'm not smelling nutsack breath all morning long."

"Dieter, would you just shoot the bitch?" Gunter asked. "We have to get out of here!"

"Gentleman?" Her voice went sweet, soft velvet over case-hardened steel. "I command you to put down your guns."

"Like…" Gunter started to say before he felt himself complying with her orders, finishing with, "hell?"

John, keeping his pistols on them, walked over and kicked their guns behind him.

"Bethany Anne, we do need to go. Where are the people in the house?"

"Colorado." She turned to look at her car. "Fucking ape-titties!" she yelled, exasperated. "That was my new Ferrari, you cooch-virgins!"

John glanced at it and had to agree. The car's body was messed up from the explosion. It wasn't looking too good.

She breathed slowly. "Well, that settles it." She walked to the first man, who was still looking at her. "Hope no one has video going," she mumbled and slapped him. The slap's *crack* was loud, and the man she had hit disappeared

"What the hell?" Gunter exclaimed as he was whacked on the back of his head and also disappeared.

She told the last, "Don't say a fucking word, and if you and your two goons want to live, I would suggest not walking far from where I send you. I might not be able to find your useless asses."

"Send me whe…" was all Klaus was able to get out before the back of his head exploded in pain and he disappeared from view.

Ashur chuffed behind her. "Yeah, good point." She turned to John. "Pod?"

"Up above us."

"Leave it." She turned to look at Ashur. "Let's go, boy wonder," Ashur chuffed again. "No, I'm not your damn sidekick, you four-footed walking rug." She grabbed John. "Now come here, or I won't get you a date."

Ashur trotted up and chuffed to her again. "I don't care," she replied. "I won't help you with any female, and we won't go on the internet to search, either. So take that and chew on it, my dear opposable-thumb-lacking pain in the ass."

ADAM, find and destroy their surveillance equipment if you can.

>>If I can?<<

What if it isn't connected to the internet?

>>I was surfing the radio waves…<<

TOM, take care of the Pod and the car, please.

Yes, O Wife of Trophies.

TOM.

Yes?

Doghouse for you, alien-for-brains.

TOM snickered in her mind.

She grabbed Ashur, and the three of them disappeared. The Ferrari took off into the sky, leaving behind a mess, a lot of questions, and not many answers.

CHAPTER TWO

John shook his head as he walked into the Pod bay. Gabrielle, striding behind him, was continuing her tirade. "Why are you going instead of me, or why not you _and_ me? At least answer _that_ question, you poor excuse for a walking mime!" She huffed in exasperation.

John grinned. The last four hundred feet, all the way from the Bitches' quarters, he had been listening to Gabrielle complaining about not taking her along. He allowed his go bag to slide off his shoulder, and he put it into his Pod before turning around and looking down at the vampire. "Because I've got one beautiful female to deal with out in public. I don't need two, especially since you just got nominated to be here to represent Bethany Anne."

"Who the hell told you I was the best option for that role?" Gabrielle retorted.

"ArchAngel. She said Bethany Anne would most likely choose you since you had the role when we all went to China." John continued his staring contest.

Gabrielle glared up at John for ten seconds. "Shit," she finally spat, then started walking back out of the bay. "Don't think I'll forget this, John!" she called over her shoulder.

"No, that would make life too easy," he agreed.

Gabrielle yelled right before she stepped through the doors, "I heard that!"

John looked back to make sure the doors had closed. "Of course, you did. You can hear an ant fart in a hurricane." As John settled in the Pod and started locking in, the Pod's doors closed and sealed. "ArchAngel, how is Gabrielle?"

"She is telling me I need to discuss 'girls sticking together' with her sometime."

John chuckled. "Does she not realize you could just as easily look like a guy?"

"Probably deep down, but since my avatar is Bethany Anne, I doubt it comes to mind."

"No, probably not." John finished clicking his straps. "Take me out." He paused before asking, "Why did you want her to stay behind?"

"Because I've analyzed the data, John. You will go and support Bethany Anne. You won't judge her, and you won't condemn her. In all things, you are her rock, and she leans on you. You are the best choice."

The Pod slipped through the gravitic shield into space. In moments, it was streaking through space eighty miles above Earth.

"You might as well take me to the address, ArchAngel."

"Understood, John. You will arrive in eighteen minutes."

One-half Day's March from Shennongjia Peak, Hubei

Bai leaned against a tree, pushing his pack into a small space between the branches. That allowed him to take some of the weight off his back. Zhu nodded to his friend as he came up.

Bai asked, "Any idea if our trackers have a clue where we are going?"

Zhu nodded. "Yes. We were chosen to follow the second group who left. I listened in on the conversations, and it seems our group met up with another group. The new group stopped for a little while, then left."

"That's good, right? That means our group slowed down, and we won't have to follow them too far?" Bai asked.

Zhu shook his head. "Bai, they stopped and had a meeting with something that joined them. That something left cat prints, our tracker claims. He wasn't happy about it."

"Why not? We know they can turn into some sort of werecat, so what is their problem? We all have silver rounds on us."

"Bai, what do cats do more than most animals?" Zhu looked into the forest, up into the limbs of the trees above them.

Bai followed his friend's glance and thought about it. "They hunt."

Zhu nodded. "They hunt. And now, they are hunting us with the intellect of both a human and a cat."

"That's not good," Bai agreed, peering harder into the foliage above them. "You think they are setting up a trap?"

Zhu looked at his friend. "Jian told Shun and me to count on it."

Bai nodded and checked his rifle, making sure his silver rounds were loaded for the fourth time this morning.

CHAPTER THREE

Etheric

"I'm saying," Gunter ground out, "how do we know she wasn't lying to us?"

"Do *you* know where the fuck we are?" Klaus asked, looking into the grayness in every direction. "I can't see shit. Neither can either of you. She said she would find us unless we moved."

"Like I trust that woman with anything! Have you finally figured out who she is?"

"Yes, I know where I saw her face," Klaus admitted.

"And?" Gunter pushed.

"She is the head of TQB." Klaus looked into the distance, but nothing changed. He still couldn't see anything; it was like looking through the fog on a cold morning.

"What kind of tech does she have if she can send us to some other part of Earth," Dieter snapped his fingers, "like that?"

"What makes you think," Klaus asked, turning to Dieter, "that we are on Earth?"

TQB Base, Colorado USA

Mason accepted a cup of coffee from Jasmin. She had taken him and his daughter from the room where they had appeared after the gray...place.

Now he was sitting at a table, with Anne asleep in the chair next to him, her head on his shoulder. Her arms were wrapped around his, making sure he didn't move while she slept.

He knew his job was incredibly secret but honestly hadn't thought it would ever affect his wife or his child. Now, the reality of how casually he had played with their safety shamed him. The last week and a half had been a nightmare.

Given some of the secret technology he worked on, he had never expected to be so easily awed by the abilities of anyone besides the people with whom he worked.

Mason wished he had some paper or something to write his thoughts down. He kept going through the events, trying to sear them into his long-term memory. Maybe one day, he would understand the technology she must have used to accomplish the act.

He had let her into the house when the dog had taken off upstairs. He couldn't let Anne off of her bed, or the bombs would go off. He had run after the dog and stumbled on the steps as if he had been pushed aside.

Pushed *aside*.

His face tightened. Had she run past him that fast?

He made it up the stairs to see the woman already in the room, speaking in a quick, clipped voice to the dog. She hadn't moved Anne yet, but she saw him enter the room. She popped him on the forehead, and everything went gray. Then, she was there with Anne and the dog. "We have to go," she told him and handed Anne to him. When he took her, she grabbed his arm and the dog.

Then the four of them were in a rock-walled room. "Wait here," she commanded. "Someone will come to get you."

Then she was gone again.

Where the hell was he supposed to go? He was holding Anne tight to his chest, just holding her as she cried, when there was a knock on the door, hard enough to get his attention. He opened the door, and a woman asked him to follow her to this room, and then brought them some breakfast.

Anne fell asleep, and here he was, wondering what would happen to Sheila now.

The three men heard the voices before they could discern the vague outlines of two people walking toward them.

A woman insisted, "I'm saying that killing them here is easier to clean up. As in, there isn't any cleanup."

A third figure trailing the first two resolved, and the dog's chuff emerged from the mist.

The gargantuan figure beside her seemed to be trying to argue for the three of them.

"I understand you didn't like returning and getting singed in the fire."

Another chuff.

"You either, Ashur."

"I might have been unlucky enough to come back into a broken piece of wall, and that would have been a real downer."

They were getting closer.

"How come you guys didn't?"

"I can peek out now. I've figured out how to barely look and make sure. The fucking fire was still damned hot. That shit burned like a motherfucker." She was close enough for the three men to discern her features. "Ah, here are my three camel-humping tea-baggers now."

The dog stopped and laid down on the ground.

"So, where is the wife?" she asked them. They kept their mouths shut.

"Oh? You are so out of your league, penis tips, that life as you know it doesn't exist. You aren't even grade-school athletes against a pro. This is like a pro team against a tank full of goldfish."

She looked them over and amended, "Dead goldfish."

She reached under her jacket and pulled out a scabbarded short sword. "You know, for some reason, there is this misunderstanding that good people should be nice to *Schweinehunde* such as yourselves. Personally, I don't agree, and since my overly large friend here," she jerked a thumb at the man next to her, "really isn't my conscience, and this isn't a good-cop/bad-cop routine like you're thinking, you can all kiss my ass." There was a chuff behind her. "I know. Stay back, since you hate getting blood out of your coat."

She took the scabbard off. "Eenie meany miny moe. Dieter, my friend, you can go." She was ten feet away, and then Gunter and Klaus jumped back because she had stabbed Dieter through the gut with her sword. Her left hand was choking him, and she easily held him off the ground while he struggled. She looked over her shoulder and spoke to the man behind her. "I told you—much cleaner here."

The big man shrugged. "All I said was, it would be easier to get the wife's location from people who were alive, even if you had to leave them alive."

When she turned around, Gunter and Klaus took another involuntary step back. The figure in front of them was from a nightmare. Her face had red glowing eyes, her teeth had grown, and she smiled at them like they were snacks. "I never said I had to have live people to get my answers, John. I can always ask them when I kill them the second time."

"She's in a warehouse!" Gunter screamed. "On the east side out by Green Valley in Vegas, I swear!"

"Shut up, Gunter," Klaus hissed. "That is our only negotiation card." Scared or not, Klaus knew the woman was the only thing that might get them out of this predicament.

Dieter had stopped struggling in her grip. His lifeless body was still hanging above the ground, his blood puddling at her feet. She seemed to finally notice he had expired. "That was uneventful," she muttered, acting annoyed as she tossed the body aside. Both men were shocked. Dieter's lifeless body had been thrown twenty feet away into the mist. She hadn't even noticed his weight.

The frightening woman took a step toward the two men. "Who paid you to do this?"

Klaus spoke up. "Will you let us go if we tell you what we know?" His voice, usually assured, was cracking.

"Klaus Weber." Her voice changed, softer but unyielding. "Stand still and tell me what you know. Who paid you to do this?"

Klaus bit down hard, trying to keep the information to himself. He kept hearing her command resonating in his mind, and he played what he would say to her over and over and finally stopped thinking about it when she announced, "That's enough. You don't need to tell me multiple times."

Her companion cautioned, "Bethany Anne, we don't have time to track all of this down right now. We need to get back to the *ArchAngel*. We have a meeting with the Japanese pretty soon."

She looked disgusted. "Okay, fine. I don't think this prick knows anything anyway. Sounds like a typical dark web merc job. I know someone bored who needs something to do."

Why? What do trophy wives do except check on truant children and blow up houses?

Shut. Up. TOM.

Klaus, aghast that he had been talking the whole time he thought he was keeping the secrets to himself, never saw the flick of the blade that cut his head off.

Gunter, his mouth open as Klaus's body dropped to the ground, finally recognized she was cleaning her sword on Klaus's shirt. Her face, eyes normal, looked up at him. "And now, we come to miny moe."

———

Mason Jayden woke up, his arm numb from Anne's tight grip. He heard people coming down the hall outside his room. His mind foggy, he tried to remember how he and his daughter had ended up in here and realized he must have nodded off for a few minutes.

Then he heard it; he heard her voice. "Sheila?" he whispered. He couldn't quite make out the words the voice was speaking since she was still too far away, but Mason thought it was his wife. He looked down to figure out how to extricate himself from his daughter, but she was already waking up.

"Mom?" she called, eyes half-closed. "*MOM?*"

She pushed her chair back when they both heard a "Baby?" come from down the hallway and another, louder, "Mason?"

Mason's chair shot back to the wall, and he grabbed Anne's hand as they reached the door, to see Sheila running down the hall, crying. The family reunion was intense as the three hugged, all crying pretty loudly.

"Ma'am?"

Bethany Anne turned around. She and John had left the three some personal space to reunite. "Yes?"

The woman, one of the base logistics and planning employees who had been helping, smiled. "Ma'am, what do you want me to do for the family?"

Bethany Anne turned toward the family. John noticed she frowned and whispered to herself, "I hate this."

Her eyes went vacant for a second. "Well, fuckity fuck." She sighed. "Call ArchAngel. We need this family with us. John and I will grab Ashur from the cafeteria and head out. When Mason asks, tell him the Queen has said she will be able to protect his family much better than those who failed him."

"Yes, ma'am," she said.

"C'mon, John. Let's fetch the white wonder dog and get back to the ship."

They walked past the woman, who continued to wait patiently some distance from the reunited family. She listened to Bethany Anne and John talking as they walked down the hall.

"Did I understand," John started, "that Ashur is looking for a bitch, or is that your idea?"

"Nice. Nice play on words, Mr. Grimes."

"I try my best." he smirked, "when speaking to trophy wives."

"John," she heard Bethany Anne say as the two went around a corner, "I swear, if you keep up that shit, payback will be a bitch."

"Oh, you pray to him, too?" His voice trailed off.

QBS *ArchAngel* above Japan

Tabitha's Pod moved slowly through the gravitic shield holding the air in the Pod bay on the *ArchAngel*. Barnabas was waiting for her as the doors cracked open. She unclipped herself and smiled at him.

"Hey, Big B!" Her grin widened when Barnabas frowned at her new nickname for him. She had decided that if she was going to live for a few hundred years, she was going to do her dead-level best to tweak him every chance she got.

Her latest choice was pet names since you always have to be hacking and testing what you think might work. She wasn't sure if this new name was going to last for more than a couple of months, or hell, it could last well into the next century.

Barnabas turned his grimace into a smile, understanding that she had just laid down a challenge. "Hello, Tabitha. I trust your trip was enjoyable?"

She followed him toward the Pod bay exit. He looked over his shoulder at her and asked, "Do you know why we wanted you to join us here on the *ArchAngel*?"

She shrugged. "Honestly, Big B, I figure you've got something that needs doing, and you need just the right sass and ass to get the job done."

Barnabas hung his head. Tabitha might be more of a challenge than he had ever encountered in his many, many centuries. "I don't recall many ladies ever telling me that they have the right, and I quote, 'sass and ass' to get the job done. Usually, they tell men to stop looking down there and that their faces are up here."

Tabitha shrugged. "Hey, I can't help it if European women don't understand just how over-empowered they are compared to men. We not only have the brains, but we also have the bodies to confuse the best of them, and, in the fog of war, men are putty in our hands." She thought for a second. "Okay, some women have the brains, not every one of us."

Tabitha finally caught up with Barnabas so that she was walking beside him. He glanced sideways at her and asked, "'The fog of war,' Tabitha?"

"Sure. Anytime a man is around an attractive woman, it's war. You might not think so, but their wives know it, and their girl-friends know it. It just happens. It's chemical. Do I have to pull up the physiological books to discuss this with you? I would think after a thousand years this would be old news to you. Hell, you're practically a talking cadaver who's walking around."

Barnabas snorted. "I am not, nor have I ever been, a cadaver," he stated.

Oh, this was so delicious. Tabitha gave herself three points and figured she was up five to two so far. Barnabas had earned two secret points for making her catch up with him.

"Big B, I bet I wasn't even alive the last time you got hori-zontal and did the mambo. I'm willing to bet you weren't even assaulting with a friendly weapon when my parents were children."

"Tabitha, please remember I lived in a monastery until relatively recently. What are you talking about?"

"Buttering the biscuit? Checking the oil? How about doing squat-thrusts in the cucumber patch? No? Damn, Number One, just how long *were* you in that cave? All right, let's try filling the cream doughnut? No? Posting a letter? Of course not, you probably don't even remember or know what letters are."

Barnabas grunted. "Yes, Tabitha, I know what letters are. You do realize letters have been used for many centuries, yes?"

She had to be up twelve to two, at least.

"Fine, I'll try to see how far back I can go. Latina women are good at euphemisms, and I have a ton. I'm just trying to remember which ones an old dried-up husk of a man like you might know. So, let's try this, Dr. Acula. How about shrimping the barbie? Oh, crap, that's something from Australia, never mind. Slamming the clam? Taking old One-Eye to the optometrist? Sorry, I forgot an optometrist is the last couple of hundred years. How about something more fantasy driven? Taking the bald-headed gnome for a stroll in the misty forest? No? Taking the magic bus to Manchester? Here's one for someone your age. How about cleaning the cobwebs with the womb broom? Fuck, Big B, didn't you ever just screw a chick?"

Tabitha finally realized that Barnabas was barely able to contain a smirk. His eyes, however, gave him away. "How long have you known what I was talking about?" she asked, annoyance coloring her voice.

He finally let loose with the smile he had been holding back. "Since five to two."

"What?" she asked, confused. "Hey, I didn't say that out loud…" She stopped in the hallway. Barnabas kept walking. She closed her eyes. "Fuuuuuck!"

She had forgotten he could read minds.

She jogged to catch up with him and find out about her new case, right after she tried to apologize…if only a little.

. . .

TQB Base, Colorado, USA

Mason held his wife's hand and carried Anne. For a twelve-year-old, she was still quite small and light.

Thank God.

His arm was dying a second time.

"Mason," Sheila whispered, "what's happening?"

The family had time to spend together, to just enjoy being a family. The lady here at the base had given them all the food they wanted. Anne had sat in Sheila's lap the whole time. No matter how much Mason tried to convince Anne differently, she was sure her mom had been taken because she'd been ugly to her. Mason had tried to tell her arguing with moms was what girls her age did.

Now that Anne had her mom back, she was being the most obedient daughter ever. Or at least until she wasn't scared anymore of her mom being taken a second time.

Which led Mason back to Sheila's question.

"We're going to TQB's home base," he equivocated. "I'm to speak to the CEO."

"I thought the lady said you need to talk to the Queen?" Sheila asked as they followed Jasmin out of the main office's doors into the early evening's darkening skies.

"Same person, apparently," Mason replied. "Her group has pulled off of Earth, so she's setting up a monarchy."

"Why does she want you?" Sheila continued.

Mason saw the black shipping container and two men, both with weapons, standing at the back, one door open.

"I think she wants answers," Mason admitted.

"Why did they help us? Is it your job?" Sheila asked. "I know I'm not supposed to ask, but you have to give me something here. Those men were looking for information from you."

"Yes, they were, and no, I don't think they are helping us because of my job. I don't know why."

Anne squirmed in his arm and lifted her blonde head. "I

asked."

"What?" Mason looked down. "Asked who?"

Anne flipped her hair, blew on some errant strands, and then used her left hand to pull the last hair out of her face. "I sent a letter to Ms. Bethany Anne, asking for help."

"How did you do that?" Mason asked.

"I heard the men talking to you when Mom first disappeared. I used my crayons to write a letter and send it. No one at school asked me about it. Well, Josephine made fun of me a little and said I was writing to Santa Claus."

Sheila chuckled. "I imagine she did."

Jasmin nodded at the two men. "These are the three the Queen wants to speak to, VIP soft delivery."

"Aye, ma'am, VIP soft delivery," answered the first guy. He was blond with huge arms, Sheila noted. He smiled at the family.

"My name is Scott." He pointed at the other man. "He's Darryl. Trust me when I say you will absolutely be safe with us."

"Not to be rude," Mason asked, "but in a container?"

Scott grinned, turned his hand over, and pointed up. "No. The Queen said VIP soft delivery."

Mason and Sheila looked up. Four sleek fighters were hovering a hundred feet in the air. "Are those..." Mason's question stopped.

"Yes, those are Black Eagles." Darryl spoke for the first time. "There's nothing on this Earth I'm aware of that's going to get through our guard. The Queen wants you safe, and we tend to go overboard for her."

"I see that." Mason was awed. His group had tried to pull as much information about those ships as they could. From what he did had found out about them, and what he knew about his own people's abilities, he had to agree with Darryl.

These four planes could probably decimate a small country.

Darryl spoke up again. "Sorry, we don't have our best quality multi-seat Pods yet. Those are in production. But, if you would jump on board? We need to be on the *ArchAngel* in about twenty-five minutes before we all drop back in."

"Drop in...where?" Sheila asked as Mason stepped ahead of her into the large black rectangular box.

"The gravity well," Darryl answered. "We need to be prepared for Bethany Anne's introduction in a couple of hours."

Scott closed the door behind them as Darryl made sure everyone was getting clipped in correctly. This container, modified for larger groups, had fifteen seats on each side of the long walls.

"Sorry, sweetie," Darryl murmured. "But we can't let you sit on your dad's lap. It's against regulations."

Anne stood up and sat between her parents. "Am I going to get to meet Ms. Anne?"

"Hmm?" Darryl asked as he carefully belted in the fragile-looking little girl. "Ms. Anne? Oh, sorry, her full name is Bethany Anne."

"Well then, what is her last name?" Anne asked. "I thought my first name was her last name. That's kind of embarrassing."

Mason noticed how huge the man was when he stood up. "No, you share parts of your first name," Darryl told the child. "Trust me, your letter got to Bethany Anne just fine, young lady, and I'm sure she'll speak to you sometime soon. Unfortunately, she has meetings right now."

"Who is she meeting with?" Anne asked as Darryl crossed to the other side and buckled into a seat next to Scott, who was talking with someone sub-vocally.

"The Japanese leadership and royalty," Darryl answered.

CHAPTER FOUR

QBS _ArchAngel_

Barnabas slipped behind the desk in his office as Tabitha sat in the chair facing him. She asked, "Why aren't you outside with the Queen?"

Barnabas shook his head. "We don't want all of our faces on video cameras, so we're only showing the minimum number of people necessary."

"Is that why I haven't seen Stephen lately?" she queried.

Barnabas smiled. "No, you haven't seen Stephen because he spends his off-time with a particular lady. It seems he has lost a battle due to those assets and the 'fog of war' you were speaking about earlier, and is enjoying life even more than he thought he could."

"No shit?" She sat up in her chair. "El Stevo has a woman? Who is it?"

Barnabas grabbed a folder. Moving it in front of him, he opened it and set it down. "Let's not try to do research for 'As The _ArchAngel_ Turns' right now. We do have a case to discuss."

She slumped back in her chair. "Wow, you _have_ been catching up. How do you know about soap operas?"

Barnabas glanced at the ceiling in his office as he murmured, "Please give me strength. Bethany Anne would be upset if any accidents happened to Tabitha."

Tabitha smiled. "Uncle B, you know I'm just playing with you. There's no need to get stressed out. I'm sure I can set up a nice relaxing Friday-night date for you if you'd like."

He eyed his female Ranger. "No, let's not. Let's not and say we didn't. In fact, let's not and never suggest it again. Now, focus," he told her, giving her such a frown that Tabitha understood she had pushed enough.

Fun time was over.

"What we have is a little bit of information. Three names you can track down, and a request to find out who hired them," Barnabas explained.

Tabitha chewed on the inside of her cheek. "If I find out who hired them, what am I supposed to do?" she asked, her head cocked to the right.

Barnabas looked at her. "You are a Queen's Ranger, so that decision is up to you."

"Oh." The mantle of responsibility suddenly weighed heavily on her shoulders. "I kind of like it when I'm just told to kick their ass, not when I have to decide if the ass-kicking is warranted."

Barnabas shrugged. "Get used to it."

Nara, Nara Prefecture, Japan

Bethany Anne stood waiting for her team to leave the ship. The noise in the stadium was loud. Very, very loud.

>>Yuko has hugged her father. This is good, right?<<

Yes, ADAM, that's an excellent sign. She wondered why he was asking her to confirm something he could look up for himself. She added another mental mark in the "becoming human" column.

There had been a number of conversations about what

Bethany Anne should wear for this event. Once the women got involved, what they were thinking bordered on the ridiculous.

While the women knew Bethany Anne would very rarely read minds, they failed to realize that Barnabas did it as a matter of course. Therefore, when Bethany Anne happened to have Barnabas join them during one of the talks, the ladies weren't guarding their minds, and he quickly discerned they were having fun at her expense.

Bethany Anne simply told the women that they would be required to wear whatever she did. Even if it was, perhaps, in an annoying canary yellow or cloying pink color.

Their suggestions suddenly became practical.

Bethany Anne put a stop to the discussion after a few more minutes. "I am a very reasonable person. I'm not going to go into meetings without weapons, even if they're hidden. I prefer black or darker colors. If you try to dress me in bright colors or pastels, I'll consider tying you upside down and using you for shark bait. If you want me in high heels, I better not have sore feet because of them."

The team ended up choosing an outfit with a tailored jacket and pants instead of a dress. She might have pants with hems that ended above her ankles showing off her shoes, or some that almost hit the floor hiding the shoes. Today, her outfit was comprised of lighter fabrics, but she had similar outfits that had more leather.

All in all, she liked the general style. With her hair up as it was, the silver hairpins added a nice touch. Jean Dukes was working on individual small rods that would spit tungsten slugs, yet didn't look like pistols.

Bethany Anne loved Jean's devious mind. The lady was truly a master of kinetic destruction. Her team, probably already working on their team name, came to work with a purpose every morning.

"Looks good, TW," John vocalized. She pressed her lips

together. That damned audio recording with Mason had been all over the ship before she got back. John told her he considered it a penalty for leaving without her Guards, and she should take her punishment with grace.

Bethany Anne about tore another strip off of him until he reminded her to think about what he felt when he thought she had died in the blast.

She stopped arguing, thought about it, and kissed him on the cheek. "I'm sorry for making you fret. You get seventy-two hours," and that was the last of it. She wasn't allowed to say anything about the jokes for three days.

Three. Long-ass. Days. Bethany Anne was going to kill someone, maybe herself, if this kept up. The grapevine on the ship reported that it was open season on the boss for three days. She noticed a countdown clock in the forward cafeteria on the ship.

Fucking hell.

Oh, yes, she was now a firm believer in praying to Saint Payback-is-a-Bitch.

She started walking out on the stadium floor, and the noise was moderately deafening.

She concentrated to reduce the impact—and the pain—from the audio overload until she could handle it better.

It took only a few seconds before she was climbing the steps to the stage behind John and Eric, with Darryl and Scott trailing her. A few women called the guys' names from the audience.

Bethany Anne started shaking hands until she got to where Yuko was standing with her parents. Yuko bowed to her, followed immediately by her parents. Bethany Anne bowed back slightly.

"あなたには、美しくて知的な娘がいます。彼女は、私の個人のチームの大切なメンバーです。あなたは誇り高いはずです。"

She left the family. Yuko's father's mouth was open, and a tear trickled down Yuko's face. For the next few minutes, Bethany Anne was introduced to the local and national political representatives on stage. Then she was shown the microphone and asked to speak to the crowd.

ADAM, I want you to connect to the stadium sound system. Translate my English into Japanese, and let me know if you have any questions on the translation.

As Bethany Anne spoke, she would pause a moment and allow ADAM to translate and interject the audio through the sound system. The first couple of times Bethany Anne did this, there was a murmur behind her on the stage as the VIPs realized she wasn't using an interpreter and they did not know whose voice was coming through the stadium speakers.

Bethany Anne smiled. "Hello to those here in the stadium and those who are watching on television or via video on the internet. I am Her Royal Highness, Queen Bethany Anne. I am also known as the CEO of TQB Enterprises, among other things. As you can see," she waved gracefully at the ship in the middle of the stadium and then pointed to the *ArchAngel* in the sky.

Bethany Anne continued, "We have advanced our technology to the point where even space is achievable. Many of our employees and my personal retinue love Japan's people, love your culture, and admire your resilience in the challenging times our world faces right now, so it was decided to connect with your country and your people. We hope to be able to increase our official diplomatic relations with countries around the world, starting with Japan."

She had to pause as the audience in the stadium roared their approval.

She finished by speaking in Japanese.

"ご支援に感謝します、ユウコのような強い娘が、ニール州から、私たちの世界をより安全な場所を作り、助けることができる国であるためにあなたに感謝します。貴重なお時間をいただき、ありがとうございます。"

She had to dampen her hearing another fifty percent. It was

complete bedlam in the stadium, driven by the younger people in the crowd.

As Bethany Anne turned away from the podium, she saw tears streaming down Yuko's parents' faces.

QBS *ArchAngel*

"Excuse me," a good-looking man interrupted Mason as he and his family were eating in the cafeteria on the ship. He was holding a tray. "May I join you?"

To say Mason had been shocked when they had arrived on the ship would have been a complete understatement.

Once they landed, and Darryl and Scott had unclipped them, Mason found he was not prepared to answer Sheila's question, "Are we in space?"

The family came around the corner of the container and saw what looked like an opening leading into the darkness of space.

The only one who wasn't afraid was Anne.

"It's completely safe," Scott told the family. "ArchAngel only allows Pods through the gravitic curtain. Anything human would find themselves pushed back whenever they got within twenty feet of the opening."

"Did you say gravitic curtain?" Mason asked, trying to catch up to what he was seeing and what he was being told.

"Well, that's what we non-propeller heads call it. Marcus has finally decided it was close enough to stop bitching about our name. Oh." Scott looked down. "I'm sorry. I should watch my words around young adults."

"It's okay." Anne looked up at him. "The kids at my school curse all the time, and the boys are the worst. I'm just thankful no one's smoking in the bathroom, trying to act cool."

Scott glanced at her parents, a quizzical look on his face.

"Words of a wise woman," Sheila answered his unasked question. "Unfortunately, it hits her at random times, never when I'm telling her what she needs to know."

Scott shook his head in recognition of something he accepted but didn't necessarily understand.

He put up a finger, and his eyes lost focus for a split second. "Okay, ArchAngel has given me the location of your suite. Let's get you guys settled, and then, after our conference in Japan, I'm sure we will have more conversations."

Mason and the family had enjoyed their large VIP suite, relaxing together, and now eating dinner in the cafeteria. He nodded at the man. "Certainly. I'm Mason." He nodded to his left. "This is my wife Sheila, and our daughter Anne."

"Barnabas," the man introduced himself. His plate only had an apple and a ceramic mug with a lid on it. He set the plate down and seated himself.

"So, are you doing okay here on the *ArchAngel*?" he started the conversation while using a knife to peel the apple.

"It's cool!" Anne jumped in. "Do you know the Queen?"

Barnabas looked down at the young girl. At first, Mason was concerned that she had offended the gentleman. "Yes, young lady, I do know the Queen. In fact, she sent me to speak to you and your parents, to help us understand a few things."

The click-click-click of nails on the hard floor caught their attention, and they turned to see a huge white German Shepherd come down the aisle between the tables, heading in their direction.

Barnabas heard Sheila ask her husband, "Is he safe?" There was a note of fear in her voice.

"Yes, Ashur is completely safe to anyone who doesn't attack the Queen," Barnabas answered.

"Ashur is his name?" Anne asked. "May I pet him?"

"I can't answer for Ashur. Why don't you ask him?" Barnabas answered.

When his name was spoken, the dog's head had turned and

honed in on the table talking about him. He had stopped three tables away as if he were waiting to make sure they felt safe around him.

"Um, why did he stop?" Anne asked.

"He's waiting to make sure he doesn't scare you," Barnabas answered.

Anne turned to look at Barnabas. "Are you fibbing to me? He knows what's going on?"

"My Queen assures me he's much smarter than any dog you have ever known."

"Does she ever fib?" Anne asked.

"Well..." Barnabas paused and scratched his chin. "If you mean would she fib for a joke? Yes, absolutely. Would she lie about something like this? No, she wouldn't," Barnabas finished.

Anne turned back around in her chair. "Ashur, can I pet you?" She raised her voice a little. He broke into a little jog...*clickclickclickclick*...and in a second, he was next to Anne.

"Oh, my," Sheila whispered. The dog's head was as high as Anne's shoulder while she was sitting on the chair. He was huge.

Anne put her hand on his neck and started petting him. "Momma, he's so soft!" Sheila gasped when Anne reached around and held on to Ashur's neck in a big hug. "Thank you for coming to save me, Ashur."

Ashur chuffed to her. "Oh, sorry." She let up a bit on her hug.

"This is the dog that was with Bethany Anne?" Mason asked. The sweetness of this dog was at odds with the decisive animal Mason's memory was telling him was a hunter-killer. His memories were getting foggier and foggier on the details.

"Yes, this is Ashur. He joined a, uh, disagreement between Bethany Anne and a few others in South America a few years ago, and has been with her ever since. If there was ever a more spoiled dog in this solar system, I don't know who it is."

"No, he isn't spoiled, he's treated well," Sheila replied. "I've seen teacup dogs that are spoiled brats. Ashur here deserves everything he gets."

Ashur chuffed in response.

"It's almost like he's answering us," Sheila added.

"He is." Anne's muffled voice came from Ashur's back. "He said you're right, he does earn it."

The two parents chuckled at Anne's imagination but saw Barnabas hadn't joined in their amusement. "What?" he asked as the two parents stopped laughing. "According to Bethany Anne, he does communicate. We just have to be willing to listen." He shrugged and grinned at them. "I'm not saying she's right or wrong since I don't understand him yet, myself."

Ashur chuffed, and Anne giggled. "Ashur said that's because you are an old fart with a brain as malu...malubable," Ashur chuffed again. "Mal-u-a-bull as a rock."

"Mason," Sheila whispered, "I didn't think Anne knew the word 'malleable.'"

"Uh, I'm certain it must have come up in a science class. I'm sure it did," he stammered.

The dog chuffed again and Anne released him, turning to her parents but leaving a hand on his neck. "Can I go with Ashur? He says there is a workout place where I can throw him stuff to fetch. Please?" Anne's blue eyes opened as wide as she could manage.

"Um, is it safe?" Sheila turned to Barnabas, not knowing what to expect.

He smiled and reached into a shirt pocket. He put a small tablet on the table and slid it across. "ArchAngel?"

The little tablet lit up, and the five of them heard a voice come out of it. "Yes, Barnabas?"

"Is there anyone using the workout room near the forward cafeteria?" he asked.

"No."

"Would you please display the video of the room?"

The little tablet showed a large room with soft padding on the floor and workout equipment along the walls.

"If you give permission, then I imagine we'll see the two of them show up on the screen about twenty seconds after they leave the table. You can ask ArchAngel to pipe your voice into the room, and they can come back when we're finished here."

Sheila looked at her daughter and squeezed Mason's hand as she answered, "Okay, you can go."

Her mom's permission wasn't complete before Anne was out of the seat and running behind Ashur, who had taken off out of the cafeteria. Ashur waited at the entrance for the young girl to catch up, and the two disappeared from the room.

Barnabas saw the anxiousness around Sheila's eyes relax when her daughter and Ashur appeared on the tablet. Sure enough, Anne picked up what looked like a tennis ball and threw it. Ashur took off after the ball, and they heard her giggle and call his name.

"I still don't know if I believe the dog was talking, but they're playing," Sheila mused, watching her daughter interact.

"How do you have gravity up here?" Mason asked, turning away from the tablet.

"TQB implementation of Kurtherian technology," Barnabas answered. "Not Vril, certainly. The energy required for that, I'm told, is several orders of magnitude less efficient."

"How, um, how do you know about Vril?" Mason stammered out.

"Well, I didn't know much, although ADAM gave me an update. I decided to ask someone who might have a better understanding, and he did."

"Who is this?" Mason, his scientific curiosity taking over.

"The Yollin scientist Royleen," Barnabas answered, a tiny smile playing around the edges of his lips. Sheila watched this man reeling in her husband like a fish after a lure, baiting him with little tidbits of information.

"What's a Yollin scientist? Is that one of TQB's companies?" Mason asked.

"Mason Jayden, you know about Vril, you are part of a group that answers to MJ-12, with technology not even the highest officials in your country's government know about, and yet you can't differentiate between one set of aliens and another?"

Mason's mouth finally opened, and like a fish, it gasped for a moment or two before answering, "Vril wasn't ever proven to be a viable energy source."

"No, because Thule Gesellschaft Maria Orsitsch of Zagreb didn't handle the information given to her correctly. However, the communication *did* work with the Aldebaran aliens who had settled in Sumer thousands of years ago, so the Thule UFOs and the later Nazi UFOs your group have hidden are based on technology from the dawn of our technological birth. This," Barnabas waved around the room, "is advanced—very advanced—compared to Aldebaran, or at least, that is what I've been led to believe."

"How do you know so much about our work?" Mason asked. "The President isn't even supposed to know."

"Oh, he doesn't, I assure you," Barnabas agreed. "Although he suspects much, as do many of the leaders who have been on this ship. We're tracking down the people who attacked you. The three we fought were mercenaries, and the ones who hired them used untraceable connections. Well, untraceable so far," he clarified.

"You think you'll be able to find them?" Sheila interrupted. "Those men aren't going to be able to get off due to having the right lawyers?"

Barnabas turned to Sheila. "My lady, those people have already been judged. They will not be dodging their punishment, I assure you."

"Good." Sheila squeezed Mason's hand.

Mason looked at Barnabas, thinking over his words. He caught Barnabas's eye. "Ever?"

Barnabas looked unflinchingly into Mason Jayden's eyes. "Those men are permanently banished. They will not be able to bother your family, or any other human, again."

Mason nodded his understanding. They had kidnapped his wife and put explosives around his daughter. His desire to flip the switch and watch them fry in an electric chair was not ever going to happen, but he wouldn't lose any sleep over their apparent deaths, either.

Mason considered his next words very carefully before speaking. "I need to talk to the Queen. There are three more families who are likely going to be in jeopardy."

CHAPTER FIVE

West Wing Deep Underground Command Center (DUCC), Washington, DC, USA

The President nodded at the two men, both military but only one in uniform. The other gentleman, retired, was uncomfortable in his three-piece suit.

Passing strange, that.

"Gentleman." He sat down. "Why do I suspect I'm about to get a history lesson?"

Jimmy, the President's behind-the-scenes military liaison, spoke first. "Because you know I don't bring people here unnecessarily, Mr. President. Henry Wells is stronger on military history than almost any other individual I know. That history covers both what's in the books, and what never made it to print. He's even stronger on history than he is uncomfortable in his business clothes."

"Annoying," Henry commented grumpily. "Suits are for young men trying to get the eyes of the ladies or the power brokers here in DC. I've been married for forty years, and she likes me just fine in shorts and tall white socks."

The other two men smiled as they both applied mental

erasers to the visual that flashed in their brains. The risk you took when you asked someone who did not play in your arena was that sometimes you had to accept different kinds of behavior. When you needed the best, and the best was strange, you took what you could get.

Even if it made you want to drink afterward.

Jimmy closed his eyes and unsuccessfully trying to shake the memory away. "So, the military plan to go to Antarctica and look into rumored technology."

"Why would there be alien technology in the ice?" the President asked. "Did it happen so long ago the ice wasn't there yet?"

"No," Henry took up the conversation. "This is actually something that started during WWII."

"Nazi?" the President guessed.

"Yes, sir, but not exactly what you think," Henry told him. "Unless you know much about the Thule Society?"

The President shook his head.

"Okay, then I'm going to have to give you a bit of a history lesson. Is that okay?"

Another nod from the President.

"There is a significant amount of misinformation regarding whether Hitler was an occultist or not. Most of this has to do with the head of the Nazi SS coming from the Aryan Pool Society and being quite an occultist himself. Furthermore, there are rumors that Nazi Germany started a base in Antarctica during 1938. When you add the Thule and those who believed in communicating with aliens to the mix, it becomes quite far-fetched, until you realize two interesting pieces of information."

The President nodded. "Go on. I can see where one of these is going to play out."

"Indeed, we now know there are aliens, so the claim that people were communicating with aliens is not so crazy anymore. The second was Operation Highjump in 1947."

"Highjump? I vaguely remember something about that. It had

to do with a Navy expedition to stop the Russians?" the President asked.

"Yes, that was the explanation given for it," Henry agreed. "But in this case, the rumors about the real experience are closer to the truth than the lie we told. The lie was frankly more believable, too."

"How so?"

"The official title of the operation, which was organized by Rear Admiral Richard E. Byrd, was 'The United States Navy Antarctic Developments Program.' It lasted from 1946 to 1947 and was led by Rear Admiral Richard Crimson. It started in August 1946 and ended in late February 1947. Task Force 68 had forty-seven hundred men, thirteen ships, and thirty-three aircraft. The stated goal was to establish the Antarctic research base called Little America IV."

Now that he was in teaching mode, Henry didn't look uncomfortable in his suit anymore. He didn't look like he remembered how he was dressed.

"Almost all of the deaths and lost ships have been blamed on the inclement weather in Antarctica, but there are a lot of fictionalized versions where Task Force 68 encountered superior technology, mostly from Nazis, who had been building an Antarctic base in Schwabenland. The truth, not recorded anywhere, is that the task force was attacked, but not by flying saucers. Rather, by people using some sort of highly advanced weapons. Our planes and helicopters down there couldn't provide effective air cover. The attackers seemed completely impervious to the cold that was debilitating our men."

"So, they didn't have a bunch of flying saucers running around blowing up all of the ships?" the President asked.

"No." Henry laughed. "Although I do have information that proves those from Antarctica did arrive in Washington DC to have a conversation in July 1952, using what we believe were flying saucers to travel. If you go back to the newspapers at the time, it was a big story. Their leader is, or was, a pacifist by the name of Maria Orsitsch. Within fifteen years, the government had no communications with that group any longer."

"We didn't try to go down there again?" the President asked.

"No, we had captured a few examples of Nazi technology of our own, and the Thule leaders didn't want to provide any alien technological insights to a belligerent country such as the US. Because of the scientists we pulled out of Nazi Germany during Operation Paperclip, the US was making some pretty heady advances. If they want to visit, they will. If we go knocking without an invitation, we will be met with the same result as last time, or so we were told."

"Okay, so what has changed?"

"When all this alien stuff came up, someone remembered we had a small project that sent out a coded message every month to Antarctica. Every month since 1967, we have received a reply. It became routine—boring, if you will—and I'm surprised it even continued. But sometimes you do something because it has always been done, and this was the same. Two weeks ago, a researcher found the small group responsible for sending this message and documenting the results." Henry shrugged.

"And?" the President urged.

"Four years ago, the replies stopped," Henry answered.

QBS _ArchAngel,_ over Tokyo, Japan

"Two meetings, two locations," Bethany Anne muttered as she and John walked briskly down one of the long corridors in the _ArchAngel._

John grinned behind her. "What was that, my Queen?"

She looked over her shoulder. "Is 'my Queen' your version of 'BA' today?"

"No?" John answered. "Maybe? Maybe I'm trying it on for size to see how it fits you. I mean, you can't exactly get mad at me since you admitted to the whole world that you're a Queen."

"Yes." She turned back around. "I did. It needed to be done to get others used to the idea that we aren't part of any country. It might prove to be a speed bump in the future."

"Oh? How so?"

"It will be us against them," she admitted. "So even if that happens, it will still prove to everyone we are separate from all countries. But our disagreements are likely to get a lot bloodier."

"Well, if it would help, instead of calling you my Queen, I could go for TW."

Bethany Anne's left hand popped up over her shoulder, flipping her Guard off.

The ten chosen business leaders sat quietly around the table. Bobcat, William, and Marcus had entered, and there had been introductions, but everyone was waiting for the big arrival.

The room was large, and could easily hold a couple hundred in the surrounding seats. But the table at the bottom would only accommodate fourteen, tightly packed.

The doors opened, and everyone turned to see a young Japanese woman enter. Some of the men around the table dismissed her before they noticed the man who arrived right behind her.

Then, everyone at the table went from polite inactivity to actively being very polite.

Bobcat raised an eyebrow. He hadn't expected Akio and Yuko to join them for the meeting, so he straightened up in his chair. The Queen was up to something. He tapped William, who nodded slowly and passed the alert to Marcus.

Marcus looked up and saw Akio and Yuko sitting on the front

row of the auditorium. He turned to William, his face confused, mouthed a "What?" and shrugged.

William winked at him, so Marcus turned off his tablet and set it down. Apparently, his friends wanted him to pay attention.

Akio whispered, "You represent our Queen. You are no timid flower, Yuko, and you will not dishonor us both in this effort. Are we in agreement?"

Yuko nodded and whispered almost inaudibly, "Yes, understood."

Bobcat was still making mental notes when the doors opened a second time.

John came in first. His presence never failed to bring about a reaction, but Bethany Anne coming in behind him made most of the attendees forget about the large man.

The study in minor facial movements by the people around the table was starting to fascinate Bobcat. He watched as many of the men as he could while Bethany Anne strode to the single chair waiting for her at the head of the table. When she didn't sit in it, he could almost feel the men's calculations running rampant in their heads. Bethany Anne didn't sit; rather, she stood behind her chair, resting her hands on the tall back, and looked down the table at those sitting.

"I understand," she started, "that there is a particular way of communicating and adhering to customs when working on business deals with professionals in Japan." She paused for a moment before continuing, "Unfortunately, I'm not polite, nor do I have a desire to follow formal ways. I have to be in another meeting with another representative from your country who is also 'not' presently here on our ship, just like the ten of you are 'not' here right now."

She looked up and down the table. "I am her Royal Highness, Queen Bethany Anne. My lineage is varied, and in a way, I'm both from this century, and from the centuries before me. I understand you have all been individually instructed about how we are going to work with your companies?"

She received ten short, sharp nods.

"Excellent. Now, here is something not in the original download."

She turned to her side and raised an eyebrow. "Yuko?"

This time, those who could watched as the young Japanese woman strode down from her seat, affecting an air of competence and assurance she had not exhibited when she entered earlier. Bethany Anne pulled out the seat and offered it to her as she spoke. "In your country, the Emperor appoints the Prime Minister. In these transactions, Yuko is my designated representative to confirm all things, and speaks with my authority to accomplish the goals I and my team," she nodded to Bobcat, William, and Marcus, "designate."

She looked to her side again. "Akio?"

As Akio came down, Bethany Anne stepped back and to the side, allowing Akio to stand behind and to the left of Yuko. "I am not blind to the potential problems that can affect a project such as this one, so Yuko has the wisdom, guidance, and protection for her person and her project of my Elites' leader and half his team. Trust me and believe you have no idea the amount of wisdom Yuko now has at her fingertips, should she feel the need of it."

Bethany Anne paused and pursed her lips. "I trust every one of you gentleman will provide the appropriate level of respect to all of my representatives on this ship and in your country. I will not be pleased should either side fail to act honorably. Akio will accept any complaints that originate from those on my team. He will take those issues up with you personally if there is a problem with any of you or your representatives. Have a fruitful discussion."

And just like that, Bethany Anne left the room. Bobcat wished he had a handful of antacids to give out to his new Japanese partners.

Apparently, having Akio as part of the group had just thrown a William-sized monkey wrench into their negotiation plans. He wasn't sure, but Bobcat had an inkling that these guys were screwed.

Yuko started the discussion. "I am very aware…" she began, forcing her voice to remain calm. Years of trawling the dark web hadn't prepared her for this, but this was what her Queen wanted. "That you may be personally affronted by being required to deal with a young woman. You will have the opportunity to make your displeasure known in a few minutes. First, I have something to say, and something for you to watch."

The men, expecting the young woman to force her title and authority, were curious. They had been notified that working with the Queen was potentially dangerous, but all had laughed it off. As leaders, almost conquerors in the business world, what did they have to fear from a thirty-year-old Queen? Now, she substituted a woman ten years her junior.

"They say knowledge is power." Yuko's voice turned cold. "And in the realm of knowledge, you are but swaddled babies compared to me."

All of the men's eyes narrowed in annoyance, but then a feeling of fear hit. It wasn't strong, but it was real.

"Pull out your tablets and read the email I just sent to each of you. The information I am sharing is what I found out about each of you in the last twelve hours. This is my effort, not even asking for support from the team of which I am part, or my friend, who could have helped me."

The men, a few cautiously, some quickly, pulled out their

phones or tablets and went to their emails. Sure enough, each had an email with an encrypted document.

"What," Shimizu Yuma asked, "is the password?" All of the men noticed the tiny smile on the young woman's face.

"Why, what would you expect from someone who hacked your computers? It is your own, of course."

A few were annoyed. A few stared in disbelief. In a few seconds, however, all believed.

Then the reading, the annoyance, and the irritation occurred.

"This," Shimizu Yuma spat, pointing at his phone, "is not honorable!"

Yuko spoke in a calm voice. "That is what I do. I point this out because I am here to save you from yourselves!" Yuko's voice rose at the end, and Akio placed his hand on her shoulder. She calmed down. "My Queen cares nothing about our country's long history and the proper ways to do things. She cares about results and time. In her mind, you get results more quickly without the attempts to hurt each other, whether that means in business or personally."

Yuko waved a hand toward them. "I can hurt you by releasing this information." She turned to look at her watch. "But in four more seconds, it will not exist." The annoyance of a couple of the men turned to astonishment when the very documents they were reviewing disappeared.

"I do this not to upset or dishonor you. I seek to make a point. A point, I might add, that is only known here within these walls. My Queen does not know I did this, although you can feel free to tell her if you would like. But here is the second and more important lesson you must know."

Behind her, Akio touched a button on his watch. He had been introduced to the technology by Yuko, and it appealed to the stoic warrior.

The lights in the room dimmed, and the main screen behind

the table lit up. Those with their backs to the screen turned in their chairs.

"Wow," Bobcat quipped. "I didn't know we were doing Friday movie night. Who has the popcorn?"

William chuckled, but that was the only response from anyone in the room.

The screen, dark, showed a very tiny point of white in the center as a female voice emerged from the loudspeakers. "This information has been brought together by Ms. Arakawa Yuko for those who have been invited to participate in the exchange of technology and knowledge."

The white dot opened, and multiple scenes showed Bethany Anne fighting using swords or guns. A few times, the video seemed to be coming from her eyes. At one point, Bethany Anne's voice, cold with menace, spoke. Those at the table saw it was at night in what looked like a Middle Eastern city. A man was in front of her, scared. "Jahannam is calling for you Dawid! Jahannam is CALLING!" She screamed the last word, and the man got back up and continued running. The cameraperson was walking toward the man as he turned to look back. The voice continued, "Dawiiid, the blood of the innocent is on your palms!" The man suddenly stopped running and turned back. He backed toward her, obviously fearing something in front of him.

Then the man stopped moving. There were muscle contractions that suggested he was trying to run, but he couldn't.

The man, blocking the sight of the body in front of him, let out a sob as the camera moved behind him. Two of the men sitting at the table jerked when the cameraperson thrust a katana through Dawid.

The view changed, and the person leaned forward and put her lips near his ear. "The cries for justice of the dying have been heard! The dead have come to claim you, Dawid. France's children shall have their justice!"

She yanked the sword out of the man, who fell to his knees.

She pulled him back up by his hair. "Tonight you are the lesson, Dawid. Tonight you are the note!" She pulled the man up. A fraction of a second later, her blade sliced through the night, leaving the man headless. She kept the head, the body falling to the street. "You, Dawid Zadeh, shall not have a proper burial!" With that, she *pushed* the head, and it disappeared into the night.

A few of the men realized they didn't hear it hit the ground.

The lights came back on, and the men turned to Yuko again. "Do not believe that Japan is the only country that understands honor or justice or retribution. You do not wish to upset me by your actions, but you had better pray you never, ever make my Queen get involved."

Yuko paused and spoke calmly and slowly. "She doesn't have any patience for bullshit."

The fear receded.

Yuko smiled, looking like a young, fresh-faced Japanese lady. "Now, do any of you feel dishonored by working with me?"

None of the men were fooled. School was in session, and as old as they were, they were the students.

There was no dishonor in learning from masters, even if they came with young bodies and beautiful faces.

CHAPTER SIX

<u>China</u>

The four friends stayed as close together as they could during the march.

"How come," Bai asked, "we are in the front hacking at plants again?"

"You aren't holding the machete correctly, Bai," Zhu told him. "You are going to tire your arm out too fast."

"That is because those of us born in the cities don't learn how to use a machete to get to work!" Bai snapped, hacking a second time to clear out the vine in front of him.

Second Lieutenant Zi Shun turned around and spoke to his two men. "Bai, Zhu is just trying to help. Don't let your frustration cause you to dishonor his help. And everybody," he spoke a touch louder, making sure to get their attention, "keep your eyes open for anything above us." He punctuated his command by using the machete to point up. He turned around and continued working his way through the undergrowth.

Bai looked up as he pulled out his canteen and took a drink of water. "Have I mentioned how much I hate jungles?"

Zhu answered, "I stopped counting at thirty-two."

The army men were loud. Geming twitched his tail in annoyance at the poor sport. From the four kings came the command to eradicate those trailing their people. The Army had tried to use air power, but it had been fruitless in the deep of the forests and the dark of the night. The Army's plan then switched to tracking the clan through the forest.

Now, he and eleven others were waiting to cause as much damage as they could to this group following their king.

Another soldier's voice reached his sensitive ears, causing another irritated twitch of his tail.

They had already scouted the men and knew there were two trackers in this group. Those two were the first targets. Two of his clan brothers lay in the undergrowth, waiting. Three more were hiding behind the trackers, along the path they had hacked from the jungle. Those in the back would attack first in swift, lightning-like strikes to get the group focused on the rear so that those in the front might turn and not see the killing hits so close to the guards up front.

Otherwise, healing was going to be a pain.

They had heard the talk, the whispers, the prayers even, as the Army men kept checking their guns and their silver ammunition. A concern, to be sure, and it pushed this from easy to at least challenging, and potentially deadly for a few. However, the kings needed the time to hide the four treasures. It was decided the best of their people, the smartest, would eventually bring the pieces together and work to continue the prophecies.

Because the Sacred Clan was patient if nothing else.

Shun's arm, tired as it was, swung hard to chop through the limb in front of him. The trees were small and thin but still took up space as their branches connected, making it very difficult to walk.

He slid his machete into the scabbard and pulled around his canteen. While he was drinking, he looked into the canopy above them and noticed two yellow eyes looking down at them through leaves from over forty feet away. "*Xiǎoxīn!*" he cried and dropped the canteen, reaching for his rifle.

At that same moment, there were the growls of wild cats and screams from those in the back.

"Look forward!" Shun commanded. He saw Jian move up beside him on his left. The two trackers were pulling back, but one of them had turned to run, and he made it maybe three steps before he screamed as he disappeared into the undergrowth.

The second had a pistol and a blade out, and was looking for his attacker and taking backward steps.

"We are coming up beside you," Shun called. The terrifying screams from those in back and the other tracker off to their left cut through the shouting of the men as they continued to look out into the jungle, growls causing many of the men to fire their precious ammunition.

"They are making you shoot at nothing!" Shun yelled. The only ones who listened were his men.

Except for Bai. He had already shot off some of his ammo before he turned, embarrassed. "Jian, we pull Hulin in with us."

Jian nodded.

A small tree bent ever so slowly. Shun had punched three shells into the brush before he thought, and a primal scream greeted him. "Now!" Shun and Jian took four steps and grabbed the tracker, and the four men made a circle around him.

"We have the scientists to protect!" Zhu yelled.

Shun grimaced. Tactically, that was going to be a challenge. "All face out, and Hulin, watch our back trail."

There was occasional fire now. The men, some probably

down to their final magazines of silver ammo, stopped firing indiscriminately.

It was quiet—too quiet—Shun and the men kept looking around, trying to see if any more bushes or trees moved that shouldn't. Shun searched his quadrant, heart racing when Jian shouted, "Up!"

The four men turned, and Hulin got one shot off before a hundred pounds of Northern Chinese leopard landed on the tracker from the limbs above, dragging him to the earth. The man's screams became gurgles as his throat was torn out. Bai got one shot in the leopard before it screamed in pain and leaped at him. The cat raked his right claws across Bai's face and used his left to slice open the man's neck in multiple places. Digging his rear claws into Bai's body, the leopard jumped backward, causing Jian to duck as it flew over him. The three remaining men turned as one and shot into the brush until Shun commanded them to halt.

Shun could hear that the shots had mostly stopped. He turned to see Jian holding Bai's head up. Zhu kneeled by his friend and held his hand as Bai tried to smile, his face too messed up to understand the words that his bloody lips were trying to form as his one good eye slowly closed for the final time.

Shun's lips pressed together, his head turning to search the forest, willing a pair of luminescent eyes to be looking back at him.

He desperately needed something to shoot.

Dulce Lake New Mexico, USA

"Explain this to me one more time?" Clean-shaven with short-cropped hair, Patrick M. Brown looked like you could have taken him off of a military poster and stuck him in the chair behind his medium-sized desk. Well, except for his right eye, which was blind.

"We have lost Mason Jayden. He didn't arrive this morning, and we, of course, went to track him down. Half of his house is burned, and witnesses are saying there was an explosion on the second floor. Only one old lady admitted to seeing anything, and her eyewitness report is odd."

"Go on," Patrick urged. "I suspect this will be good?"

"Oh," his second, Bruce shrugged and took one of the two seats in front of the desk, "it's either perfect, or she's a loony."

"In our business, loony is more likely."

"True." Bruce crossed his legs. "The lady says she was walking to pick up her paper when the explosion happened. She looked to see three men lying in the yard across the street from the burning home and the neighbor's roof raining down. The three men got up, raced across the street, and had what looked like guns in their hands."

"Looked like?" Patrick asked.

"Six houses and she's old. Eyesight problems."

Patrick nodded.

"So, assuming pistols, they run across the street. Then something kinda round drops right out of the sky and a huge guy jumps from about a second-floor distance down to the ground. She can't hear anything from the round thing. Then, a woman and a dog come up behind the three men. Little old lady says the guys laid down their pistols, the woman goes up, and she swears this is true, she hits each man once and they disappear. Then the strange lady, the dog, and the huge guy disappear as well. She had a car..."

"Oh? What happened to the car? It disappear too?" Patrick smirked.

"No, it flew away."

Patrick's eyes narrowed. "What kind of car?"

"She claims a sports car, maroon."

"Fucking A," Patrick exploded. "Fucking A! It's got to be that bitch CEO of TQB Enterprises. She's the only person with a sports car that flies. They have those Pods, so her man could have come down and jumped out. Her guards are huge." He thought for a moment, then asked in a calmer voice, "Why were they there?"

"Running hypothesis is the three guys with the guns were doing something with Mason. I've done a quick check of the logs, and he has accessed secured data areas he wouldn't normally go into. Not something that trips our systems, but odd. No one has seen his wife in a few days, and we have the explosion upstairs."

"Bedrooms?" Patrick asked.

"Where you would think—upstairs."

"Wife is gone, the child is home, and Mason is checking into stuff he shouldn't." Patrick leaned back in his chair and thought about possible scenarios. "Okay, if we assume the guys were bad, they took the wife, and maybe did some sort of dead man's switch on the child, we have someone trying to mine our data. That means we have a mole, or someone who has figured out who our people are."

Patrick leaned forward and put his elbows on his desk. "If we assume TQB were the hostiles, I can't make that work. They could easily come get us here if they wanted. I'm sure they have more technology than they're showing. That she can do something to move someone into another dimension is believable, if barely. I hadn't considered it, but I can believe it. Further, from our own people who have tried to hack their computers, it can't be done. All psychological reports indicate they would never take a wife to get Mason to steal data."

"What if they changed?" Bruce asked.

Patrick shook his head. "We could what-if the hell out of anything. No, go with the knowledge and see how it fits. What it tells me is we almost had a data breach. We have three additional families that leave us vulnerable, so we need to pull in our reliable people and disappear and take care of any loose threads. We aren't nearly ready to produce our tech at scale yet, nor can we fight the government."

"A government who funds us." Bruce smirked.

"Well, yes. But we don't really work for those civilians anymore, do we?" Patrick looked at Bruce, his good eye reflecting the question to his subordinate.

"Nope," Bruce agreed. "The sheep are clueless."

South America

Tabitha's Pod dropped her off at home, or rather, at Michael's old home.

Just not the same anymore.

Hirotoshi and Ryu were both standing outside in the dark shadows. "Hey, boys," she greeted. Hirotoshi gave nothing away, but she did notice the aggravation Ryu displayed at being caught.

"Don't get your tighty-whities in a bunch. Wait, do you guys even wear banana hammocks? I mean, I suppose it could leave your cherries in a bunch and all. Or do you let the grapes of wrath just swing as God intended?"

Hirotoshi dipped his head in acknowledgment and went inside the house first. Ryu brought up the rear and answered, "Yes, we use the German *ein dickenhammaker* variety," he whispered, completely straight-faced.

Once inside, Tabatha went to the sink, filled a glass, and started drinking before she pieced together what Ryu said. Then, as Ryu watched, she spat out the water and started choking and laughing at the same time as she slapped the granite beside the sink. *"Ein dickenhammaker! PRICELESS!"* She started choking again and had to try to stop laughing for a minute.

Ryu turned to Hirotoshi, who winked at him while Tabitha kept sputtering, "Guys!" Cough...cough... "Guys, dammit, that shit is..." cough... "funny! Oh my God, *dickenhammaker!*" She finally got herself under control and turned around and smiled at

Ryu. "Okay, we're one and one. I found you guys in the shadows, but you nearly killed me with a joke."

She walked past them into the dining room. "Come join me here. We have an assignment."

Ryu lifted an eyebrow at Hirotoshi, who gave a tiny shrug, and they followed their leader to the table and sat down.

Tabitha pursed her lips. "Okay, we ain't got much to go on so far. We have three mercenaries who are no longer with us but were hired by parties unknown. We, of course, need to put real names to 'Unknown.' It, perhaps, might have been nice to see if these guys had overheard anything, but I understand our Queen was short of patience. I am totally behind this, and support her one-woman effort to rid the Earth of dipshits and dingbats who harm kids."

There was a long pause. Hirotoshi eyed her. "But?"

She shrugged. "I just wish she would get a little more information between judgment and execution."

Tabitha sucked in a large breath and released it in a rush. She turned to her right. "Let me ask this question, Hirotoshi. Do we need this location any longer?"

"This house?" he asked. Tabitha nodded. "No. We can operate from anywhere. Since the Queen fixed our sun weakness, nothing is keeping us indoors any longer. We can work wherever we want."

Tabitha's eyebrows drew together. "Are you saying we can stay out in the woods?"

"Easily," Ryu responded. "Most of our team learned to live off of the land as little kids. As vampires, we often would need to go underground to hide from the sun. You lose any fear of bugs, snakes, insects…"

"Stop!" Tabitha had her hand up. "I'm South American, and we deal with lots of stuff. However, this PYT is not into creepy crawlies anywhere near my hair, or anyplace that can be considered an entry point. So, let's focus on leaving disgusting methods of sun aversion for the history books and figure out how to get what we need to sleep above the insects, not with them."

Tabitha was so intent on watching Ryu she failed to see a very small smirk form on Hirotoshi's face.

She took control of the conversation again. "Okay, if we don't need this location, then I want you guys to work with me on how we can stay mobile. We will designate any semi-permanent location our base of operations, and I want us to be able to leave anyplace within fifteen minutes. I know you guys are lean so that probably isn't your problem. However, I need to teach at least one of you, maybe two of you, computer hacking skills. Do we have anyone on the team who would be interested?"

"Most would be interested," Hirotoshi answered. "When you live a few hundred years, you learn that curiosity solves a lot of problems."

"Okay, who has the most proclivity to learn it?"

Hirotoshi and Ryu stared at each other. Tabitha pretended she could see the mind meld the two must be doing. It was a shame, she conceded, she couldn't jack into it.

Or could she? It was worth testing.

Finally, they broke their staring contest. "There are two," Hirotoshi replied. "If you permit me, I will ask them personally but discreetly, so their answers will be considered dishonorable if they do not desire to do this. May I?"

"Sure," she agreed. "I learned my lesson before. If you seek permission, it's usually an honor thing. Okay, make it so, Number One."

Damn, Tabitha thought, she was sure she was going to get Hirotoshi tweaked just a little by calling him Number One. She had spent two weeks setting up the plan to get him to accidentally see *Star Trek: The Next Generation*, and now...nothing.

Dammit!

"Next question," she continued. "What do we do with this house?"

This time there was no pause. The men chorused, "Burn it down." Tabitha shocked, stared at both of them, then one, then the other. "Burn it?"

Hirotoshi nodded at Ryu, who answered, "Yes. There has been too much evil and loss in this house. Further, we have not found any secret cache of the drugs used to change people. But just because we have not found it, does not mean it isn't here."

Tabitha pursed her lips. "One second."

My Queen?

What? Oh, Tabitha! Wow, hadn't expected you to be calling. What's up?

Can I have permission to burn down Michael's house...or rather, my house?

It's yours, so you make the decision. But I'm curious as to why.

My advisors, Tweedledee and Tweedledum over here, suggest it because it's a house full of evil. And, there's a slight possibility there's serum we can't find still hidden somewhere in the house.

Tweedledee and Tweedledum? Have you called them that yet?

Oh, HELL, no! I'm Latina. We might get excitable every once in a while, but we do know there are lines you don't cross.

So, what you're telling me is that you're just waiting for the right moment?

Well, yes. But how did you know that?

You're Tabitha.

Oh. Well, when you put it that way, it makes sense.

It's a gift. Was that all you needed?

Yes, thank you.

And then Tabitha was alone in her head again. She was a little lonely after she broke the link. Talking like this could become a drug if she overused it, she thought.

Or Bethany Anne would give her a mental bitch-slap and her head would ring for days.

Never mind, potential problem solved.

She spoke to her guys. "Bethany Anne is good with the

suggestion to burn this house down, so I'll spend the next few hours sleeping, then search the dark web. Let's get your questions about who's going to learn hacking answered, and they can start with me tomorrow morning. Have the rest go through the house, and let's pull out what we want to give away or sell and stash the cash or whatever. Plan on us finding new digs and always able to move our headquarters at any time."

She looked around, taking in the room one last time. "Let's do this."

CHAPTER SEVEN

QBS _ArchAngel_

"What is that?" Bethany Anne asked as she sat down at the table. Scott, Eric, John, and Darryl looked down at themselves.

"What?" They chorused together.

Bethany Anne's eyes narrowed. "That!" She pointed to John's neck. "The silver trophy pin on your lapel?"

"Oh, this?" John answered, so smooth ice wouldn't melt in his mouth. "These are just, ahh…" He faltered when he noticed her look. "You want to see it?"

Bethany Anne's face turned happy. "Sure!" She held her hand out. "Let's see all of them, shall we?"

The other three guys' eyes darted to each other. Perhaps they had overplayed their hand?

The men each dropped the little silver symbols into Bethany Anne's hand.

TOM.

Yes?

Is it possible to change the energy I pull from the Etheric and turn it to heat?

Sure. Wait, why?

I want to make a point.

You know that molten metal would burn into your hands and your healing would or at least should heal over the wound, making it a problem to get out, right?

Okay, how do I melt this metal?

Ummmmm. TOM went quiet for a moment. **Probably need an iron crucible, and you would use the Etheric to create an electromagnetic induction wavelength causing an eddy current to heat up the metal.**

Bethany Anne looked around the room and spotted a small mug used for decoration.

Grabbing the small cup, she lifted, but apparently, it was strictly decoration, and some smart individual had decided to glue it down so it wouldn't fall off if something happened to the ship.

TOM, is this thing good for me to use?

TOM explained what she would need to do to create the correct field, and it took only a couple of seconds before she felt some heat in the mug.

Yup, the right stuff.

The guys winced when Bethany Anne ripped the decorative mug off of the sideboard table. "Someone should fix that." She brought the gray mug to the table. "So," she started and dropped the four pins into the mug. "I know these might have looked like little trophy pins, so quaint and cute."

She looked around and spotted a towel. "Scott, would you mind bringing me that towel?" He turned to see where she was looking and stood up from his chair. A couple of steps there and back, and they were good to go again as Bethany Anne held the mug in her right hand with the towel between her and the cup and her other hand on top.

Then, it got weird...er.

She concentrated, and the guys quickly smelled melting metal as little wisps of smoke escaped the lid of the mug.

Fuck, fuck, fuck, FUUUUCK that's hot! Bethany Anne screamed mentally.

To the guys, it looked like she just casually put the towel and the mug down on the table. John and Darryl leaned over the table and looked into the mug.

Their four trophy pins were nothing but a puddle of metal at the bottom of the cup.

"Those," she exclaimed, "are not approved Queen's Bitches' uniform pins. Are we clear?"

"Sure, sounds good," Eric chimed in. He noticed her look. "I mean, yes, ma'am?"

She nodded. "Now that we have that little discussion out of the way, I understand you have all spoken to Barnabas?"

"Yes," they replied.

"Suggestions?"

"Two of us go and protect each family. If they are attacked, step in and stop it," Scott replied.

"There are three families, and who is going to stay with me? Or, are you guys willing to leave me alone?" she asked.

"Not likely." John grimaced. "I pulled the short...uh, I mean, I am the designated lead on your protective detail."

Bethany Anne ignored his comment. "Who makes up the three teams?"

"Darryl and Nathan for the Switzers." John pulled up some notes on his tablet. "Scott and Barnabas get the McWhorters, and Eric and Gabrielle have the Gants." He sat down his tablet.

"Barnabas is going?" she asked him.

John shrugged. "It's not like it wouldn't be a good thing. The old man needs to get out and play sometimes, too."

"So." She smiled and waved her hand in a circle. "Those who on guard duty are looking forward to it, right?"

"Hell, yes," Darryl exclaimed, his eyes fairly sparkling. "We get to hide in the shadows, and take out bad guys who have horrible intentions, and completely fuck up the unsuspecting assholes."

Bethany Anne's smile stayed on her face as the men laughed at Darryl's enthusiasm. She turned to John and asked, her smile falling, "And you drew the short straw, right?"

The guys' grins all faded.

John shrugged and smiled back at her. "Hey, we can't leave you alone by yourself. Otherwise, you go blow up houses and shit."

Bethany Anne shook her head and reached out to the mug, turned it over, and knocked it against the towel on the table. After a few blows, a small lump of metal dropped onto the towel, and she put the mug to the side.

"Your pins, guys."

She winked at the four men and stood up. Then she disappeared.

"Awwww, shit," Eric complained. "I don't think she enjoyed the little trophy pins."

John scratched under his chin. "I wonder what she's going to do when everyone in the ship wears theirs?"

Tokyo, Japan

"I know." Yuko spoke softly but Akio could hear her over the train. "You are not happy leaving the sword. But I am very appreciative that you allowed me this chance to walk outside without fearing someone's arm might get cut off."

Akio smiled. "I think you have more concern than is warranted, little Vicereine."

Yuko's lips compressed. "That isn't funny. I'm not anyone special."

"You are now, so learn from it, Yuko. I have plenty of knowledge to impart, and I am willing to do so. You can choose to receive it in a manner that is easy to bear, or you can learn from your mistakes. Either way, you will learn," Akio told her, his voice firm. "There are no other options. The Queen commands it, and we will obey. That is the title she has bestowed while you lead her people in Japan in her place."

"She gives me too much responsibility," Yuko argued.

"She gives you what you can step into, not that with which you are comfortable. Notice how much support she has offered. You have internalized the knowledge you have acquired from your many efforts to seek information, and now you must do so again. This time, we are here to protect, to defend, and to make sure those who would look down on our Queen by looking down on her representative are taught otherwise."

"Honor in life," Yuko replied. "And Honor in death." Yuko closed her eyes and thought about what she had learned. She reached up and touched a button on her dress collar.

"ADAM?" she subvocalized.

>>Yes, Yuko?<<

"Are we confirmed?"

>>We are, Vicereine.<<

"Oh, not you too!" she hissed. Beside her, Akio allowed a small smirk to show as he continued surveillance.

>>Why not me, too? You are still my friend, are you not? A title is a title. It could be Secretary Yuko or High Janitor Yuko, could it not? Think less of the title and more about the project.<<

"ADAM, what would I do without your understanding?"

>>Whine a little more to Akio, would be my guess.<<

Yuko was silent for a moment. "Okay, both of you, I will stop whining and do my best. This is another challenge, but one in the Outernet. I am Vicereine Arakawa Yuko for her Royal Highness Bethany Anne to Japan. I will not dishonor my charge by failing to give it my best effort."

>>And always be my friend.<<

"Always," she whispered.

The train pulled into the station, and two people stepped off. Around them, a cushion of space occurred without any obvious explanation. Those walking subconsciously felt a strong desire to stay away from them. The woman, in a fashionably cut suit, followed the taller man, dressed in a fashion that was contemporary, and yet felt centuries old. He kept his attention focused toward the front and the sides.

Few would notice the three men who followed closely in their wake, blending in. They seemed to slide through the crowd, keeping up with the two in front of them easily.

They were the three Elite backup, protecting the Vicereine's back.

There were two operations in play right now for the Queen, and Yuko's was but one. Akio had a second, and soon a third would join them.

Their Queen never did anything half-assed.

Unless, Akio thought, you count going out to search for and rescue a small child without her Guards. You could always depend on her to let emotions run those operations.

And, Akio wouldn't change Bethany Anne in the least if he could.

She helped keep life interesting. Like now.

Gangnam District, Seoul, South Korea

The two Chinese men stepped out of the limousine and nodded to the driver, who closed the door behind them. The streets were alive, since Gangnam had turned what was once a low-rent district to one that equated to Beverly Hills with a mixture of New York City or Tokyo thrown into the mix.

They were shown through the door of the club, past those who waited to get in, and then ushered around the huge dance floor, thus avoiding the young people listening to the K-pop beats and dancing.

Neither of the two men nor the gentleman leading them to the back spoke. Had they wanted to, it would have been a mostly unsuccessful effort to yell at each other.

Chaoxiang hated clubs, but this was where he and his partner had been told to come and do business. His Chinese bosses, those working in military intelligence, wanted the technology it was rumored the Japanese would get to access, and no Japanese Yakuza member would collaborate with the Chinese directly.

They hated each other.

It wasn't that the Japanese liked the South Koreans either, but the two countries had a formidable enemy in China. As the local eight-hundred-pound gorilla, they suffered doing business with a less distasteful ally.

Now, Chaoxiang needed to hire Japanese Yakuza for a major operation, and also needed a cutout to hide any knowledge that China had had a hand in it.

One major mountain range demolished was a suitably large warning, so his bosses didn't want to risk another direct attempt. Plus, if the Japanese ended up pointing the fingers at either their own people or the South Koreans, it would be bonus points.

The man leading them into the back pushed on a piece of the wall that opened, outlining a door that had been hard to see in the darkness of the club.

Once the three men got through the door, their ears were happy to be saved from the constant pounding of the music.

The back of the club was clean, and Chaoxiang and his partner were shown into a small room. Inside, they were met by a young, attractive lady with long black hair and a ready smile. She took their orders for drinks and left. Chaoxiang noticed that crystal methamphetamine and ecstasy were available as selections alongside the liquor.

Moments later, two members of the local criminal organization stepped in. Once the introductions were accomplished, Chaoxiang got down to business.

He wanted information from a certain group in Japan, and he wanted the response to stay in Japan if the project went bad.

The two South Korean gentlemen smiled. They both understood this could be a nice operation. The group the Chinese wanted to hit was their enemy as well, and the potential value of the information was millions. The Chinese would expect the information, but, they understood copies would be made, right?

If they would be able to make the Japanese take the fall for the crime? Well, that would be considered a job bonus. His group might have to work with the Japanese, but liking them was entirely another matter.

Las Vegas, NV, USA

"Now, I'm not complaining, exactly." Nathan sipped his coffee while waiting for the light to change. "But our little girl has a sleep schedule from hell, I swear it."

Darryl followed the instructions from the GPS on his phone. They had stored the F12berlinetta in a rented garage and now drove an all-black Mercedes S550. It kind of pissed Darryl off since he had been looking forward to using the flying car, but all they had gotten to do was come over from Colorado in it.

"Too easy to spot," had been the reasoning, and Darryl agreed with the assessment, but didn't like it. It took away from riding in the car.

Still, the S550 was a sweet ride, and he did admit it was fast as hell.

"Eyes on the targets?" Darryl asked.

Nathan turned to look at his little tablet. "Still good. Arch-Angel's little techie spies are on the job. In another," he looked up at the time, "five minutes, we can tell overwatch we got this."

"Sounds good." Darryl turned into a pleasant neighborhood. It wasn't, according to John, as nice as Mason's, but it was new, and fortunately, it didn't have a security post.

Well, good for them, not so good for Mr. and Mrs. Switzer.

———

"You going to eat that?" Gabrielle asked, watching Eric lovingly pat the large styrofoam container sitting between them in the car.

"Yes, I am going to eat that," he agreed. "I'm going to open the lid, inhale the delicious aroma, and sip the broth like the golden, delicious nectar of the gods it is."

"And then?" she asked, eyeing the cup like it might have a snake inside that was waiting to bite her. "What is it called?"

"*Posole*," Eric replied, turning left down a side street. "With an 'e' at the end."

"Okay, *posole* with an e," Gabrielle repeated. "Just know that you are eating a kiss-blocker until your mouth smells better."

"Seriously?" Eric asked, jerking his hand away from the cup.

Gabrielle took a couple of extra-loud sniffs and nodded.

Twenty seconds later, Eric pulled into a stop-n-rob, and Gabrielle looked around. "Why are we stopping?"

Eric jumped out, ran inside, and was back out before her voice had finished echoing in the car. He slid something in a brown bag into the spot next to the styrofoam cup.

"And that is?" Gabrielle asked.

"Kissing Roto-Rooter," Eric told her. "Cinnamon schnapps."

"What?" She looked at him. "You're covering the *posole with an e* with alcohol?"

Eric smiled. "No, it's mouthwash."

Gabrielle shook her head and punched him in the shoulder. "Have your cake and eat it, too?"

"No, I wouldn't dream of that," Eric replied, pulling into the Gants' neighborhood. "I want my posole and your kisses, too."

Gabrielle reached over and patted Eric on the arm where she had slugged him. "Well played, Mr. Escobar, well played."

Nice muscles, Mr. Escobar, nice muscles indeed, she thought.

"So, you haven't driven in how long?" Scott asked Barnabas, the two of them heading to North Las Vegas.

"It wasn't that long ago. In fact, I had to drive here in Las Vegas. Well, outside of it," Barnabas answered.

"That's right, you took care of the assassin, right?"

Barnabas snorted. "Not so much an assassin as a gravedigger and trigger-puller. He played on the stupidity of those sent to him mostly. Once or twice, he shot someone from a distance, I didn't dig too deeply to get the details."

Scott shrugged. "Dead men tell no tales. Didn't you use that last grave for him?"

"Karma," Barnabas replied.

The two men settled into an easy quiet as Scott drove their car to a street one over from the McWhorters and slowed to a stop next to the curb. With ArchAngel watching the house, Scott decided they would run from one street over if anything looked amiss. That way, no one was going to see them casing the house.

And no one could possibly imagine how fast they could arrive.

CHAPTER EIGHT

QBS *ArchAngel*

"Did you say twenty-one fucking *years*?" Bethany Anne asked, her voice pitched an octave higher than normal. John and Peter both stopped in their tracks, turning around when Bethany Anne stopped walking.

Peter raised an eyebrow at John, who shrugged in return. By the look on her face, it was obvious she had just been surprised by either ADAM or TOM. Peter gave John the sign language for "A" and John shook his head, signed back "T."

The bet was on.

Bethany Anne's eyes rolled. "Why the hell didn't you tell me?" Her shoulders dropped. "Yeah, I do remember that. Dammit." She started walking again, and when she came up even with the guys, they kept pace. "When the fuck am I ever going to remember to stop being so impatient?"

This time, the comment seemed to be directed at herself, not one of her mental roomies.

"What happened, boss?" John asked.

She turned to look up at him. "You know how I demanded seven years of servitude from Captain Kael-ven T'chmon?"

"Yes," John replied. "How did twenty-one years come into play?"

"How did you know it was twenty-one?" Bethany Anne's eyes went distant for a fraction of a second. "I said that out loud, didn't I?" Both men agreed she had. "Dammit." She paused and sighed. "Seems that he agreed to seven solar years. My impatient little ass didn't listen to TOM when he tried to explain that their solar year isn't equivalent to our solar year. So, the translation stuff changed everything to the normal solar year, which is—"

She got cut off as John jumped in. "Three of our years." He snorted. "Leave your home, travel the galaxy, become the Earth's first alien slave." He chuckled. "Perhaps you should take a couple of lessons in negotiation."

"Perhaps," Bethany Anne agreed. "Or maybe I should allow TOM to interrupt me and actually warn me next time."

They reached the conference room doors, and before she walked in, Bethany Anne hissed, "Perhaps then, I wouldn't have alien tagalongs for the next twenty-one fucking years!"

The room was large and had two specially made seats, more like small couches without backs, in which Captain Kael-ven T'chmon and Scientist Royleen were sitting at the moment. Presently, Kiel was working with the Wechselbalg in another part of the ship. He got to learn about fighting Wechselbalg and how to take a beating for killing Coach.

Often.

Apparently, half the Yollin crew supported their captain and took his oath as their own. Now, she had half a damned ship's worth of vassals she didn't want.

Fuck my life, she thought.

On the other hand, Team BMW and most of the people based in science and mechanical loved the new toys. Royleen, when he saw those who were waiting for repatriation were going to live, had decided to give his oath of obedience as well. It wasn't a bad place, but it didn't have much to do for a scientist who needed to continue learning.

The *G'laxix Sphaea*, or as she found out the translated name, the *Dawn of a Golden Future*, was being worked on right now by a large team. Some were going through and making sure they knew what was what. Others were seeing what technology they could acquire or use, and a third group was updating the ship for Bethany Anne.

When Bethany Anne got a good look at the sleek craft, she blurted, "That ship is beautiful." She paused for three seconds before adding, "Mine!"

It wasn't long before the scientific and research teams started working on the new ship. So far, they didn't have a clone of ArchAngel to install in the craft, but Marcus and others were working on that as well. The biggest challenge had been locating a viable place to work on the spacecraft. This time, Stephen had come to the rescue. He still owned a number of warehouses, and those who worked in them still understood Stephen's requirement for secrecy.

So, Team BMW got working on it. Pod shuttles raced from the asteroid belt with the best workers for the new technology. They had filled three huge warehouses with the new ship under cover of night and a meteor shower.

The team dropped some very small meteors—they got the idea from the Chinese operation—and lit up the Mediterranean sky. A little subterfuge with the satellites by ADAM, and the Queen's people and one alien spaceship were safely hidden inside the warehouses, which were guarded by some very, very deadly people.

The first attachments to the space ship were temporary gravitic plates that could be controlled by TOM or ADAM in case they needed to get the ship out of there.

Once they accomplished this first step, the orders were changed to have everyone stop attackers long enough to load into the ship, and the antigravs would take most away.

The remaining Wechselbalg were stationed to harass attackers until the ship was away, then they would disappear into the surrounding area and be picked up later.

Once the plates were in place, plans for gravitic shields and the gun emplacements were drawn for installation.

Then everyone got down to some serious work.

"Gentleman, ladies, and aliens," Bethany Anne began. "We need to discuss what it is going to take to move forward with our plans so that people can go through that Gate." She sat down at the head of the table. "Talk to me, Michelle," Bethany Anne told Dr. Brown-Williams, who was in charge of the food production, while accepting a Coke over her shoulder from Peter and twisting the top off.

Dr. Brown-Williams nodded. "We have more than enough production for plant and protein, with the new growth containers based on the fully nutrient-focused setup. We have the right fish in the tanks to create the fertilizer that goes through the system to feed the plants that in turn clean the water fed back into the fish tanks. With the corrected light systems, the fish are breeding now as well. We've added the crustaceans some of the teams have asked for."

"Oh, God!" Bobcat blurted. "I'm going to get crab in outer space?"

Dr. Brown-Williams smiled. "Yes, Bobcat, you're going to get crab in outer space. Perhaps not a large variety, as we are dealing more with the farming of shrimp, but crab is in the plans."

"What about wheat, corn, and such?" Bethany Anne asked.

"If you can provide the space, I can grow them. With the light amplification systems, we can now generate the right wavelength to feed the growth systems, and the gravity plates help tremendously. I've talked to Marcus about water, and he confirms that we can change the water D to H ratio on the comets we can grab and use the water available from them for personal use and foodstuffs."

"How much space do you need?" Bethany Anne pressed.

"I'm modifying the needs now based on growing fungi and yeasts and using the new 3D printing to make them palatable. We've stocked up like crazy on some items, such as spices. They just aren't something we can produce effectively. I've got enough of the nutrients to fill a small moon."

"Yeah, funny you should mention 'moon,'" Bobcat interjected. Bethany Anne put up a hand and he stopped, allowing Dr. Brown-Williams to continue.

"So, for the massive number of people you have asked me to consider, and with the systems we can use based on the latest Kurtherian technology for energy and gravity, we can stack food production like crazy. We're going to have more of a problem with protein, except for the 3D-printed stuff.

"But we can use the droppings from the livestock as fertilizer for the plants. I'm going to need many square kilometers of land with a pretty substantial height to create hydroponics for growing our food. One kilometer gives me a million square meters to play with. Not including walkways, the higher we go, I get another million cubic meters to play with per one and a half meters of height. For animals, I need to grow twenty pounds of greens for each pound of beef we raise."

"Good thing Nathan isn't here, or he would be crowing how the Wechselbalg will have to start eating more vegetables." Those who knew Nathan was the only Wechselbalg who truly enjoyed eating vegetables chuckled.

"We can easily get over a hundred thousand plants a week from the hundred and twenty Freight Farms growtainers we have. Plus, with the enhancements we've been adding, we expect to triple that output," Dr. Brown-Williams added before summing up her findings. "You find me enough space to easily get into the containers or duplicate the technology outside of the boxes, and I can feed a million people."

"People are going to need to start porking each other to get us to a million." William grinned, but Dr. Brown-Williams only caught some of the comment.

"I'm sorry, I didn't plan on pork in the mix. Should I?" she asked, oblivious to the chuckles from Bobcat, William, and Marcus, who kept his face straight while his friends smiled.

"No. Maybe, although some will miss bacon once our stores are depleted," Bethany Anne replied.

"Not necessarily true," Dan interrupted. "I've spoken to those in charge of food for the Yollins, and they have a similar saying to our chicken."

"What, everything tastes like chicken?" Bethany Anne asked.

Kael-ven T'chmon chuckled, the sound coming out more like a raspy clicking of mandibles around his mouth. When he spoke, everyone with the new translation software and the embeds for communications could understand him. The rest had translation hardware and a single earpiece. Both of the Yollins had a similar setup for communication.

"I have had your chicken." Kael-ven grimaced. "It is rather plain, like a talik, which is everywhere. I have had your pork, and it is pretty tasty, similar to our bistok-barook. There are plenty of the animals on the southern plains of many of our continents."

"If it's so tasty, why don't you eat it?" Bethany Anne asked.

"We do eat them, just not very often, since they are expensive. Bistok-barook are very aggressive and have no herd mentality, so they are a very poor choice to use as a food animal. They are considered a sport kill within the third and fourth tiers of our society. However, you have to be willing to take the limitations to actually claim a bistok-barook kill, or you will be sent back out with a knife to kill one. Society will shun you forever for having tried to gain the prestige dishonorably."

"What are you allowed to kill them with?" John asked.

"Anything you can hold in your hands, but you cannot have on powered armor," Kael-ven replied.

"Wait," Bethany Anne asked, "how big is this animal?"

Kael-ven turned to the scientist. "Would you care to explain?"

The Yollin scientist nodded. Royleen had been lambasted substantially, and in a few areas bettered, by the human scientists he had previously wanted to use as test subjects. The humans, meanwhile, had to try to realize that to him, humans were equivalent to the monkeys people had been using for test subjects for centuries, and in some societies, still did.

"The bistok-barook is a six-legged sinewy creature when young, and can travel a great distance. They grow up to over three thousand of your kilos. They are omnivorous but prefer meat. Most of them are what you consider dominant, so they are not herd animals, and simply recognize that they should not stick together for any amount of time, or fights occur. At least, outside of mating. As they get older, their ability to travel long distances wanes and they fatten up. They are still incredibly quick for a shorter distance, say a..." the scientist faltered for a moment, calculating, "couple of your kilometers, and of course, they are able to stand their ground quite well. They have some protective carapace around their shoulders and heads, but most of the body is unprotected. They do have horns, usually around this long." He held his two front arms out in front of him, separated by about two feet.

He continued, "In our society, it is considered too low an activity for a second-tier member to make an effort to kill one."

Here, Kael-van interrupted Royleen. "That is because someone in the past decided it was stupid to do so, and made a tier-level decision that it was beneath anyone on our level to go on these hunts. Personally, I think they had an offspring who was going to try, and therefore, it was decreed to be beneath us. Most likely because it would show that we get ourselves killed by foolish means as often as the third tier if we did this publicly."

Bethany Anne raised an eyebrow and considered Kael-van's declaration. He had mentioned on more than one occasion his criticisms of the tiered society of the Yollins and their desire to "do it this way because this is how we always did it" belief in moving society forward.

"Okay, sounds like the Wechselbalg will have something to do to help fill up the larders with meat," Dan announced. Everyone turned back to the conversation at hand, and Bethany Anne nodded her agreement.

"Thank you, Kael-van and Royleen." She added, "Okay, food seems to be on track. However, we need a base...no, a fortress, to protect our people if our ships are in battle."

"Well, about that," Bobcat started before Marcus interrupted.

"What they want to build," Marcus pointed at his two friends, "is a Death Star." His look told Bethany Anne that this time, he thought the two guys were asking for something over the top.

"Complete with a planet-destroying laser?" she asked.

William smiled. "Well, I wouldn't turn that down, but who the hell destroys a planet? Anyone realize how wasteful that is?"

Bobcat took up the conversation. "Yeah, I mean, the poor little bistok-boorokies would be killed too."

"And there goes our bacon," William added.

"Can't have that," Bobcat replied.

"Word," William agreed. Bethany Anne saw Marcus's eyes roll up to the ceiling. She was going to have to get this conversation back on track.

"Guys?" she interrupted them. "Can we focus on what you want to create rather than the latest imagined bistok-barook recipe?"

"Sorry, boss," Bobcat replied. "But I loves me some pork, and the thought of laughing my ass off at a bunch of Wechselbalg who have to go kill the pork is funny. Okay, we want to grab a large nickel-iron asteroid and get inside the thing and drill it out. We'll use the outside to store the massive number of shipping containers for a while, until we've drilled enough inside to move people and content in, and then we'll use the gravitic drives in concert to move the asteroid."

"Excuse me for being dense, pun intended," Bethany Anne asked, "but isn't nickel-iron rather hard?"

"I can answer that," Royleen spoke. He was getting used to having the ability to interrupt outside of the caste system. These humans seemed to have a system based on roles, but when it came to conversations, it was appropriate to add and interject as necessary without being considered rude. Rude, Royleen found out, was a type of hierarchy filter in conversations. "Nickel-iron is hard. However, the Yollins have been working in outer space for many of your centuries, and have methods to drill into the asteroid and produce valuable products at the same time as we hollow out the inside."

"It isn't quite like slicing through butter with a hot knife," Marcus admitted, "but it's very fast. It's approximately like us drilling through coal. The difference is that their mechanicals will eat into the asteroid and then send it through a processing core that will separate a lot of the metals for us. It helps move the production forward. We can, of course, turn that piece of the machine off, and it will create stackable bricks for speed."

"So, it drills and separates the metals into the constituent ores, and prepares them for final smelting. Do I understand this correctly?"

"Yes," Marcus agreed.

"You have one of these?" she asked.

"Oh, no," Royleen replied. "We do not. However, we do have the schematics for three different sizes of the machines in our databases."

"How fast can this machine be built and tested?" she asked.

"Probably about six months, boss," William answered her. "I've gone shopping for the best machining and fabrication machines the Japanese have, and if we get the right stuff, we can start by getting some of the components created on Earth in different countries. But some of the stuff is advanced tech we need to make ourselves out in the belt."

Bethany Anne thought about it for a second. "How many of these machines are you looking to build?"

"At least four," Bobcat answered. "Always running two, one for immediate backup, and a third for separate operations outside of the core. Then, we'll create self-replicating machines to start the second stages of the building of parts. Using an M-class asteroid, we would have a lot of the basic material, but we'll need to add in the more complicated items as required. They, in turn, continue mining as we expand."

"Separate operations?"

"Sure," Bobcat answered. "We'll want dock areas. Somewhere ships can connect with us and have interactions, but easily separated from our inside area and safe. Probably two, actually. One for our own ships to dock if we want to keep it separate and far apart. No need for anyone to easily attack our ships as well and try to gain entrance inside."

"Okay," Bethany Anne agreed. "What about light?"

"We're good there," Marcus answered. "We have enough energy through the Etheric to power what is effectively a large incandescent using a version of a Yollin heat source. The light it usually produces is in the red spectrum, but we can tune it to something closer to our yellow and tweak for heat output. We'll have about four different cutouts to make sure it doesn't super-nova inside the base—"

"A bad result for everyone inside, I'm sure," Bethany Anne interrupted.

"Yes, it would be," Marcus admitted. "If they didn't fry immediately, the cold would get them soon after.

"So, how safe is this going to be?" she pressed. "I don't want to be worried about a fake sun going supernova inside my people's base."

Marcus hummed a bit before answering. "Honestly, I think we wouldn't need but one cutout. I've worked four various safety breaks to continue the heat and light, each one progressively separating the power into smaller and smaller sources. That way, at the end, we have twenty-seven small heat sources, and if any of them malfunction, they just go dead. The chance of a catastrophic failure after level four is less than our own sun dying soon."

Bethany Anne thought about it. "Okay, but triple check those numbers, please." Marcus nodded. Bethany Anne pursed her lips. "Right. We have food, shelter, power, and water covered at the moment. I've seen the plans to have the rails and regions broken out like a city. Confirm we have protection capability and figure out how we're going to deal with attacks from the outside. I have reviewed the idea of making it large enough for ships to pass into, but I'm not sure about that idea yet. Let's discuss the ships, the warriors, and the new toys Jean Dukes wants to play with…"

CHAPTER NINE

Nathan nudged Darryl. They had moved the car to a spot outside the neighborhood because they had been passed during a patrol sweep by the local police. They decided that not getting asked questions was better than sticking closer. With *ArchAngel* overhead, they hoped to get some advance warning, and it looked like they had it.

There was a black van pulling into the subdivision. Darryl started the car. In seconds, he had pulled into the main street and was quickly catching up to the van, which was keeping to a sedate pace inside the neighborhood. As the vehicle made its third turn, traveling deeper into the community, it was evident this wasn't a false alarm.

They passed the main entrance to the subdivision and turned down a side street that paralleled the neighborhood. Down at the end, the guys pulled off the road. They jumped out and ran, easily vaulting the six-foot fence, to dodge through the children's toys strewn about the backyard, then vaulted the fence one more time. This brought them out on the street across from the Switzers' house. Nathan and Darryl quickly backtracked into the bushes beside the neighbor's house and watched as the headlights from the dark van pulled onto the street.

"Looks like we get to play tonight after all," Nathan murmured.

Darryl looked at his friend. "You sound like a man who's been cooped up inside too long."

"That's because I'm a man who has been cooped up inside too long. I know Ecaterina tries her best to understand, but even with the workouts with the other guys, it isn't the same as going against someone who really doesn't mean you well."

"Yeah," Darryl agreed. "I get that. She tell you anything important before you left?"

Nathan smiled in the dark. "Yeah, she won't forgive me for getting killed and leaving her to raise our baby all by herself. Apparently, that wasn't enough of a warning, so she told me she would raise the little lady to be a Steelers fan."

Darryl whistled. "Damn, went right for the nuclear option, didn't she?"

"Yeah, can't let little Christina grow up a to be a Steelers fan. Or even worse, a Coke fan, too." Darryl smiled.

"God, no!" Nathan spat. "A Coca-Cola drinking, terrible-towel-waving female? Hell, I'd be prouder if she danced on a pole."

"No!" Darryl laughed.

"Well, not really, but it was funny, right?" Nathan grinned. "Looks like our fun has arrived."

"Let them go in?"

"Yeah, that's part of the agreement," Nathan replied. "When the first set goes in, we need to hit any left in the van."

"Modified BA blood for the win," Darryl agreed as he checked the gun, confirming the sleepy darts were locked and loaded and just waiting for a trigger pull.

"They work better than the name-brand sleepy darts," Nathan replied. "Looks like we have three...no, four leaving the back of the van. Nicely outfitted in all black with head cover. Seems like they got their gear from the same store."

"What, Terrorists-r-Us?" Darryl asked.

"Well, I'm not sure you could call them terrorists so much as Black-Ops-r-Us." The guys could see, on their protective glasses, the input from ArchAngel's drones. Two had split off and were heading around the back of the house. The Switzers had a dog that got off one bark before it was silenced.

Permanently.

"Okay, that's good enough for me." Nathan's eyes went yellow as he started running, but he found he was already late to the game. Darryl had bolted across the street and flung open the van door. Nathan heard two *pffts* from the pistol as he passed the van, running all-out on his way to the backyard.

Those two assholes were his to play with.

Nathan saw the two enter the back door, setting off the internal alarm the guys had installed to help hide any noise as they came into the house behind the attackers. ArchAngel would immediately shut down any communications coming out of this group to their home base once the alarm went off.

Nathan had always sought to overcome, to be better, to find new ways to accomplish goals, and under Bethany Anne's tutelage and with tweaks with the Pod-doc, he had accomplished his own version of enhancements and upgrades.

He could mutate just parts of his body. Like, for instance, his chest and arms, and his oh-so-gloriously-destructive hands and nails.

The two jerk-offs had just entered the downstairs hallway and were heading quickly to the main floor bedroom. That was where the adults would have been if they hadn't been warned by Mason and Sheila.

Now, there were a couple of mannequins under the sheets. Nathan had just arrived at the master suite door when the two he was following unloaded three taps to each body in the bed.

Jack Caton didn't like his orders, but he had decided years ago that the group's best protection was secrecy, and he and his teams knew having to silence those who had a life outside the project was a possibility.

Silencing those who had needed a normal life. Wife, kids, and soccer games on the outside. Basically, crutches and millstones around their necks.

Risks.

He hated the damned alarm, shrieking and forcing him and his team to do this without the professionalism he would have preferred.

Jack raised his suppressed Beretta M9A3 and fired a three-shot burst into his targets. He wasn't sure if Switzer was sleeping on the left or the right when he fired. He started to move forward to check his kill. Alarm or no, something didn't seem right. Then he heard a scream from right behind him.

Nathan, his right hand sprouting five-inch claws rammed his arm like a jackhammer through the first guy he came to. He got off a scream as Nathan lifted him into the air and flung him sideways, blood spraying the walls in an arc as the body slammed into the wall.

Jack turned to his right, bringing his Beretta around as he watched Kolman's dead body flung easily into the wall.

SHIT! He tried to get his gun on point, but his hand was caught in a crushing grip as the half-man, half beast smiled at him. "I don't like those who kill animals indiscriminately," the thing told him, his yellow eyes penetrating the gloom.

Jack's arm was caught in a vice-like grip as his own pistol was turned and the barrel placed under his jaw. "Life for a life," the guttural voice growled, and a furry hand pushed his trigger finger back.

The blood splatter hit the ceiling, and Nathan dropped the second commando. He smelled Darryl and turned around.

Darryl was looking around the room. "Damn, you Wechselbalg are so fucking messy."

"Incoming, contact in seventy-two seconds," both men heard from their implants.

"Time to skedaddle." Darryl turned around. Nathan started running, knowing he wasn't going to catch up with the man, but he would be there by the time Darryl tossed him a body as he passed the van.

They easily carried the two from the van as they jumped over the fence to get back to the car.

"Sure wouldn't have been able to pack these assholes in the F12," Darryl agreed as they tossed the sleeping bodies into the car and pulled back onto the road, avoiding the arrival of the first responders by thirty seconds.

Berlin, Germany

Terry nodded to the taxi driver and stepped out of the cab. He had been on a minor bender for the last week. Melissa had slapped him one last time, then she left him in New York after the American government brought them back from the aircraft carrier where TQB had dropped them off.

Apparently, his military mindset, which he wasn't changing, still concerned her deeply. She fanned the flames of a small argument into a raging inferno and left town, going back, he supposed, to her university.

Never calling him back.

Still, he couldn't drink her kisses away, or her eyes, or her smell.

Damn. He had tried. Oh, lordy, how he had tried.

He sighed and walked toward the hotel, on another mission to retrieve something no one should probably be trying to attain. He sure hoped it wasn't back to the Sandpit again. That sand always got in the wrong crevice, and there isn't any polite way to get it out in mixed company.

The first call came in, warning him about a second call and suggesting he would want to drink some coffee. The second opportunity was the same as last time.

He had exactly forty-six minutes to wake up and slug through two cups of the nectar from the god of life and goodwill before the second call came in. The voice had a German accent and it promised an interview, all expenses paid, to get him to Germany and back if it didn't work out.

He sighed and told them he could be at the airport within four hours.

That had been yesterday morning. Now, Terry was in Germany looking at a hotel that was probably built two hundred years ago and would be here two hundred years after he died.

Sliding through the front doors, he made his way to the front desk and received instructions about how to get to the conference room. He was surprised when the door was guarded by a pair of men who were competent, brisk, and experienced. The hard kind of experience.

These guys were either still in the military and on loan for this, or recently retired. His ID was checked, and then he was allowed inside.

Good thing he had left his weapons back in his hotel room.

This room was arranged a little differently than his last job. There were people sitting at the front behind a table, and about twelve people in the first two rows of chairs. He was the first to sit in the third row, with two empty rows behind him. There were five seats on each side, the main aisle down the middle splitting them.

Most of those here seemed to have tasks, so he pulled out a tablet and started to see if he could figure out who these characters were.

By the time the meeting started, four more people had entered.

There was some rustling of papers, and Terry put down his tablet to give them his attention.

There was a woman in red on the left, an older gentleman in the middle, and another on the right, both men in suits. The gentleman in the center stood up. "My name is Dr. Schäuble, and I appreciate all of you joining us on such short notice. We seem to be missing two people, so either they have decided not to join us, or perhaps traffic has not worked in their favor. Either way, we will not hold you up because they have been rude."

He took a drink of his water and then set the glass back down. "This expedition, and trust me, it will be an expedition, is a research effort comprised of private companies in concert with support from the German government. The support is not as overt as perhaps we would like, but we do have deeper pockets and access to information we might not have had otherwise."

To Terry's right in the corner was a screen, and Dr. Schäuble pointed to it and pressed a small button. A slide came up, and Terry's blood went cold.

The title was Operation Highjump.

"We are looking to sail a ship to a particular location in Antarctica, where it is rumored, backed up by information the German government has shared, there is a base started by people from here in Germany in the 1930s. There were many in…" Dr. Schäuble's voice droned on about the location, but Terry was already tuning him out.

If there was anywhere he hated going more than the Sandpit,

it was into the cold. They could take this operation and shove it up their asses as far as he was concerned.

No fucking way was he freezing his testicles off in the Antarctic.

No way, no how.

The door opened behind him, and a light melodious voice interrupted the speaking man. "I'm sorry for being late. I was caught up in traffic."

Terry hung his head, his shoulders dropping. He knew that voice, and he also knew his choice of whether he was going to go to the Antarctic was now in someone else's hands.

Specifically, it was in her hands. Melissa had apparently been called in for the very same project.

God, he was going to need some good thermal underwear.

Terry was surprised when she tapped him on the shoulder. "Move aside, TH. You can't be allowed to go on this trip without me. You'll just get in trouble." He was trying to come to grips with her even talking to him when he slid to his left, one chair over.

She sat down and bumped him with her butt. "Move a little faster, soldier. I ran the last four blocks to get here."

Terry slid quickly into the next seat, his emotions completely fubar-ed by her actions.

"We shall talk," she hissed to him, "about how you failed to call me back. You military guys have no idea how to act around women. I cried for a week, you ass!" she practically spat.

"*I'm* to blame?" Terry's anger started to get the better of him when a couple of people in front of them turned to look at them. Both he and Melissa mouthed "Sorry" and held in their conversation.

It seemed she was right about one thing. He had no idea how to act around her.

. . .

Las Vegas, NV, USA

When Eric and Gabrielle were notified the hit was happening on the Switzers, they drove the eight houses to pull up in front of the Gants' house. They got out of their car as the Gants came running out of their home.

The teams had placed a couple of monitors and piped in the video of the three locations for Robert, who was having trouble believing his group would kill them.

"Just stay around and park at the small mall," Eric told him. "We'll slip into your bed, and if this is a false alarm, you can drive back here, jump back in bed, and nothing happened, understand?"

Robert nodded and slid into the car. Gabrielle had already closed her door, shutting Mrs. Gant inside. They walked into the house as the Gants drove off.

"Incoming, one minute thirty-six seconds," ArchAngel warned them. Gabrielle shut the front door.

"Not bad, but a little messy on their timing," she qualified as the two of them walked into the master bedroom. Eric was already yanking the power plugs for the monitors and set them on the floor next to the wall.

"Come to bed, baby?" he asked as he slid into the bed and patted the other side. "I promise you a good time." He twitched his eyebrows at her.

"Wow," she replied, sliding into the warm sheets. "You know just how to sweet-talk me into the horizontal position, at least—" Her voice cut off when he slid across and kissed her. "Oh…" She paused for a moment, regrouping her thoughts. "Good call on the mouthwash." She ran her hand up his chest, enjoying the feeling of the goosebumps she was causing on his skin.

"Four exiting a dark van in front."

"Seriously?" Eric turned to look at the door, his eyes starting to glow red.

Gabrielle decided she liked that look on her man. She snuggled against Eric. "Shall we take care of these annoyances and plan another night together, hmmm?"

Eric smiled. "I suppose it would be rude to use someone else's bed. Well, I'm sexually frustrated now, and pissed as hell. Care to take care of the riffraff?"

"Now you are talking like a vampire, Mr. Escobar, and I like it," she purred, and the two turned as men came down the hallway.

"Go, ArchAngel," Eric subvocalized. The alarms started shrilling, and they darted out of bed in the darkness. Eric tossed a small ball that exploded into light, blinding the four men, who had on night vision goggles.

That was when the shouts, yells, and dying began. Eric passed Gabrielle as he streaked out to the street, seeing what kind of fish he had to catch out there.

Moments later, with the driver sedated, Gabrielle came up with one over her shoulder. "He seemed to have a clue, so I decided to bring him along. The other three are done."

Eric closed the van door after shooting the extra guy with a sleeping dart. Gabrielle got into the passenger seat as Eric walked around the other side and got in. They drove off into the night.

CHAPTER TEN

<u>Tokyo, Japan</u>

William was in heaven. Well, if heaven was a large warehouse with some of the latest computer-controlled CNC mills, lathes, and other machines for mass manufacturing. Some of the new machines included contraptions with capabilities he hadn't even known existed yet.

The Japanese had pulled out all the stops to impress the hell out of Bethany Anne.

William had arrived the previous night, and he'd immediately started trying to figure out what his group had, and what they needed to get moving on the project that would result in a new home for Bethany Anne's people.

The base they needed once they went through that Gate.

Might made right in Yollin space, and while Bethany Anne had promised the opportunity for the Yollins in the home system to allow them safe passage, no one, human or alien, was expecting them to take her up on it.

So far, Bethany Anne and the core team believed that only the Yollins had Earth's home location and frankly, the Yollins she had captured had admitted no one was expecting much from them. It wasn't until the end that those on the *G'laxix Sphaea* understood just how much opportunity the little backwater solar system represented. By then, it was too late.

They had been trapped, and couldn't get back out of the system.

Now, William was taking a sabbatical from space to get everything he needed to mass-produce the tools and technologies the teams required to bore out a nickel-iron asteroid about eighty kilometers in circumference.

Moving the big-ass sonofabitch wasn't his problem, thankfully. Marcus had spent many nights yanking his hair out with TOM and others as they figured out using the enormous numbers of the smaller gravitic plates from the shipping containers to help move it. It wasn't like this was going to be speedy. In fact, it was going to take a few years to move the asteroid to the Gate. First, they had to accelerate it, then slow it down as it approached. The ships and the asteroid would go through mostly together. The way he understood it, they had thirty minutes for everything to get through once the first passage happened.

As long as the first passage was an approved ship, that is. Good thing they hadn't blown the Yollin ship to kingdom come or their plans would have been screwed.

Three hours later, his eyes drooping a little, his ears caught the first noise that had struck his mind as being misplaced, but he had been too tired to care much about it.

Akio was walking down the street. He was coming back from making sure Yuko was protected. He had two men with her, and one watching the warehouse at the moment. He was three blocks from the warehouse when he received a signal that a break-in was happening. He started running.

The pistol shots were fired when he was but a block away, and Akio's eyes went red.

The screaming had started as he saw Eiji attack. Something was wrong. Way wrong.

There were too many here.

Not only was this warehouse supposed to be a secret, but there was also no way a hit with this many people involved should be going down. Many of the people weren't fighters but looked like thugs or landsmen. People used for muscle.

Eiji was doing his best, but the sheer mass of people was allowing some to run past him even as he cut down many, dodging as others tried to shoot him, often hitting those in their own group in the process.

Akio ratcheted up his fear projection as he slammed into the back of the group, his sword swinging like a scythe through wheat as he sought to maim and not kill.

If he saw a weapon, however, that person died.

His fear had the desired effect. The people trying to push their way into the warehouse stopped and then started to turn and push their way backward, often finding Eiji or Akio.

"Let them pass!" Akio yelled to Eiji, who nodded his understanding. They certainly had enough people incapable of running to answer questions. Akio was able to grasp from the frightened men that they were Yakuza, or hired by the Yakuza, to hit this warehouse and grab everything they could carry off that didn't look like conventional technology.

That was when Akio heard William yelling from inside the warehouse and two pistol shots.

Akio's eyes flashed completely red, and he pulled a separate knife and started slashing at anyone who dared slow him down as he raced into the warehouse seeking his Queen's friend.

"This stuff has to be worth something, there!" Goro pointed at the large black man, who was writing on a clipboard. He turned around, looking at the trio first in confusion and then in anger.

"Who the fuck are you?" the big black man yelled. "Get the hell out of here before you lose your fool lives."

Not only did the black man look annoyed, but he also didn't seem concerned that Goro and his two buddies had pistols out and pointed at him.

"Not us, you," Goro replied. "Which of these have non-human technology?"

"What the fuck are you talking about?" the black guy responded. "These are all CNC mills and lathes, and over there," he pointed with the clipboard, "are microprocessor manufacturing machines."

"You lie, American!" Goro spat, fear coming over him. His hand jerked twice. "Let's see how well you answer now as you beg I don't shoot you again!" Goro practically yelled at the man. The fear was becoming overwhelming, like it was growing on them. The other two with him were looking around.

Goro kept his attention on the black man, who was leaning back on a large container, blood running down his shirt. "Oh, now you done gone and fucked up," the black man cautioned weakly. "You can kiss your ass goodbye, you poor excuse for a second-rate villain." He paused as he watched Goro striding toward him. "For the record," William coughed, "this shit hurts." He dropped his clipboard and slid down the container to land on his ass.

"Fucking hell!" He groaned. "If I can't eat after this because I'm healing, I swear to God I'll kick your scrawny little Asian ass."

Goro stepped over to the black man and pointed his pistol. "You will tell me where the technology I need is, or I will put this next bullet between your eyes!"

"Motherfucker," the black man wheezed a little, "you should

turn around and pay more attention to *him* than my black ass."
He nodded behind Goro.

Goro looked over his shoulder and watched in alarm as his friend slid off the sword of the person the black man had just warned him about. A man whose eyes were glowing red and looking in his direction. His voice, centuries old and full of anger, spoke, harsh and clipped. "You have hurt my Queen's friend and my charge. He is in pain that you will atone for. You will provide the energy necessary to heal him."

Goro, overcome by fear, couldn't move as he watched the vampire, his teeth growing, walking toward him. "You have come to the end of your life, and you will scream as it ends. This, I promise!"

"Damn." William, squinting, winced in pain. "I wish I had some popcorn for this shit."

Akio dropped the body to the ground, its mouth frozen in pain, the eyes dead.

He walked over to William and pulled up his sleeve. "I am dishonored, but through healing, I may restore you. Will you accept my blood as part of my restitution to make things right?"

"Of course, Akio," William replied. "But if you can do something to help me when you need to get the two slugs out, that would be a fucking beautiful thing, man."

Akio nodded and looked William in the eyes. "Well, hey," William backpedaled. "I didn't mean we needed to go all man-on-man here, brother, you know I like you and all..." William's head slumped as Akio smiled.

Americans, always thinking that every gay guy liked them.

Akio grew his nails, searched, and found both slugs and pulled them out. He slit his wrists to share the nanocytes. He pursed his lips and then slid his finger lengthwise, jabbing the bleeding digit into each of the wounds to push the nanocytes in as far as he could.

Ripping off William's shirt, he wiped down the bleeding area to see if he was healing. Satisfied, Akio pushed awareness back into William's mind, and William slowly started to wake up.

William blinked a few times and grinned weakly. "Did I like it?"

Akio chuckled. "If I didn't know you, William, I would have to kill you for that disrespect."

"Akio," William put his right hand on Akio's left shoulder, "that was no disrespect. That was me treating you like I would treat any brother of mine. That was me speaking to family. If I offended, I'm sorry, but this is all I have to offer you without being false. Just me." William shrugged. "I can no more change me and my smart mouth than you can change what you feel, so can you accept me as well?"

Akio stared at William and considered his explanation. Then Akio put his right hand on William's left shoulder. "I needed to protect you since you are my Queen's dear friend. Now, I will protect you because you are my brother, William."

William smiled. "Good. Now that we got that male bonding bullshit out of the way," William paused dramatically and looked Akio deep in the eyes, "did I like it?"

They laughed together. "You, William," Akio got next to William to help him stand up, "are such an ass."

"Music to my ears, brother." William grunted. "God." William pointed at the very dead Goro. "I would have paid good money to have had some popcorn when you tore him a new asshole."

The two men had taken a few steps before Akio answered, deadpan, "I left his asshole alone, William. He isn't my type."

William busted out laughing and grabbed his midsection, causing them to stop walking. "Oh, God, Akio!" William cried out. "You're killing me again, you jackass!" He laughed and wheezed, trying to catch his breath, his insides still painfully tender.

The two were making their way to the front when Eiji came back. "Clear, and I hear sirens. Do I need…" He looked beyond the two men. "Oh, I need to get rid of some evidence." Akio nodded, and Eiji stepped around the two men and grabbed Goro's dead body.

"They were here for our technology," William explained as they walked. "The dead asshat behind us was looking for our Kurtherian tech. We need to figure out who gave them this location and send a proper response."

Akio nodded sharply. "That I will do gladly. It is time to remind the cockroaches that there is something to fear in the night."

"Oh, fuck me!" William exclaimed. "I'm going to miss the good stuff, aren't I?"

"If you mean the killing and the destruction, I'm afraid so, William," Akio agreed as he helped William sit down in a chair. "I didn't give you enough blood to heal you all the way." He paused in thought, then continued, "I've got some of Bethany Anne's blood back in Yuko's room that would be better for you, plus you have some of her nanites already, correct?"

William nodded, he did.

"We don't want to mix them if we can help it, I understand," Akio temporized.

"Probably not," William agreed as he looked down the hallway at all the dead or moaning bodies. "Fuck, it looks like a Cuisinart went through here."

Akio looked down the corridor. "I should probably have the Vicereine come." Akio grimaced, thinking about her response to the blood. "She will need to be here to represent the Queen."

William chuckled and turned to Akio. "I'll give you ten to one odds she'll throw up at least once."

Akio smiled, looking back down the hallway. "I'll take that. How about an ounce of gold?"

"Huh?" William responded. "Oh, yeah. I guess humanity's money is going away, isn't it?"

Akio nodded. "We are going to go to another system of credits, I understand. But you can always trade gold."

William smiled. "Okay, ten to one, and I bet an ounce of gold."

Yuko bit down hard as her guards Takeshi and Nario brought her through the first set of the wounded, dead, and dying. The stench of the dead mixed with the cries of the wounded as her eyes sought to hide from all of the police strobe lights flicking around in the night.

Her stomach was queasy and threatening to rebel. She did not wish to embarrass herself and therefore, her Queen by vomiting in this place.

She saw Akio and walked over to him. "What happened?"

"We were hit by Yakuza. They understood we had some special technology here for a transfer to the government. Apparently, the information was planted by someone, and they struck earlier due to lack of complete information."

"Is William okay?"

"He was shot twice." When she put up her hand to her mouth, her eyes large, he quickly added, "He will heal and be healthy again, but he will also be tender for a couple of days at a minimum."

Yuko put a hand on Akio's shoulder. "You have blood all over you. Are you and Eiji okay?"

"I am fine, and Eiji is fine as well, but I had him change clothes so it looks like there was only one of us fighting. Many of these," Akio waved at the bodies, "are known criminals, so they are already trying to figure out what to do. As the Queen's

Vicereine, you are the representative." He looked at her, and she gave him a sharp nod.

She understood.

Turning around, she scanned for the clot of important-looking police. She paused a moment and covered her mouth.

"ADAM?"

>>**Yes?**<<

"Find out who the top level officer at my location is, please. Also, I need to have access to anything you can discover about what the police already know or suspect."

>>**Presently, we have local police, but there are two additional agencies on their way here. One is the special investigations team, and the other is public security intelligence, who are arriving without much fanfare. Further, there are others who are trying to limit the press who are also coming at this time. The Japanese press are usually the ones who report on police misdeeds.**<<

Yuko turned and started into the building. "Akio, you and Eiji need to step inside. We must not be seen outside at this time." She walked boldly into the warehouse but wanted to gag at the stench in the hallway. She stepped carefully over the gruesome parts.

Akio came up behind her. "Allow me to carry you over this... mess." Yuko nodded, and Akio gently picked her up and moved through the hallway. He set her down on the other side and William spoke, surprising Yuko.

"Dammit, Yuko." She turned to him as he watched her from his chair. "Why can't you be a normal female just once for me?"

She looked back at Akio, who was smiling. "What is he upset about?"

Akio looked back into the hallway. "We had a bet, and I just won."

She turned to William. "What was the bet?"

He shook his head. "I'll tell you later. Now would be unfair to you and Akio."

She shrugged and looked around, seeing two more dead bodies down in the warehouse. "Are those the two who shot you?" she asked.

"No, that one has left, permanently. But we didn't want him around, so the answer we are giving is 'yes.'" He grunted and added, "ADAM has already pulled the necessary video and stripped the shit we don't want getting out, so we have that to give to the police."

Yuko nodded. "I'll work with ADAM while we wait." She turned to Akio. "How many names do you want?"

"All of them," he answered, his lips set in a firm line.

She nodded and walked to a small desk a few feet from William. "All that I can find, I will give you."

CHAPTER ELEVEN

QBS _ArchAngel_

"So, you two had fun." Scott was drinking his coffee in the cafeteria. "Nathan and Darryl had a good time too, but Barnabas and I got to sit in our car and drink coffee and shoot the shit."

"Not my fault." Eric sat down across from Scott as Gabrielle waved and then headed toward her room.

Scott nodded. "Yeah, we waited all night for someone to attack our location, but we figured the other side losing two sets of team communications caused our hit to be a no-go. Our bait left after the video from Nathan and Darryl's takedown anyway."

"Where are our new guests now?" Eric asked, blowing on his coffee.

"Second set of guest quarters, but I understand they are going to either be repatriated to Earth if they want or moved to quarters in the asteroid belt if they don't. As you can imagine, the men are for it, and the wives are completely undecided. Lots of family down there."

"That will do it every time," Eric agreed. "How's it going with Cheryl Lynn?"

Scott snickered and looked behind Eric.

"She's behind me, isn't she?" Eric asked and received a thump on his head. "Ouch!"

"Yes, she is!" Cheryl Lynn came into view and pulled out a chair next to Scott. "Cheryl Lynn is fine now that Scott is back, and she is happy that nothing happened. I know this is what I get for signing up to care about one of you guys, but I can't say I like it a lot." She sat down on the chair. "I saw Gabrielle going down the hallway. She looked tired."

"She is. She didn't sleep during the operation, and while she drinks coffee just fine, she didn't do much drinking on the trip. The damned nanocytes kinda take the caffeine buzz down a notch. I've worked on pulling Etheric energy to help keep me up, but she needs to do the same now. She was pissed I was one up on her ability-wise, but I'm sure she'll figure it out soon enough," Eric finished.

"After she sleeps," Cheryl Lynn added, to Eric's nodded agreement.

"So, answering your question," Scott slipped an arm around Cheryl Lynn, "she's fine. Just a little tweaked with worry when I go on an operation."

"I'm right here," Cheryl Lynn told him, then laid her head on Scott's shoulder and closed her eyes. "You guys go ahead and talk. I'm just going to take a nap." She lifted her head and pushed on Scott's muscles. "Couldn't you be just a little flabby? It's like sleeping on a rock." She laid her head back down. "Never mind. I'll just find me a small pillow. You keep those muscles hard, dear."

Scott glanced down at her hair and smiled, then looked up at Eric and winked.

Eric raised his cup. "I guess that means you'll be at the workout at sixteen hundred?"

"If I'm not," Scott moderated his voice, "I'll lose these muscles, and then where will I be?"

Cheryl Lynn reached across with one of her arms, her eyes

still closed, and snuggled closer to him. "I'll still care for you, even with muscles that are kinda flabby. You still have a cute butt." She paused before adding, "Don't lose the butt."

The two men chuckled.

"What's on tap for today?" Scott asked.

Eric answered, "Uh, I think it's Thunderous Thursday, so we go back to the classics."

Then both men started singing, *"I've got big balls, you've got big balls, but SHE'S got the biggest balls of them all!"*

"Seriously?" Cheryl Lynn complained, voice muffled from speaking into Scott's chest as the two guys laughed. "You guys sing about Bethany Anne?"

Eagles Nest Rocking Country Bar, Virginia Beach, VA, USA

PO2 Harmon tossed his five bucks on the table and grabbed the waiting beer, taking a sip before wiping the suds off his mouth. "Damn, that was what I needed."

PO3 Neil moved the five-dollar bill to the end of the table so Melissa, their waitress, could grab it the next time she passed.

Harmon raised an eyebrow. "She spotted us the beer, knowing you were running late," Neil told him. "I told her I'd pay it if you failed to show up in," he leaned forward to look behind Harmon, "another ten minutes."

"Got called back by Senior Chief Needledick to dot the Is and cross the Ts on some paperwork. Can't believe I missed that shit. Didn't get too much of a talking to. I guess I looked pissed off enough at myself. Damned embarrassing."

"What, no one told you that the Iranian Navy has openings if you keep fucking up that bad?" PO2 Ronnie asked, grinning. "That's what I was told by my chief."

"Uh, no," Harmon admitted. "No Iranian Navy offer, but if the rumors are true about where we're going, I think I might have taken them up on the offer."

"The big 'A'?" Ronnie asked, and Harmon nodded.

Neil turned to Ronnie. "Alaska?"

"No, dumbass, Antarctica," Ronnie replied. "Alaska would be nice. At least they have people living there. Fucking Antarctica is nothing but ball-busting cold covered by freezing sleet and winds they say will throw your ass off of the ship."

"Make those pansies from *Wild Catch* squeeze their sphincters tight enough to drop ball bearings after eating raw metal," Harmon added.

"What's the group going to be?" Neil asked.

"Frigate, Cruiser, LHD, I'm hearing," Harmon answered. "Go in, let the Marines land, and check out a couple of interesting satellite locations, and if we find anything, dig in a little and get more backup. If not, we sneak back out. Everyone is going bat-shit crazy wanting to do Indiana Jones stuff all over the damned world. I'm hearing some really highly-placed people have been up on the QBS *ArchAngel*, and everyone knows that they have alien tech."

"And they aren't sharing," Neil interjected.

"Shit, would *you*?" Ronnie replied. "Fuck, if I had their tech, I sure as hell wouldn't."

The men saw Melissa heading in their direction, so Ronnie grabbed his mug and finished the last couple of swallows. His mug hit the table just seconds before Harmon's banged down empty as well.

She smiled as she dropped off three freshly filled mugs. "I'll take that as yes, you'd like these?" In seconds, she had their empties on her tray and had turned to move back to the bar.

"God, I'd..." Neil started.

Harmon put up a hand. "Don't say it," he told his friend. "We all think it, but just don't say it. She's had a tough life, and even if we think we wouldn't do anything ugly to her, we all know Uncle S calls the shots for now. She won't date Navy, and it has every-thing to do with her father leaving and never coming back."

"He was Navy?" Neil asked.

"No," Ronnie replied. "He was just a loser who couldn't handle the responsibility. She likes us, but won't date us. Them's the breaks sometimes," Ronnie answered, and then stopped watching her and turned back to his table. "So, we leaving soon?"

"That was the call I expect to come down, but we need to get a few things loaded, at least on our ship," Harmon answered.

"Damn, I'd hate to be the Marines on the LHD. That is going to suck mosquito balls, out in the cold like that."

"I'm sure they'll have some sort of wonderful stuff that keeps them all toasty and warm." Harmon snickered. "Right before it breaks down on their asses and they have to walk the rest of the way."

Ronnie replied, "They do have a way of getting shit for equipment at times. It makes you wonder if the brass is taking it in the ass on the budget, or they just can't find a supplier that can make stuff that doesn't break."

"Or someone is pocketing the money," Neil added. "Although I kinda doubt that. Every one of their guys started with a rifle in their hands."

Ronnie looked at his watch. "Okay, gents. It's time to accelerate our lives and go be a global force for good."

"And freeze our nuts off doing it," Neil added.

"Just make sure you look fantastic with icicles hanging off your eyebrows," Harmon told him as he held up his mug. "Keep them nuts warm, guys. Let's do our jobs and get home safely. One of these days, there will be a Ms. Melissa waiting for us."

The three guys clinked their mugs together and downed their beers. Each dropped a ten on the table and waved to Melissa on their way out.

Tokyo, Japan

William sat in his chair, wincing slightly but otherwise fine.

"Does it still hurt?" Yuko asked him.

"No, this time, it's the small chair assaulting my rather rotund ass." He grinned. "Sorry, I should probably think about my language around the Vicereine."

Behind her, William saw Akio nod in agreement.

"Don't worry about it for my sake in private company. You should see what I sometimes read on the boards when the guys don't know I'm female."

"Does it get better when they know you're female?" William asked.

"Depends on the group. Occasionally it will, but usually, there is a jerk troll who decides I represent all the females who have mistreated him in life. Like somehow I am to blame that as hackers, we are usually introverts who rarely eat well and don't take care of ourselves, and therefore don't look too attractive."

"You look good," William offered.

"I'm Japanese. I have very good genes," she replied. "Plus, I've been working out since I was in Australia. Akio and the guards are pushing me hard. I've never been in better shape or in more pain."

"It is good for you to handle all of the challenges. It allows you to grow," Akio told her. William noticed she didn't roll her eyes like he would have expected.

"How can I help the negotiations?" he asked.

"The delegation is expressing that they want the ability to protect themselves much better in the future from a belligerent China, and they believe puck technology is the way to go."

"Well," William started, then stopped. He wiped his face with his hand and started again. "I think the better technology would be the railgun stuff we have, with a second layer of larger pucks that can strike at a distance. The problem with the pucks is, anytime they're planning to hit something large enough, the puck will be destroyed in the process. I know for a fact we aren't going to give them the knowledge to make their own pucks, so that's a no-go."

"Will they be able to reverse-engineer their own pucks?"

"Not possible. The pucks will explode if tampered with, and you need to make that very, very clear to them," William warned. "I have some videos showing what happens when you try to open a puck case. If they pay attention, they won't do it anywhere near a populated place."

"You still expect them to try?" Yuko asked.

"Of course. I would. They'll put it in a bunker somewhere with a sacrificial robot and a bunch of sensors and high-speed cameras. Not that it will gain them much since the explosion is so fast they will get a very small amount of data before anything near enough to record will be consumed. I'm providing the video to prove my point, but they won't believe it until they test it themselves." He shrugged. "It's how scientists are."

"What else can we offer?" Yuko asked. "If the pucks are going to be off limits?"

"Well, the pucks are off limits to them, but you guys are planning on staying here after we leave, aren't you?"

Yuko nodded. "I've been asked what I want to do, and Bethany Anne is setting something up for us to stay here in Japan. Akio and our team, plus another will be remaining behind. We will be representatives of the Queen."

William explained, "I imagine you'll be left with a defensive suite and other toys as well, so you'll have pucks and the ability to control them outside of the Japanese government. As long as they provide you land and support, your capabilities will be a strong force multiplier for theirs, so negotiate well on that aspect. Bethany Anne isn't going to leave you weak, I'm sure."

"No, and we will have Pods for travel and secondary locations if we have to run. But my plan is to stay in the background as much as possible, and go underground if I can."

"It's the hacker in you wanting to hide, isn't it?" William asked.

"I am trying to think strategically," Yuko replied. "I have asked Akio and the others how they stayed hidden for so long, and they believe hiding has many benefits. Also, when Akio finishes with his response to the attack, we will have many additional relationships, some owing us favors."

"So, not quite the power behind the throne, but power the throne can call on?" William asked.

"Yes, I believe that is what we are working on. The Japanese government, of course, is the throne in this case. Not the actual royal family, but the idea is there."

William nodded. "With everything going on in the news, it's becoming more and more obvious we're heading for a showdown, aren't we?"

Yuko thought about it for a moment. "Yes. Most likely. We see it on the dark web, where you can buy and sell names for pennies on the dollar. Thieves in countries you can't locate on a map steal from banks in the biggest cities in the world. The largest nations are preparing to destroy each other digitally each day, so anyone with half a clue should probably at least pay attention to it."

"God, who needs the aliens to do us in? We're doing it to ourselves." William grunted. "Well, there are always bright spots, right?"

"Sure," Yuko agreed. "We have new ways to generate power, which feeds into exciting ways to produce food, which is one of the biggest problems we have. Then there's shelter, but with the 3D printing of cement coming along, I understand they will be able to 3D-print a house. With all of the sand in the desert, it seems likely we have some use for it."

"Agreed, the promise is there. We just have to turn ourselves toward something other than trying to beat each other up, but that isn't why Japan is helping us." William chuckled.

"No, they are setting up defenses, and we," she nodded at

Akio, "are here to establish a hidden safe house for the UnknownWorld."

William smiled. "That would be a big surprise for any country trying to attack, to run smack-dab into the Empress's own First Battalion of Wechselbalg. Those fuckers don't know when to lay down and die!" he laughed.

"Well, sure, but covertly," Yuko added.

"Of course. Let me show you some technology. We have a room-temperature superconductor that will make their scientists cream in their... Ahhh, sorry!" William covered his face with his hands. "I blame Bobcat," he muttered behind his hands. "He doesn't teach me how to speak in front of ladies."

"No," Akio agreed from behind Yuko. "He does not."

CHAPTER TWELVE

<u>Berlin, Germany</u>

Terry kept quiet as he watched Melissa discuss the particulars with the other scientists. He and Melissa had had a long, hard talk about a working relationship between adults.

Which was to say, Terry fought hard about acting like an adult until he got hard, then he capitulated to all of her demands.

Every. Last. One. Of. Them.

Shit, he couldn't even remember everything he promised to do. The only thing on his mind at the moment was how was he going to protect this damned expedition. They weren't bringing along any of the German government's special operatives because there was a chance they would run into the American Navy and they didn't want an incident. Plus, this was supposed to be led by the industrialists, not the eggheads, which was a nice change.

Perhaps. Maybe. Well, depending on the Idiot In Charge.

Fuck all, he needed to make a phone call.

He turned and nodded to the two guys manning the door. "Phone call, be back in ten."

He stepped out into the street and walked a short way. He pulled out his phone, hit a shortcut, and waited.

It went to voicemail.

"C'mon, Robert, you owe me," Terry mumbled, and hit the number again. This time, it was picked up on the second ring.

"Okay, buddy, you are getting in between me and some possible action. This had better be better than fucking good," Robert complained in his ear.

"Love you too, sweetheart, and between you and me, your palm isn't a hot date," Terry replied.

"Ass." Robert laughed. "What do you need, bro?"

"I possibly need a small group of mercenaries for a trip similar to the one I took recently, but this time going south."

"How south?" Robert asked.

"All-the-way-'til-hell-freezes-over south." Terry rolled his eyes when he heard the snicker. "Yeah, freezing nuts and all."

"Wait, don't tell me," Robert asked, his grin coming through loud and clear in his voice. "Melissa is involved?"

"Yes."

"I thought she broke up with you?"

"I didn't get the message," Terry replied.

"The message that you were supposed to chase her?" Robert asked. "Didn't you get that message with what's-her-name back in school?"

"Apparently not, asswipe, and would you be so kind as to not mention previous flames anywhere near her?"

"I'm not. I'm in America, and you're in Germany, right?"

"Yes, and frankly, that isn't far enough."

Robert singsonged, "Terry, my friend, you have it baaaaad."

"Tell me something I don't know. I'm going to fucking Antarctica for her, so yeah. I know nothing fun is happening in Frozen Popsicle Land horizontally-speaking, and I'm still willing to go. Plus, I'm suffering this phone call and all of your ridicule as well."

"Not enough protection?" Robert asked.

"No, they got my name from somewhere, and they learned the German government isn't lending any ops people, so I get to go hiring."

"We aren't cheap, buddy." Robert grinned.

"Fucking double-dipper!" Terry replied. "Don't give me that shit. Your, uh, previous employers would stand around in a circle-jerk for this opportunity."

"I love it when you beg." Robert laughed. "Man, I'll check, and they'll probably okay it. Give me a couple of hours to get the right permissions, and text me the dates and details. We'll do a pickup on your way down south."

"Great. I'll owe you one, Robbie," Terry answered.

"No, I've got that feeling. You still got something to pull out of the hat?"

"Same one as last time," Terry admitted.

"That was the best one I've ever seen, so it would be pretty hard to top it," Robert pointed out.

"That's true. Okay, I'm going to go back in. Send me your merc outfit credentials and details so I can sell you guys."

"Game on, brother." Robert hung up.

Terry looked at his phone and then looked left and right down the street. He slipped the phone into his pocket and started walking back to the building. "You got that right, Robert. Game on, brother, game on." He straightened his back as if his worries had been lessened, shared, among those who had been there, done that, and walked out together.

Tokyo, Japan

Special Liaison Investigator Jiro Dai parked his car and sighed. Another assignment to hand-hold someone wanting special information on criminals. Someone who would probably want to hug the criminals and sing religious songs.

Not his type of people.

He grabbed his laptop and badge and walked into the hotel, nodding at the people at the desk and taking the elevator to the top floor. He clarified his thinking. These were rich touchy-feely types.

Even worse.

The elevator dinged and he stepped out, surprised to find someone on guard in front of the only door in the hallway.

Dai got the impression he had already been judged as a non-threat. It was a little annoying to be dismissed so quickly.

The door opened, and another man stepped out. He had a sports bag filled with something light over his shoulder, and canvas covering something long held in his other hand. He turned to the guard. "The Queen's trust is in your hands, understand?"

"*Hai!*" the guard agreed, and the man turned his eyes toward Dai.

Dammit! Now he felt twice-judged, and he was an ant. What the hell had his boss gotten him involved in? The man nodded and started toward the elevator Dai had just exited. "We will have a long night, Inspector. I hope you slept well?"

Dai looked at the guard, then shrugged and followed the new guy back into the elevator.

Dai got in, and the new guy hit the ground floor button. "My name is Akio, and tonight we will see the type of justice you have wanted for years, Inspector. I hope your stomach is up to the challenge of your desires."

"What are you talking about?" Dai finally found his voice. "I was told to come to this address and help the person who wanted to communicate with criminals?"

Akio looked at him. "Investigator Jiro, this night will be about communication, but not equal communication. It will be about sending a message from the Vicereine, who receives her instructions from my Queen for those who attacked her people. Attacking is never permitted without a response."

"What? Who is the Queen we are talking about? Vicereine?" Dai was trying to get his wits about him.

The elevator dinged, and Akio stepped out and nodded to a man Dai hadn't seen earlier. So, they had a watchman at the bottom. No wonder the upper guard hadn't been worried about him.

It took Dai a few seconds to realize that Akio was retracing Dai's steps right back to his car. "You will need to drive us back to your home."

"What? Why?" Dai asked, sliding into his seat and popping the locks so Akio could get in.

Akio got into the front seat and closed his door. "So there is a record of you being at home this evening. You do know you have a tracer on your police-issued car, yes?"

"Well, yes, I guess. I hadn't thought about it before." Dai pulled out of the hotel's superstructure and started driving back to his house. "Why am I doing this again?"

"Because you are not the only one who is tired of the criminals hiding behind the law, and I will send a message they will understand for decades."

"What message?" Dai asked, turning onto the freeway.

Akio answered, "You do not mess with the Queen's people, or she will reply in kind."

"Do I want to know her response? I understand you don't wish to talk nicely to them." Dai was surprised to hear the grim man chuckle.

"No. My Queen does not talk nicely to those who attack first. She just responds."

"You are talking about the incident from last week, aren't you?" Dai asked, finally cluing in on the vague rumors and comments around the office. He had been working his own cases, so he hadn't listened too hard to office talk.

"Yes."

"Then isn't your response a little late?" Dai asked, turning off the freeway and taking another turn down a side street.

"No. One does not create a night that will be remembered with hurried planning," Akio told him.

That sounded ominous. "Just what are you going to do?"

Akio turned to Dai. "Deliver her response, of course. And make sure that it is understood and agreed something like last week will not be tried again."

"How are you going to do that? I can't do anything without special permission, and the NPA isn't going to give me that."

"No, all the NPA has done was allow you and me to speak for a few minutes, making sure we understood that you were doing your best to handle the case. Then you drove home. The information in your car's GPS will corroborate your story since the data is sent in real time back to your headquarters."

Dai slowed, pulled into a small, narrow two-story, and pushed the button for the garage to open. Pulling into the garage, he hit the button again to close the door.

Akio got out and grabbed his bag. "Now, as they say in America, this is where you decide if you want to take the red pill or the blue pill."

"What?" Dai asked. "You mean *The Matrix*?"

"Yes, Inspector. Do you want to go to sleep and learn about this in the morning like everyone else, or do you want to participate?"

Dai looked at the man's two bags. "What is in those?"

Akio lifted the sports bag. "This one is my uniform." He lifted the other gear. "These are my weapons."

"Just you?"

"Inspector, you are ignorant of just what I am, or you would not be asking."

"Okay." Dai was agitated. "Tell me who I just let into my house for reasons I've yet to truly understand to do what to people I probably would agree need stuff done to them."

"Inspector, I'm retribution for my Queen. She has a message, and when she wants one of these messages sent, she sends the very best."

"And you are?"

"I am," Akio told him, "a Queen's Bitch."

Dai couldn't believe what he was doing. He watched as Akio changed into his uniform with a fanged skull emblem on the shoulder. He unrolled his pouch with two swords inside. One was very, very old, but obviously well kept.

Akio had asked him one more time, "Red pill or blue?"

"I'll stick with red and see how far down the rabbit hole we go," Dai had replied.

"Then you need to get on your protective gear. I don't expect you to fight, but if someone shoots at you, you need to make sure you are as protected as best you can be."

Now he was putting on his bulletproof vest for maybe the second time in his career, and his blood was starting to pump. This was happening. It was really happening.

He was going underground and helping someone who was going to take the fight back to those who flouted the law.

He was going all Dirty Harry on the criminals. The American police movies were some of his favorites.

He pulled out his SIG P230 and strapped it on. His colleagues, those fighting the Yakuza, were the few who carried the automatics.

"If we do this right," Akio told him, "you will not use that tonight. We want to limit any proof you are anywhere but here. Keep your holster, but leave the SIG here. I have something in the Pod for you."

Dai pressed his lips together, but Akio made sense. He put the gun down.

"How do we get to the roof?"

Dai stopped asking why all of the time. He sounded clueless, which he was, and he would find out soon enough.

The two men stepped outside and then made their way up the back steps that took them to his roof. Dai's eyes widened as he realized there was a large black object hovering above it.

"Let's go, Dai. We have messages to deliver tonight," Akio urged. Dai walked around to see Akio open the Pod doors and then reach behind the two seats and pull out a metal box. He pressed his thumb on the lock and it popped open, then he pulled out a pistol and handed it to Dai. The inspector took it and tried to see what it looked like in the dark.

"Look at it in the Pod. That is a Dukes' Special. It fires metal slivers using railgun technology. I'm going to lock it to a maximum power level of four."

"What does it go to?" Dai asked as Akio put the box back and directed him to sit in the left chair. He sat down after holstering the pistol and started locking himself in as Akio sat, strapped himself in, and shut the doors. The screen lit up with holographic controls.

"The pistols," Akio explained as the view out the window showed the neighborhood disappear beneath them, "go to ten, but your wrists would most likely shatter at six."

"Why do they go to ten if they will break anyone's wrist at six?" Dai asked.

"They will not break everyone's wrist, although I will admit they do cause pain at ten."

"You've shot them at ten?" Dai asked.

"Of course. Jean won't allow you to have the pistols until she checks you out on a pair and confirms you know the dangers of using them. I've modified mine to allow you shooting access for the next eight hours."

"What happens after eight hours?" Dai asked.

"It won't fire, and it will go terminal if someone tries to take it apart, so I wouldn't suggest that. If you do, make sure you let me know so I can be somewhere else."

"Where would you go?"

"Preferably the moon." Akio had no humor on his face.

QBS *ArchAngel*

"Kiel." Eric nodded to the Yollin, who was resting on a couch at the side of the large fighting room.

"Bitch Eric," Kiel replied. "Please tell me it is not your turn to fight me?"

Eric smiled. "No, it isn't. But I *am* curious. Why do you ask?"

"Because I have had my Yollin excrement location beaten, and I will admit, I am tired."

"One second, Kiel. Computer, note that the verbiage translated 'excrement location' and now use ass, please."

"UNDERSTOOD."

"Well, you did kill someone that people here knew, so they all wanted a piece of your hide."

"Yes, I understand that, and I understand that you humans care for your friends at a level we Yollins would not know outside of family, most likely."

"Well, to be truthful, I'm sure some of the Wechselbalg just wanted to try you on for size, since you're a little taller and bigger and carry your own damned armor."

"Yes, I've had to shed a layer to get rid of the cracks. I couldn't fight for one solar day while it hardened again. My exoskeleton was very damaged."

"Who was the worst?" Eric asked.

Kiel chittered in laughter. "Are you asking who was even close to the Queen's beating? No one. She kept her promise and I survived, but she made me wish to be dead. I will not harm one of hers without thinking again."

"She does have a way of making sure we learn her lessons," Eric agreed.

"She is not afraid to get into the warrior's area and fight. Why is that?" Kiel asked.

"I thought your king fought?" Eric asked, surprised.

"Yes, when he has an armada at his back or a thousand soldiers in front of him. Plus, he only considers it a proper fight if the person is in his tier," Kiel answered.

"Wonder what level he would find Bethany Anne?" Eric asked, not expecting an answer.

Kiel chittered again. "He would not ascribe a level to her, and that is a good thing. I am pretty sure he would get his Yollin ass kicked, and he would have to give up the throne. That is why he has so many fighters in front of him."

"Why doesn't someone just bomb him, then?" Eric asked.

"That is not the Yollin way. It has to be trial by combat. You are only allowed the weapons and armor you sleep with."

"Wait, you guys sleep with weapons?"

"No, the translation software must have messed up. I meant you are only allowed to go into the fight naked. You can have nothing else with you."

"Oh, Bethany Anne would just love *that* precondition."

"She would want to fight without a cover?" Kiel asked.

"No, sorry, I'm making a joke. I doubt she would like the condition. She can be a little prudish sometimes and prefers black over *au natural*."

"It would not bother her to fight without weapons?" Kiel asked.

"Kiel, Bethany Anne is never without weapons, trust me."

"I'm trying to understand this, so bear with me a moment," Bethany Anne told Marcus. "I heard Scientist Royleen just fine."

Captain Kael-ven T'chmon chittered. "It is not always easy to accept what our learned ones say. From what I understand, you humans already have this knowledge, but perhaps not the tools to manipulate it well."

"Yes," Marcus agreed. "Think of it this way, Bethany Anne: there are two types of components, one we understand, which is energy, and one we don't, which is gravity. You, me, the Yollins, your food, electricity, water—everything is energy at some level. There is much related to mass vs. matter and Einstein's equation. So, the rock we need to tunnel into is energy. The process we are going to build is going to seek to pull the different energies together into a machine. This machine is going to get most of it right, and some of it wrong. It just means we won't have perfect blocks of whatever's in the machine, but it will be really, really close."

"Usually." Royleen spoke up. "It takes a massive amount of energy to power these machines, but I understand with your Etheric connections, the power is most likely not the problem at this point. So, we can dig into the asteroid and have the materials pulled apart and set up for us. We will be able to sell this back on Earth since the raw materials will be untraceable once they smelt the product down."

Bethany Anne tapped her finger on her lips. "We're wrapping up most of our mass purchases since we are getting pushback from our existing partners anytime the government finds out about our involvement."

"Kael-ven." She turned to the former captain. "I have a question."

He asked, "Only one?"

She asked, "*Et tu*, Kael-ven, *et tu*." She looked up at the ceiling. "I've told you I will express to the Yollins that I'm seeking to pass through peacefully. You know I won't back down from a fight, and so both of us expect I'm going to get one."

He chittered his agreement.

"Fine. I expect to kick their asses, by the way. I know you didn't expect that in the beginning and I've been polite about not asking questions I felt would cause you to give up Yollin secrets. However, because of work done by Royleen here..."

"What work did I do for you?" Royleen called, shocked.

"Your effort to translate human and Yollin communications were found by my team," she supplied.

"But that was secured!" he answered, then looked at his previous captain, alarm in his eyes. "I did not provide support to the humans to get into our computers."

Kael-ven waved a hand at the scientist. "It does not matter. Humans are devious and smart. Plus, there is a Kurtherian involved, and what is our security against one of them?"

See, I told you so.

It's like a get out of jail free card for these guys, Bethany Anne griped. *Every time something happens that they could possibly be blamed for, they whip out the Kurtherian card, and everyone's like "Oh? A Kurtherian was involved? Well, bad luck and all, you couldn't possibly win against them."*

We do have a reputation. I've tried to get you to believe that.

Yeah, well, having had to live with you for so long, I forget that not everyone is as docile as you.

Thank you, I think.

"As I was saying, due to the work that was done, we have our own personal Rosetta Stone and are quickly amassing a store of your latest knowledge. What I want to know, is what will it take to create a binding and non-breakable treaty with the Yollin king?"

This time, both of her Yollin vassals started chittering. Bethany Anne looked at Marcus, who shrugged. "Okay, out with it," she finally told them, impatience winning when they didn't stop for over a minute.

"The only non-breakable treaty with our king is to become a slave system to Yollin, Queen Bethany Anne. Without besting the king in personal combat, there is no other way, or you will be at war with Yollin for a very long time."

"Well, that settles it," Bethany Anne stated. "I don't have the time, so kicking his ass will have to be the plan."

Kael-ven's chittering stopped. "What? You would assume the reins of the Yollin government as well as your own?"

"Well, the ultimate authority, sure. But I'm far too busy to be the governor of the Yollin people."

"Well, then who are you going to put in that position?" Kael-ven asked. "I guarantee that all of those connected to the throne are going to figure out a way to be pains for you. It is all on the honor system."

"I know, so isn't it a good thing I have a vassal who is already bound to me by honor and will want what is best for his race, Governor Kael-ven T'chmon?" she told him sweetly, smiling at him.

This time, the only Yollin chittering was Royleen. Marcus found it amusing that a poleaxed expression on a Yollin, in the right light, looked like a poleaxed expression on a human.

Tokyo, Japan

Dai woke up from the phone ringing. He had a splitting headache. He grabbed his cell phone and looked at the number.

It was his boss, and the time was almost noon.

He punched the button. "Yes, sir! I'm sorry, sir. I will be in shortly." He struggled to get up, his brain pounding in pain.

His boss' voice came through the phone. "Never mind that, Special Inspector. Consider yourself on sick leave for forty-eight hours. I don't want you showing up right now since it is a madhouse with the press around here. All I wanted to say was good work. Goodbye."

"Goodbye, sir." Dai barely got that out before the line went dead. He leaned back in bed and dropped the phone back on the nightstand.

Oh, God! He had a splitting headache. He turned the other way and found himself staring at a glass of water and two pills, plus a note. He noticed through bleary eyes that there was a porcelain *tokkuri* and two small *sakazuki* cups on his little table.

Oh, it was coming back to him now. He grabbed the analgesics and drank the water. All of it. He was suffering from, he eyed the *tokkuri* again, way too much sake sometime this morning.

Akio was correct: it had been a blue or a red pill decision. He might not ever be able to speak about the evening, but he would forever remember that for one night, the fear that came to those in the night from those delivering righteousness was from a partnership.

And he had been the one who had pointed out those who needed the lessons from a Queen's Bitch.

He remembered the red eyes and the fanged teeth and got out of bed, walking over to see if there was any sake left in the *tokkuri*.

There was none.

He had really needed the alcohol after the night they'd had. He opened the note and smiled. It was Dai's own personal "Call me if you need help card," complete with Akio's signature.

This was now his most prized possession. He padded to his bathroom to see if he had even tried to get all of the blood off of himself before crashing last night.

CHAPTER THIRTEEN

<u>Adjacent Kiel German Naval Base, Germany</u>

"We have contact," Terry heard on the team's channel.

"Seriously?" Terry bitched aloud to himself, then hit the talk button. "Where?"

"Twelve," was the reply.

Terry looked down at the map. They were coming from the south and heading toward the stern of the ship, where they were loading. "How many?"

"Looks like six," their lookout replied.

Terry grimaced. Unless they pulled guns, which were verboten here in the port, this was going to be a physical confrontation. Even so, he had hoped that being adjacent to the base would stop any idiotic attacks and allow them to get out of the port without incident.

It was past nine in the evening and the people were working under the sodium lamps, trying to get the ship loaded and underway.

Robert called in, "Me and the boys are moving to intercept. Got anything in backup for this?"

Terry replied, "I wasn't expecting to have anyone try to

engage us here in Germany. Seems like a stupid place. We don't even have anything yet."

"That's probably the point," Robert continued. "Someone doesn't want you to go in the first place. So, bust up some stuff, run off some of the people, and at least slow the project down, if they can't cause enough problems to stop it totally from happening."

"All right. Ask the porters to grab something and go into the ship and fail to come back out, like they're taking a break for a few minutes. Let's leave them out of this situation. You need me to come down there?"

"No. You're paying the bills, boss. You get to stay up there and let us hired hands enjoy ourselves for a few minutes."

"Fine, but I want it noted that I offered," Terry told him.

"So noted," Robert replied and dropped the connection.

Less than a minute later, Melissa came into the room. "I understand we're being attacked?"

Terry kept one eye on the monitors showing different parts of the ship and the docks. He watched the two that gave him a good view of the loading area and the inside, where the deckhands had started grabbing weapons. "How in the hell did you get that information so quickly?" he asked, not sparing a glance to see she was breathing hard.

"I was in the inside loading dock checking on some equipment when the first loaders came in with the message from Robert. You aren't going over there, are you?"

"Huh?" Terry replied, not looking at her. "No. Robert says to stay out of this one since I'm paying for their help. They want the exercise."

"Good," she murmured.

Terry didn't hear her comment. "The lucky bastards," he mumbled.

She noticed that the toughs had come into the viewscreen he

was watching. Her eyes narrowed at Terry, and she turned and left the room.

Terry was watching the screens and failed to notice when she left.

"I don't think you guys have the proper clearance to work in this area," Robert stated. The lead tough was a big man. No hair, broken nose, and tattoos on his neck. He had three guys to his left, and two to his right.

"We don't need clearance, American." His voice was rough, like too many cigarettes had been smoked. "Just earning some drinking money, boys, aren't we?" He looked at his guys, all of them fairly well built. Robert noted the herky-jerky thinner guy on the right.

"Thomas?" Robert asked, and hand-signaled the man he was concerned about.

"Got him, boss," Thomas replied and moved a few feet over to give himself a good view in case the guy pulled a knife.

"Do you guys have a favorite hospital?" Robert asked. "I mean, we aren't planning on taking you, but I'm sure we can ask dock security if you can go there. If they don't just dump your broken bodies into the water."

"You speak big, little American." Broken Nose grinned.

Well, shit. Broken nose and missing two teeth.

"Hell, I'm just waiting for you guys to ask us to dance." Robert looked at the six to five odds. "We haven't had anyone to test out our new dance moves with since… Well, ISIS, right, guys?" His team all agreed that was right.

Broken Nose spat to the side. "I'm not sure why you would be here if you had been fighting over there, but we have some drinking to do, and we can't do it until we finish our job."

"About damned time!" Craig Goulding exclaimed from Robert's left. "My dinner's getting cold, Frenchie."

"Awww, fuck!" Robert spat. Craig's putdown spurred the men to start the fight. Robert had been working on figuring out a way to defuse the situation, not incite the men, and Craig just had to add that little bit of fuel to the flame.

Ducking, Robert had allowed his annoyance to get in the way of paying attention to Broken Nose's first punch. Robert turned his move to a back leg-sweep, but he didn't have the momentum to do more than barely bend the guy's leg. He twisted and rolled away, to come back up, ready for an attack this time.

"Almost had you, little boy!" He grinned. "You should tell your friend we like to explain the difference between fighting us and fighting the French!"

Robert used both forearms to block a wickedly powerful right-hand swing and then used his right elbow to smash his assailant's nose. Blood spurted. It caused his opponent to back up a couple of steps, but the pain didn't substantially slow him down.

"Oh, fancy moves, is it, then?" Broken Nose asked. Robert looked around, and his quick glance told him his group had it under control. They practiced fast and deadly takedowns, so beating someone soundly without using killing moves took a while longer.

"Well, I don't think I'm going to just stand toe to toe with you and slug you," Robert answered. "By the look on your face, you don't care, and the ladies love how I look already."

"That's because your ladies like pretty boys, American!" Broken Nose insisted. "While mine like virility."

"Look, Jacko, it's the money you're paying them. They'll tell you anything for a few euros," Robert answered, and sure enough, after a few moments of thinking, Jacko yelled something ugly in German and came forward to grab him, arms outstretched.

The end, when it came, was almost anticlimactic.

Jacko Broken Nose got a swift snap-kick to his groin as Robert's upper arms blocked and pushed Jacko to keep from being grabbed. Jacko's head took a dive as he folded around his abused family jewels. Robert grabbed it and pulled hard so that his rising knee intercepted Jacko's face, inciting a bone-crunching sound.

By the time Broken Nose finally hit the dirt, four others were down, and one had his hands up as all of Robert's team eyed him like he was the one hamburger in front of a bunch of starving men.

Terry's voice came through his earpiece. "Robert."

Robert grabbed his earbud and stuck it back in his ear. "Yes?"

"Dock security are on their way. Probably just a couple of minutes if you need to hide anything."

Robert looked around. "No, this was just a fisticuffs episode. You got anything to show our side of the fight to security?"

"Yes, I've already shot over the beginning few seconds, so you should be okay. If not, I'll pull some more."

"We should be good, but they're going to need a forklift for Broken Nose here." Robert poked the man with his toe, but he didn't even groan.

"Yeah, okay. Well, shit," Terry replied.

"What?"

"Just noticed Melissa is gone. Well, I'm sure I've fucked up somehow, and I'll learn about it as soon as I make sure you guys are covered."

"Nah, go find her now. Tell her you went searching as soon as you figured out she wasn't with you. You'll be out here in a few."

"That's not right," Terry started, but Robert interrupted him.

"First round on you if within sixty seconds of finding her, she sends you out here," Robert offered.

"Deal, but I'll head out there immediately if she isn't in her berth," Terry replied.

"Okay." Robert dropped the call to make sure his men were good.

Two minutes later, dock security rolled up, and within another sixty seconds, Terry came out of the ship.

Robert was watching his men help the security group move the thugs. They had all been woken up with smelling salts and were being loaded into a van. He looked at his friend. "She was pissed you went and checked on her, right?"

"Yeah. What the hell is that?" Terry asked while he watched the toughs getting added to the van.

"You can't win, but you tried, so that gives you some points. You won't know you got any points, but her time to cool down just dropped thirty-three percent or more. Plus, she feels good that she told you to go do your job, which is probably what you were doing that got you in trouble in the first place," Robert explained.

"If you know so much about women, why don't you have a wife?" Terry asked, sighing loudly.

"Because that is the culmination of four serious relationships and a little therapy, trying to figure out why I failed four times in a row," Robert answered. "Looks like it's our turn to talk again."

"Fantastic! Something I can understand." Terry stepped forward and held out his hand to the security lead.

South America

Michael's house pyre had gone well. The flames had climbed high into the sky by the time the team had to jump into the waiting Pods and leave before the local emergency crews came to put the flames out.

When the fire trucks arrived, it was too late to do anything but contain the fire.

They dropped their critical equipment off on the QBS *Arch-Angel* and grabbed rooms. Their chosen rooms were similar to the Queen's Bitches' setup, with a general living room and common area in the middle. Tabitha's team, however, preferred to keep the lighting down and use indirect lighting up the walls for minor decoration. Tabitha liked the effect and the Zen feeling, so she just used a couple of lamps by the table for when she wanted more light.

With her enhancements, that wasn't often unless someone human or not very modified came in.

It had taken Tabitha and her team a couple of days to track their first lead after talking to Mason and Sheila. There was a small warehouse that also housed a business office on the outskirts of Bielefeld, Germany. After researching the city, they found the Bielefeld Conspiracy, where those on the internet persuaded others the city did not exist, and the team laughed at how gullible people were.

Tabitha got down to business.

She thought it interesting that the people she sought would be located in the same small area as the Praetoria Mercenary Group, a company most Germans would refute existed if they were told about it. War, to Germans, was often a four-letter word.

Still, the three-story building seemed to be fairly well set up. It was on a few acres of grassy land and had no trees or shrubs blocking its view for a hundred meters in any direction before they allowed local foliage to grow.

She had already tried to hack their computers, but there wasn't anything there for her to get. No databases, no servers, nothing.

It was like these people didn't trust computers or something. What a pain in the ass.

Now, she, Hirotoshi, and Ryu were dropping down in one of the new four-seater Pods. The two guys were up front while she reviewed the building's layout.

"We're going to see what kind of security they have and then do a little B and E, guys."

"Breaking and entering?" Ryu asked.

"Yeah. You watching more American police shows now?"

"Yes, I particularly like the older stuff on Netflix," Ryu admitted. "I can just watch right through with no commercials."

"I wonder if Netflix would be surprised to find out ADAM has ripped everything they have and stored it on the *ArchAngel's* servers?" she wondered aloud.

"Does the Queen know he is doing that?" Hirotoshi asked.

"Probably not. When she finds out, I figure she'll find a way to pay them for it." Tabitha shrugged. "They say you can watch as much as you want for free. ADAM being able to watch and understand it at inhuman speed kind of gets around the rules."

"I don't think the Queen would buy that argument," Hirotoshi admonished.

"No, me either. If it were me, I'd just... Well, never mind," she finished lamely. No reason to let these guys know what she would do. She needed to uphold the impression she was working for justice, not actively figuring out ways to steal movies.

They rode down in silence for the next few minutes. Tabitha was watching her tablet scroll information as they got closer to the building's location. The nearest neighbor was over three kilometers away, nestled in the hills.

"We have four walking the grounds," Ryu reported from up front, looking down at the information displayed on the windshield HUD. "Also, it appears there are multiple devices radiating something all over the landscape."

"Yeah, probably motion detection," she agreed. "They don't have anything up on the roof for some reason. Let's see why not." Tabitha started subvocalizing instructions to the AI ArchAngel had supplied her for this operation. "Ha!" she announced. "The idiots actually do have something going on the roof, but it looks like they have it on their own loop. Now, why the hell would they do that?"

Hirotoshi kept them above the trees over half a kilometer away, silent and practically invisible in the night.

"Wow, these Germans really know how to do the bunny together!" she finally exclaimed.

Ryu turned in his seat to see Tabitha holding her tablet up, twisting it sideways and muttering, "Hell, I might sign up for that..." She dropped the tablet to see Ryu looking at her. "Ah, there was some footage."

She paused, then added, "Apparently, the guards are of both genders, and a couple got freaky up on the roof a week and a half ago and never changed the security back." Ryu saw her blush just a little. "Is it me, or is it getting hot in here?" she asked, fanning her face with her tablet and smiling.

Ryu snorted and turned back around. It was rare for Tabitha to be embarrassed about anything sexual.

Made him wonder just what was in that video she found.

Tabitha slid two Jean Dukes pistols into her holsters and tied her hair back, grabbing a full-face mask from her bag. "Here's the plan. Find when all of the guards are walking away from the building and drop me. I'll get into the building and find the stuff, then exit the building, and you guys pick me back up."

Ryu turned around, and she looked back at him. "What?" she asked. "Easy-peasy."

Ryu caught Hirotoshi's eyes rolling and carefully schooled his face to not give anything away.

"We go down in twelve seconds, Kemosabe," Hirotoshi advised.

Ryu turned back to see Tabitha messing with her holsters and her breasts, muttering, "Dammit, these ta-tas weren't made for clandestine shit. I need some titty tape. I can't get my holsters to lay right around these big bazoongas." A pause and some more pushing, followed by, "Shit, that hurt the nips," then more muttering.

Ryu turned back around and faced the front, trying to keep his own blushing to a minimum.

Seconds later, Tabitha cracked open her door and dropped the ten feet to the building's roof, rolling and coming up quickly to move in the dark toward a door as Hirotoshi and Ryu quickly went back up into the night.

"Do you think she will make it in and out quietly?" Ryu asked.

It took Hirotoshi only a second to respond, "No."

They laughed.

Tabitha stopped by the door and pulled out her smaller tablet, the screen set to minimum intensity. She subvocalized, "Check for alarms in proximity."

"Alarm active on the door," came the reply in her ear.

"Can you disable?" she asked.

"Yes."

"So, disable it!" Tabitha sounded exasperated.

"Done."

Tabitha listened carefully as she turned the knob, and when no alarms sounded and nothing seemed to be amiss from either outside or inside, she slipped in and closed the door. She turned her small tablet around and allowed the dim light to give her enough to see the stairs as she went down, ending up at a normal door. According to her schematics, this opened into one of the major halls.

Time to go looking for information the old-fashioned way.

Kamilla heard the noise from the floor above her but ignored it. Jürgen must be walking his third-floor shift.

She continued looking through the new potential recruits.

Their team in America had never called back in, which was going to be a problem. Since the house they had been casing blew up, she figured something bad must have happened to them, and everything possible had been done to erase any trail from the operatives back to their organization.

A few minutes later, she heard Jürgen come into the outer office and get a cup of coffee. After another couple of minutes, he rapped on her door, and Kamilla looked up to see him smiling with not one, but two cups.

"Java?" he asked.

"Gladly, and thank you." Kamilla accepted the cup as Jürgen sat down. "How was your third-floor walk?" she asked.

"I haven't done it yet. I'll do it right after this cup." He saluted her with his coffee and took a sip. He noticed her forehead furrow. "What is it?"

"I heard footsteps up there a few minutes back, and I thought it was you. Is anyone still on three?"

Jürgen put his cup down. "No, they left for Victor's birthday celebration at four-thirty to get a jump on the beer-drinking."

Kamilla opened her second drawer. Reaching in, she pulled out an S&W 60 LS Ladysmith. Jürgen nodded and got his Beretta 92fs out, and the two of them left her office, Jürgen speaking into his headset microphone.

"Fuck me," Tabitha muttered. "Wonder-twin superpowers and all, but what I need is a simple answer to a simple question. Who hired Bethany Anne's assassins from here?" She looked around the office. It had three desks, all facing a central round table. The middle desk was in front of a large window. The room was about twenty-five-feet square, with lots of bookshelves all filled with old books, some knickknacks, and a number of three-ring binders.

She walked around the room and looked at the table, but everything there seemed to be about a project in Ethiopia.

"It's been over five minutes, and we haven't seen anything disastrous happen...yet." Ryu and Hirotoshi watched the video feed. Presently, they had four tiny video drones flying around the building's perimeter as their Pod stayed up in the clouds, out of sight.

"Give her time. I'm sure we will see her calling card, soon," Hirotoshi replied.

"If I was a book of names, where would I be?" Tabitha asked herself, walking to the first desk. "Fuck if I know. I would stick the data in a folder inside my... Shit." She put a hand on her head. "Where the hell do you think computer operating systems got the metaphors, Tabitha?" She looked around for a filing system. "Stop having a blonde moment and start moving a little faster!"

Kamilla and Jürgen crept up to the third floor and opened the door, looking down the hallway, which had several doors branching off of it.

It was empty.

"Each door in order?" Kamilla asked Jürgen. "Or go straight to the main office?"

"Let's go for the office since that's where most of the information is stored. If someone is up here and in another office, we might spook them, but they shouldn't find anything," he whispered back.

She nodded in agreement, and they crept forward toward the second to the last door on the right.

"A... B... C... Clients. Got you, bitch!" Tabitha whispered when she heard a creak outside the door. She looked around and rolled her eyes.

She hadn't been paying attention, and now someone was outside the door. She grabbed the last two months' folders and quickly rolled them, putting them inside her chest piece across her stomach. Pulling one of her Dukes specials, she flicked it to five.

"Tweedledee and Tweedledum!" she murmured into her mic. "Look out, guys, here I come!"

Kamilla held her pistol in her left hand as she slowly turned the doorknob. She mouthed to Jürgen, "Three, two, one..." and flung open the door, stepping back as glass started shattering inside the room.

Jürgen rushed into the office and aimed at a black figure that had a pistol out and was shooting the glass. He fired two shots, but the figure just...disappeared.

Kamilla was right behind him, aiming at nothing.

"What the hell?" she asked as they rushed toward the window.

The shattering glass happened at the same time Tabitha's comment came over the comm link.

"Who are Tweedledee and Tweedledum?" Hirotoshi asked as the Pod came screaming down from the night sky.

"Probably our latest nicknames," Ryu answered. "I see she has started running northwest. She is out of the fire zone already." He looked on the map and tapped the glass. "Head here. It looks like a good pickup point."

"Adjusted course," he replied.

"How the hell did they get off the grounds so fast?" Kamilla asked, the lights blazing in the night.

"Why don't you ask the more interesting question?" Jürgen admonished, pointing to the ground. "How did they land from three stories up, not kill themselves, and still run away?"

"FUCKITYFUCKFUCKSCREWME!" Tabitha bitched to herself as she ran through the trees. "Dammit, that shit hurt! When will I learn to stop jumping off three-story buildings?"

A tree limb she hadn't noticed popped her in the face. "Ugh!" She ducked the next one.

Stopping, she pulled out her tablet and checked her location. She had another couple of hundred yards to go to hit the small lake. She could feel her body popping back into place and healing as she stood there. As tempting as it was to stay, she started jogging toward the lake, wondering what grief her two Tontos were going to give her.

Thirty seconds later, she came out of the brush and saw the Pod to her left. Jogging over, she pulled open the door and slid into the back. Taking off her mask, she pulled out the folders from inside her protective vest. "Home, James."

Hirotoshi raised an eyebrow at Ryu as the Pod lifted into the night.

"Kemosabe," Hirotoshi began, turning in his chair. "Twee-

143

dledee and Tweedledum? I am no more the same as Ryu as you are the same as Gabrielle."

"Of course not," Tabitha agreed.

Hirotoshi waited for a second, nodded, and turned back around in his chair.

"Gabrielle just doesn't have the same level spank-banks as I do," she finished.

CHAPTER FOURTEEN

Zhou Song pursed his lips and nodded at the representative from his government. This information, this directive, was too delicate to be sent over wires where any of a number of governments or companies could potentially listen to or read it.

So, Ambassador Zhou now had a meeting and a directive.

"We have proof," Intelligence Agent Ho explained, "that TQB is not only using alien technology, but they are now in possession of aliens as well."

"How is this possible?" Zhou asked.

"How do they have possession, or how do we know?"

"I do not want the details of how we are aware of this. I need to understand enough to make sure I can persuade others it is true. Or true enough for now. I'm curious how they accomplished it."

Agent Ho shrugged. "From what little I understand, there was some sort of exit they needed to fly through, and they tricked the aliens at the exit using surprise and subterfuge. Either way, they now are in possession of the alien ship and technology, plus whatever technology they had before. This cannot be allowed to continue, this keeping of information away from those of us here on Earth and not allowing us to communicate with representatives from alien governments."

"So, at the moment, it is their word against ours that they have these aliens and the alien technology?"

"At the moment," Agent Ho continued, "yes, it is. Start the process to inform our people on the council and in the supporting nations so that when the truth comes out, your additional suggestions have had time to become ideas they will believe they came up with themselves."

"I understand the council's requirements and know which contacts I need to speak to, at least in the beginning."

"Good." Agent Ho looked down at his watch. "I have another forty-five minutes if you have any additional questions. Then, I must be back on the airplane since I go to Switzerland next."

"I am curious," Ambassador Zhou inserted, "what the council would answer if I should request a permanent ban on any business dealings with TQB? A ban if they do not immediately provide and turn over all technology and alien representatives?"

Boston, MA, USA

"Rook to Queen's four," David called and moved his piece. Standing up, he walked back over to the chair and picked up his laptop. "Your move, old man." He grunted as he sat down and opened his communications program.

Fred snorted. "You're older than me by eighteen months, geezer." A few seconds later, he added, "I'm moving Bishop to—"

"Well, shit," David exclaimed, interrupting him.

"What's up?" Fred asked, looking up from the report labeled *Nanotechnology Shifts Resulting from Alien Technology* and TOP SECRET printed on the first page.

"We just got a note from the Germany resources. They had a break-in at their corporate headquarters in Bielefeld."

"What happened?"

David kept reading his screen before answering. "Well, this isn't good," he muttered.

"What. Happened?" Fred asked again.

David answered slowly, "The thief took a couple of months' worth of client information, shattered a third story window, jumped out, and then ran off into the woods. The video is…well. Fuck!"

Fred set the paper down, stood up, and walked behind David's chair. David hit the Replay button, and both men watched as the video displayed a view from the tree line back toward the building. It showed darkness, then sudden light when a third story window was shattered, and a figure in all black jumped. The figure landed and rolled, then got up and streaked across the field.

"Says here," David added, "the open field is a hundred meters, and the video is in real time."

"That's not possible," Fred looked at the document he had started reading. "Oh, dear."

David looked over his shoulder. "What 'Oh, dear' are you thinking?"

Fred walked back to his chair and picked up the recently acquired research paper he was reading. "TQB could be looking for us."

"What are you basing this on?" David asked.

Fred picked up the report he had been reading. "The executive overview discusses what might happen to a human with the right modifications, including healing, killing, and," he pointed to David's laptop with the papers, "enhancements."

David looked down at his laptop. "And the only people with technology far outstripping anything we know about is TQB."

"Yes." Fred sat down.

David scratched his nose. "Well, that would put a real downer in our efforts to stay off their radar."

"We still have our cutout. We haven't been stupid." Fred leaned back in the chair, taking a small sip of his whiskey. "It isn't like they're going to be able to track us back through the shell corporation without getting inside our external base computers, and we don't have those connected to the internet."

"True," David mused. "Plus, I'll put in a call to Total Qubyte Biotech to up the budget and add a requirement to find and eliminate," he pointed to the video, "whoever that is."

Fred looked over his reading glasses. "What budget?"

David laughed. "I give them a budget to make sure they're on a leash and can't spend just anything they damn well please."

"David," Fred admonished, "don't be penny-wise and pound foolish. If TQB finds out we had anything to do with something they don't like? It's going to be our personal pounds of flesh they are going to want in reparation."

David pursed his lips and nodded. "Right. What budget?"

"Also," Fred added as he paged back through the document to where he had stopped reading. "That German expedition made it out of port. They need a better reason to stop heading to Antarctica. Who do we know in Brazil?"

"One moment, let me finish this first message." David switched applications and studying for five minutes while Fred read his report. "Okay, we have a two-cutout connection to the Red Devils in one of the *favelas*. Since the police and army have been engaged in pacification efforts for the last couple of years— since the Olympics—it's been tough. They need some cash, and something to get a little pride back. We could get them to harass the ship and anyone who is from the ship."

"Do it." Fred pointed past him at the chessboard. "I've moved. It's your turn."

David looked at the board. "Oh, didn't notice. I'll get to it in a minute."

. . .

Rio de Janeiro, Brazil

Terry stood at the bow of the ship and watched as a group of the men and women left to go into the city. Some went to acquire additional supplies, some to hit the last warm port before they hit Antarctica.

He heard the scuff of the shoes coming up behind him. "Staying on the ship?" Robert asked him.

Terry turned and nodded. "Yeah."

Robert moved his shoulders. "I've still got that itch going, buddy." He stood next to him, looking at the sights. "Where's Melissa?"

"A little seasick at the moment," Terry replied.

"Oh, damn that sucks," Robert sympathized. "She didn't take the medicine?"

"Yeah, she has now. But it took her realizing she couldn't eat the chocolate chip cookies the kitchens made to finally capitulate and start taking it. She claims she hates taking any medicine if she doesn't have to. I don't take it, so she figured she didn't need any either."

"Still thinking an academic can do anything a soldier can?" Robert asked, grinning.

"Pretty much," Terry agreed. "It pisses her off that I have the memory I do and can still operate out in the field. She's pretty competitive."

"You picked a live one, that's for sure," Robert stated. He noticed Terry's eyes shift focus and stare as a large black Jeep turned into the lane coming down toward the boat. "You expecting someone?"

Terry nodded. "You still got that itch?" Robert grunted his affirmative. "Well, I made a call, and here comes our ace in the hole."

Robert watched the Jeep for a moment. "We are well and truly fucked, aren't we?"

Terry sighed. "Yes, we are."

"All I'm saying," Richard whined as their driver pulled into the last street before a large ship at the end, "is I hate the cold."

"After the winters in Europe, you would think this would be but a spring day," Samuel quipped.

Richard turned to look at his friend. "Have you truly been alive too long?" he asked in an old language. "We will be in Antarctica, not a bad winter in the Old Country."

Samuel shrugged. "The girls needed some time off, and are resting out in the belt. Gabrielle never punished us for Mark's death. Maybe this is our penance?"

"No." Richard sighed. "I spoke to Gabrielle. She knows we never quit doing our job."

"How is that?" Samuel asked, and his eyes widened. "You allowed her access to your memories?"

Richard nodded. "Mark deserved it. So did Sia and Giannini when Gabrielle spoke to them after the funeral. They recovered the body and had the funeral back in Colorado. Mark's family was shocked to learn he had been killed by a foreign government."

"They told them?" Samuel asked.

"No, I told them," Richard admitted.

"You never shared that with me."

"I'm still hurting, a little. Mark was a friend, and I was supposed to protect him. I failed," Richard insisted.

"No, we all failed against a government hit man. We didn't know we had been targeted at that level. I appreciated the fact you left enough to ID the guy."

"No mercy doesn't mean no body."

Their ride slowed to a stop in front of the ship. Both vampires looked out the glass. "I see our new contact is up there," Samuel informed his partner.

"Yes, and the other is the military contact, Robert," added Richard.

"Too many people with names starting with the letter R around here," Samuel bitched as he opened the door.

———

Robert's profession was bringing the pain using whatever options were available, and he was usually a very good judge of abilities.

The killing kind.

He and Terry had walked over to the gangway to welcome the two guys who had gotten out of the Jeep, each pulling a large bag with them... Bags that clinked and looked heavy. Very heavy, based on how hard the straps were straining in the men's grips. Neither one seemed to be bothered by the weight.

Who the hell did Terry invite to this party, anyway?

CHAPTER FIFTEEN

QBS *ArchAngel*

Sitting at the table, Tabitha bit into an apple and studied her laptop. The suite's main door opened and Barnabas walked in.

"Hello, Big B," she greeted, pushing the piece of apple around in her mouth to speak before swallowing.

"Hello, Two." He sat down at the table. "Tell me about your latest success."

Tabitha looked at him through slitted eyes, but he didn't seem to be giving her any grief about her less than elegant escape effort. "I have eighteen clients in the past two months. Sixteen, I've confirmed had nothing to do with my case, and I've ignored them. One is probably the bad guys, and the last I've set aside for special consideration."

Barnabas raised an eyebrow, so she added, "I'm not happy with the project on the second one, so if I have time, the guys and I are going to go visit the client." She shrugged, and Barnabas didn't follow up any further.

"The problem," she continued, "is the data leads to a dead end, electronically speaking. It's a cutout company, and I can't get anything in or out of there, nor can ADAM. Another prick-ass group who has a clue about digital security."

"It offends you?"

"I'm lazy," Tabitha answered. "I'd rather just break into their company using computers and be done with it, but whoever this group is, they aren't stupid. Well, let me qualify that. They aren't ignorant about hiding their tracks, so they're probably well-connected and have been doing this a while."

"Are you trying to make the people fit the facts?" Barnabas asked.

"Perhaps, but my hacking experience says it's usually the older people, the ones who worked before computers were so pervasive, who don't have a problem figuring out ways to function without them. Those of us who grew up with them are hampered by our inability to understand what you do without computers in your life."

Barnabas considered that for a moment. "You surprise me, Two. I hadn't expected that much insight from…"

Tabitha grinned. "A package as delicious as this?" She smiled and flipped her hair.

Barnabas closed his eyes and shook his head a couple of times. "Just when I think it's safe to compliment you."

"You will find out it is *always* safe to compliment a woman. We eat it up. Try it around other ladies, and let me know what you find," she told him as she took another bite of the apple.

Barnabas pursed his lips and nodded.

She swallowed the bite. "Except when it isn't," she added thoughtfully. "Like, right after you do something she's mad at you for. Then it just feels like you are trying to butter her up."

Barnabas put up a hand. "This isn't a discussion on how to have a male-female relationship, Number Two, so let's not go there."

"Fine, but one of these days you will get back on that horse, and you will be happy I've been dropping these little tidbits of wisdom."

"I'm sure I will," he replied drily. "What's the next step?"

"Visit the den of iniquity and see what information I can find out from the inside." She shrugged.

"No third-story windows?" he asked, smiling.

"No." She looked at Barnabas with a frown on her face. "No three-story buildings. However, the latest video updates from ArchAngel show it has lots of men with guns and dogs and shit, so I'm taking in the Tontos."

"You don't think that's overkill?" he asked.

"Hell, no! The Tontos laughed their asses off at the video ArchAngel had of my last successful data acquisition, so I decided they needed their own opportunity to get out in the field. The lazy bastards."

Barnabas stood up. "Well, remember we want to track down the truth, not start another war," he admonished and walked out of the room.

Tabitha murmured, "Mmmhmmm." Then, a few moments after Barnabas left, she looked up at the closed door as her eyebrows drew together. "War?"

Rio de Janeiro, Brazil

Robert was watching through the light amplification binoculars a few hours later when he heard a couple of clicks on the ace channel. Or at least, that was what he was calling the channel Richard and Samuel were using to communicate with his team.

During the daytime, this was a pretty safe zone, and so far, they were only missing one person out of everyone who had left the ship. One of the cooks had family in town and she hadn't come back, but that wasn't totally unexpected.

Now he turned his glasses up and down the dark docks, punctuated from time to time by weak lights, trying to figure out what the aces were trying to communicate to him and his team.

Moments later, the bridge door opened, and Terry, hair messed up and tucking a shirt in, asked, "What do we have?"

"No idea yet." Robert moved the binoculars away from his face. "But those two left the ship, and I'll be damned if I can even see them. Are they even warm-blooded?" Robert chuckled. "It's as if they disappear into the night or something." He put the goggles back to his face and continued looking when a voice came in on his team's line.

"Contact, south access, two vehicles. One sedan, one old Toyota filled to the brim with troublemakers."

Terry pulled up his own light amplification binoculars and turned in the direction Robert was looking. "Well, get the guys ready to repel boarders. Permission granted for live ammo."

"I wonder what our aces are going to do?" Robert asked as he relayed Terry's commands.

Samuel, south side. Richard sent to his friend.

Moments later, a figure dressed in black jumped to Richard's roof from across the street and jogged over, his feet crunching on the roof. "Do we have something to do?" Samuel asked as he came up beside him and looked over the side of the building.

"Yes, I think this time this is something we should probably take care of ourselves. The ship's team is breaking out live ammunition, so I don't want to be downrange when they unleash. That shit hurts."

"Well, the idiots are coming up this street. It isn't like we couldn't take out those two street lights and have some fun," Samuel agreed.

"You know, I'm just still pissed," Richard mused. "I don't have much fun in me at the moment."

"Oh, really?" Samuel asked. "So, Auran is still at the surface?"

Richard nodded.

"Well then, it's *all* going to be fun." Samuel's eyes went red and his voice got deeper. "Just a different type of fun, old friend."

Richard turned to his friend, his eyes blazing red. "Yes, there are no victims tonight," he agreed as he reached down to grab some pebbles from the rooftop.

"Shit!" Robert exclaimed. The two lights on the street blew out, and he would swear he saw two figures drop from the top of the two-story buildings next to the road.

That was when the chaos started.

"We have fire, we have fire!" Victor called over the radio. Gunshots and screams began to reach the ears of the men on the boat. Terry and Robert both stepped out of the bridge to hear what they could, and it wasn't pretty.

"Fuck me," Terry muttered. "Did you see a Toyota get thrown into a building?"

"See it, yes," Robert's eyes were glued to his binoculars. "Believe it? No."

Richard tossed two small pebbles, one at each, breaking both lights and dropping the road into darkness except for the head-lights of the small Toyota truck and old brown Ford sedan in front of it. He stepped off the building right behind Samuel, flexing his legs to drop almost silently to the street.

He saw Samuel walking at an angle to the first car and casu-ally kick out, his foot slamming into the driver's quarter panel, which caused the car to turn violently and ram into the building to their left. The Toyota in the back then caught Samuel in their headlights and slammed on the brakes.

Richard walked quickly up to the Toyota and smiled maliciously.

Santiago was driving Mateo's beat-up old Toyota. Since Mateo was stuck in jail after the latest police crackdown, he wouldn't be using it tonight. He and his people needed money to get weapons again after the last raid by the cops, and this looked like it was going to be an easy hit.

None of the guys were wearing any clothing or gang symbols that would point back to them since the cops were getting smart with videos and images. Even hiding in the slums wasn't working as it had years before.

"Dammit!" He elbowed Jorge. "Keep your elbows to yourself. I got to drive."

"Like that's so hard?" Jorge grunted. "Following Miguel and shit." He moved his elbow anyway.

Both streetlights sparked, then shattered. A second later, the taillights of the car in front of them jerked violently to the right. It skidded into a building, and then Santiago slammed on the brakes as a figure appeared in his headlights.

"What the fuck?" Santiago heard from a couple of guys holding on in the back, as well as a couple of pistol shots from the car in front before the screaming started. Then they saw another figure walk into their headlights, his eyes glowing red, and teeth, vampire teeth, prominent in his smile.

"Jesus, Mary, and the Holy Ghost!" Jorge exclaimed as the man grabbed the front of the Toyota. Santiago could hear the guys in the back stumbling and jumping out of the bed of the truck. Time seemed to go into slow motion as the man twisted. The truck instantly flipped, the street turning round and round, and then, with a massive, concussive slam, they hit a building. Quiet reigned for a moment as they got their wits about them.

"Santiago," Jorge rasped as he looked at his friend, only to see that half of his body was lost under the truck, laying on its side. "Oh, God!" he mumbled when the screech of the other door being torn off assailed his ears.

"Sir, what the fuck is going on?" Robert heard from Craig over the comm.

Robert clicked the mic. "Our protective detail has intervened. Everyone stay frosty," Robert replied.

Thomas jumped on the channel. "I thought *we* were the protective detail?"

"Apparently," Robert continued, "Terry's ace in the hole decided to save us the trouble of shooting a lot of people."

Screams shattered the night, the occasional gunshot punctuating the cries of the wounded.

"Sir," Victor called in, "did you have an itch?"

Robert clicked the button. "Affirmative, guys."

"Well, we are fucked." Victor added, "Again," to a lot of laughter over the comm.

Terry, still watching to see what he could see through his binoculars, smirked. "Well, at least they still have their sense of humor."

The strobing lights of the police and medical vehicles flashed around the walls as the cop Inspector Gutierrez had sent to the ship walked back and reported in. "Sorry, sir. They say they were all on the ship when they saw the headlights. Then, all hell broke loose, with screams and gunfire and lights going every which direction." He held up a small USB drive. "They gave us the video that was aimed in this direction."

"Anything special on it?" Inspector Gutierrez asked.

"Only one thing they didn't mention, sir," the cop added. "I can hear those in the fight screaming a name when it all goes down."

"Well?" the inspector asked as he accepted the USB drive.

"They are screaming '*El Diablo*,' sir," the cop answered as he looked at the dead.

Richard watched and listened to the police from three buildings away. Samuel was watching from the building on the other side of the street. Richard spoke softly but loud enough for Samuel. "'*El Diablo*?'" he chuckled. "If only Gabrielle would give us a few weeks in the slums, I'd give them *El Diablo*."

"It was fun," Samuel agreed. "Perhaps we were growing too sedentary in Australia."

"Did you heal yet?" Richard asked. "Bad luck taking that last shot."

"The little prick was playing dead, and shot me when I turned him over," Samuel bitched. "I can't believe I fell for that trick. Promise me you won't tell Gabrielle?"

"I'm not telling her anything, especially not that I saw you drop the little prick's body off the pier after you took payment for shooting you."

"Oh," Samuel answered. "I thought I was sneaky."

"Samuel, I've been with you hundreds of years. I don't believe that you *can* be sneaky around me."

"Bah," he replied. "I'll have you know I've fooled you plenty of times."

"Like when?" Richard asked, watching medics pick up a couple of arms and drop them on the body they belonged to.

Richard wondered if they would find the head. He remembered kicking it off, but not where it went.

"I can't tell you, or you'll figure out how I accomplished it."

"'*El Diablo*.'" Richard laughed again. "God, that's *priceless*."

Robert's team, except for Frederick, who was up top keeping watch on the police, joined Terry and their boss in the team's meeting room. Everyone on the ship had seen what was going on, but most of them thought it was some gang-on-gang violence that happened to have been close.

Terry looked around the table at the men. "I'm going to ask, but not require, you stay as mum about this as you can."

When you hire a bunch of guys who get assigned to agencies with acronyms, you take your chances, Terry thought.

"The two guys are with us—their names are Richard and Samuel—and they were the people who had a field day out there." He nodded in the general direction of the docks. "They're on loan here because we're getting more attention than we should be."

"I'll say this again." Thomas sighed. "Not that I'm complaining since it might have been a pain to go through the police discussions about us shooting everyone, but I thought *we* were the protection detail?"

"You are, or should be," Terry amended. "After the incident in Germany, I reached out to the same people who helped us in the Sandpit to see if they had anything they might be able to provide."

"Oh, goody," Craig muttered.

"Hey, just be glad they're on our side," Robert interjected.

"Hey." Craig put up his hand. "I got nothing against them. We'd all be six feet under without their help with ISIS, so I'm good there. It just means we're probably on to something, and anything we find is going to get lost in transit."

"No," Terry told them. "All that stuff was returned—eventually," he qualified. "Melissa says it got back to her after a week."

"So, they probably went through it and made sure nothing was relevant and gave it back," Craig finished.

"Might have been the price for saving our lives." Terry shrugged. "I don't know."

"I've heard screams before," Victor mused. "Those men saw monsters out there."

"The police officer," Robert stated, "says not one person was left alive. Most had been torn apart, or had major slashes across their bodies and bled out. Like something a monster would do." He looked around. "Just remember these monsters are *our* monsters and be polite."

"Fuck yeah, be polite." Charlie laughed. "Because I don't care what anyone else says. Every time I'm involved with TQB, those motherfuckers get scarier and scarier."

Every man sitting knocked twice on the table, affirming their agreement with Charlie.

CHAPTER SIXTEEN

<u>TarHunt Protection Services, Kentucky, USA</u>

"Section One, move to channel Alpha Seven and report," Night Watch Leader Ryan Burrow called into his microphone as he punched in the new channel for his second set of speakers.

"Terri here. Clear outside Building Three, Base." a feminine voice spoke over the speaker.

"Roger, Terri." Ryan checked off the task. "Clear."

Ryan did this again for five more sets of outside perimeter guards watching the main building Ryan was in, as well as the other two buildings. One outside building was temporary quarters for those staying less than two weeks, and the other was for meetings with external contacts.

No one outside of the company was allowed inside the headquarters unless they were with upper management, and that was very rare.

Ryan's video system hit sixty different locations within the main building and ten inside the other two. Personally, none of the guards much cared about the two outside buildings. If something happened there, it was treated as a nuisance.

In this building? That would be a problem.

Tabitha and her guys got ready in the same room. They helped her make sure her weapons were strapped on properly.

Ryu had been selected to be her backup and would carry a backpack with the electronic equipment she would need to hack the system. Hirotoshi was with Katsu, who was Tabitha's hacking backup. They all had the electronic devices Team BMW had built especially for her team.

Small computers with Etheric communications to ArchAngel and ADAM, with the special EI the two had pulled together for Tabitha.

Named Achronyx, it was a specially-programmed subset of ArchAngel running off hardware presently staged on the *Arch-Angel*. Eventually, it would reside in the ship being designed for Tabitha's team. The Etheric connection stopped the tablet's signals from being discovered but allowed Achronyx the option to sniff and subvert the surrounding assets if possible.

Usually through poor Wi-Fi as a first choice, then through other means as available.

"Ranger Team 2 to Pod bay, Ranger Team 2 to Pod bay," Arch-Angel announced.

Tabitha and her team silently left the compartment.

Minutes later, they had boarded one of the larger Pods and strapped in. "Take us down," Tabitha directed. The video screens showed their Pod lifting off the deck and heading out of the *Arch-Angel*. Soon, the Earth was in front of them, and they were on their way.

The black Pod stayed up half a mile as the team watched the heat signatures walk the grounds beneath them.

"Here, here, and here." Hirotoshi pointed to three locations. "They are uncovered at all times."

It had taken fifteen minutes for the micro-drones to settle in and locate most of the external security sensors.

"That's because," Tabitha hit a couple of buttons to pull up the heat sensors, "they're trusting the motion and heat sensors in those areas, and the walls have no entrances." She hit a couple more buttons, zooming in on the roof. "I don't see any options for us dropping on the roof, either."

Kouki spoke up. "Why not just hit them hard, take down the humans, and power our way in?"

"We're trying to leave people alive. These guys aren't bad, they're just in between us and the information that I need," Tabitha answered. "We can't be the good guys if we do a lot of bad things to innocent people."

"I didn't mean kill them, Kemosabe. I meant render them unconscious," he clarified.

"Oh." Tabitha turned and looked at the vampire. "I'm sorry. I'm used to everything being black or white."

Kouki shrugged. "We are just as capable of rendering senseless."

Tabitha turned to Hirotoshi. "What's the downside to Kouki's suggestion?"

"I would think video," Ryu offered, and Hirotoshi nodded.

"This place is fifteen miles outside any human habitation, in the middle of nowhere," Tabitha continued.

"I thought they were in Kentucky?" Shin asked.

"Ask most people, and they will tell you that this *is* nowhere. Well, except for the fine people of Kentucky, I'm sure," she added and played with the controls again. "Achronyx, I need information about the power supply coming into this set of buildings."

"Do you want to include local power sources, or strictly those arriving from external locations?" the EI asked.

"Both."

A solid line came into the camp from the west, and a portion behind the main building was highlighted.

"Send a drone around the back of the building. I need to see what that looks like." Down below, a small insect drone, the size of a fly, sped around, heading toward the large building and then around the side to hover above a large metal skid. It had a rectangular half and a circular half.

"That half," Tabitha pointed to the side with the large pipe jutting out of the other side, "is the momentum device to provide quality electricity to the computers inside. The power is going to come into this device, get cleaned up, and then go into the building. If the electricity dies, the momentum of the massive weight spins enough to keep the power going. Then, they probably have additional batteries inside to maintain the power at least a few hours in case they run out of diesel."

"We need the power, or we can't use the computers," Katsu commented.

"Teach your granny to suck eggs, Katsu," Tabitha murmured while she played with the controls highlighting the building schematics they had been able to pilfer from the local government offices. "Here's the central office, and here looks like the primary location for the computer geeks."

"So, we hit the main office to connect to the server?" Katsu asked.

"No, you go for the computer admin's computers. If there's a back door, those fuckers will have one because they won't want to walk through the security to get to the servers if they don't have to." She spoke a little louder. "Achronyx, do we have a count of internal people?"

"I have located eight heat sources walking outside around building one. None in buildings two or three."

"Plus, count on another one or two in a control room to be safe," Ryu added.

"That seems reasonable," Tabitha agreed and stood up. "So, is the plan hit to them fast, knock them out, kill security, and then hack the servers?"

She looked at Hirotoshi, who seemed to be accepting input from the rest of the team just by looking at them. "Yes, it is."

"Achronyx, take us down as soon as you have scrambled all available security."

"Understood. One moment, please," the electronic voice replied.

Down below, seventeen small devices angled toward any wires that were available. Six of them, larger than the rest, pulled out metal pins that stabbed the cables, seeking a way to penetrate the wires within.

"Core security has been infiltrated. Please stay away from all areas marked in red since I have been unable to take control of those signals."

The team locked in the areas in their minds and nodded.

"Just keep the video off of us, Achronyx," Tabitha requested.

Ryan kicked back, sipping his coffee. It was always the midnight to three o'clock shift that was hardest for him to stay awake. On his third sip, two of his twenty monitors went to static.

He leaned forward, setting his coffee down. "What the hell?" He hit the call-all button. "Stay sharp, people. We have interference on the video cameras." He barely got out the last word when the audio squawked a piercing loud high note and he slammed his hand down on the Mute button.

"Shit!" He grabbed the walkie-talkie and hit the button. "I'm on mobile walkie-talkie, people. What are you seeing?"

"Nothing's wrong out here, boss," Terri replied. "Building Three is clear."

"Nothing here either," Deith reported.

"Where are you located, Deith?" Ryan asked. He waited a few

seconds. "Deith, where are you located?" Ryan swore. "Terri, can you see Deith?" He barely got the question out when four more of the videos went to static.

Shit, shit, SHIT! "Terri, can you see Deith? Terri?"

He double-checked his channel, and he was transmitting on the right one for the time of night. A blip on one of the videos caught his eye. Two more video cameras, these inside the building, also had something flash in front of them.

A female spoke. "Hey, boss?"

Ryan raised the walkie-talkie. "Terri, where the fuck are you?" His frustration destroyed the calm demeanor he had meant to project. "We've got people inside the building somehow. Get whoever you can and get your ass in here!"

This time, he practically yelled the demand as two more of his internal video cameras went out. He reached across and hit the prep button to warm up the final server defense system.

Then, the power dropped for a microsecond before the backup came online.

There was a rap on his door and a "Boss, open up" from a female on the other side.

Ryan pushed his chair back, took two quick steps, and pushed open the armored door. "Terri, get your ass…"

"Hi, sugar." A pretty Latina all in black smiled at him as all of the cameras behind him blanked. "Terri is asleep right now, but she gave me this to play with." She waved Terri's walkie-talkie back and forth. "So…" She stepped into the room and grabbed Ryan's shoulder.

The smaller woman easily forced him down on his knees. "You are going to take a short nap after you give me the code to the server room, honey."

"I can't!" Ryan shook his head. "I don't have the combination to the lock." He grabbed the lady's arm and tried to dislodge, then twist it. She popped him in the head.

"Stop that shit!" Ryan slammed to the floor, grabbing his head when the pain from her slap registered.

Tabitha looked back at the door, and Ryan's head moved slowly to see someone in black, face covered, who shook his head.

She looked down at Ryan. "Dammit, that makes things annoyingly more difficult." She stepped over Ryan, who was still seeing two of everything. "Put him to sleep."

Tabitha walked toward the server room, Ryu behind her. She pulled the small Achronyx device out of a pocket. "Achronyx, can you do anything about this?"

"According to location sensors, you are in front of the research area. The servers are located in a room beyond one and past another door. This door is on a simple alarm system that is bypassed. You can break it down."

"Who can break it down?" Tabitha asked, her voice going an octave higher. "I don't have bones like Bethany Anne, do I?" she turned to Ryu. "Do you?"

Ryu stepped forward, and Tabitha stepped back. He looked at the slice of glass with tiny wires six inches wide traveling up the door. He turned around, scanned the hall, and then walked to a bathroom and stepped in.

"Seriously?" Tabitha asked. "I ask him about opening a door, and he goes to take a piss?" A second later, she heard a loud screech and then a bang from inside the bathroom, and the door opened once more.

Ryu stepped out with a misshapen metal box, and Tabitha took another step back. Ryu walked up to the door and then the glass shattered as Ryu sped up and shoved the metal box through the glass. He reached in and unlocked the door from the other side.

Tabitha went in behind him, noticing that the tiny wires had cut slashes in the metal box. "Oh, those would have hurt like a bitch," she muttered.

They walked across the crunchy floor, glass not bothering them in their shoes with the leather soles. Ryu looked at the final door, a metal one with no window on it. "You need in there?" he asked.

"Yes. Maybe. Hold on," she told him and clicked the call button on her collar. "Katsu, any luck?"

"None, Kemosabe," came back. "It seems these admins are not as lazy as most."

"Fucking great. Okay, thanks." Tabitha nodded at Ryu. "I need in there."

Ryu looked around and up to the dropped ceiling. Turning to his left, he took two steps, then pushed off the nearby wall and popped two of the ceiling tiles. They fell on the floor and he did it again, but this time he grabbed something up in the ceiling, and his body and then his feet disappeared.

"Always fucking leaving when all I need is a door opened," Tabitha muttered. "Imagine what he'd be like on a date."

There was a small noise from the other side of the door and then a click, and it opened. Ryu waved her in.

"Wow, that was impressive." She saw an air vent that had been ripped off the ceiling. Its parts littered the floor.

She looked at the three rows of server systems, each twenty feet long and back-to-back. "Wow, déjà vu." She moved to the first monitor and keyboard system, then called, "I need you, Ryu, so badly," as the man came up and turned around.

She zipped open the bag and pulled out her very small laptop and two very tiny USB keys, plus three cables. "Sorry, just wanted you for your tool, buddy."

Ryu snorted and started walking around the room when she was finished pulling the electronics equipment.

Achronyx called over the team band, "We have a 911 call to the local emergency services. ETA seven minutes."

"Don't ever tell me time," Tabitha muttered.

"I didn't. It was actually six minutes and forty-six seconds. I rounded up," Achronyx answered.

"We need to work on your manners, Achronyx," Tabitha stated as she looked over to see what was happening as she tried to hack into the system. "Some other time, though. When you tell me the time on…" she paused and frowned. "Dammit, that doesn't look right." She changed ports and typed additional commands.

Moments later, her eyes opened wide. "Oh fuck, oh fuck, oh fuck, no!" She started typing rapidly, then started cursing in Spanish.

Ryu walked in when he couldn't understand the cussing—it was coming so fast—and saw she was typing much more rapidly than the computer was able to register. Finally, she slammed her hand against the cage next to her, causing it to dent in a few inches.

"*FUCK!*" she screamed. "Tabitha, you idiot! You tried amazing them with stupidity, now try a few tactics, you hack." She looked at the door, punched the lock, and twisted it to the side. Grabbing one of the USB keys, she put an arm back into the cage and turned to Ryu. "Do me a favor and fuck up every one of the cage doors so none look any more special than the others."

Ryu shrugged and started walking down the lane, punching, kicking, and delivering head-butts to the cage doors to mess them up. By the time he was done with the last row, Tabitha came down the row, chose a door midway, and opened it. Reaching behind it, she explained, "The bastards did a melt job on the primary access. We tripped something, and they fucking scrammed the main hard drives. I'm putting a USB on the back in an out-of-the-way place. Maybe we'll get lucky, and we can get access in a few days after they fix everything." She pulled her arm out, closed and locked the door, and walked back the other way, stomping on the floor.

"Maybe we'll get lucky, and the fuckers won't be so damned good a second time." She sounded exasperated as she turned the corner.

A second later, Ryu heard her voice in the room, and over the comm. "Tontos, let's shag ass. This was a bust."

CHAPTER SEVENTEEN

<u>Dulce Lake, New Mexico, USA</u>

The underground base had been around for well over seventy years. The natural tunnels under the base opened into a deep underground cavern system that went off in multiple directions. The single base entrance led to a shaft that descended over two thousand feet using a large elevator that was over twenty feet in diameter.

However, for operations, various large doors were opened into the deep cavern system, and if you had the right map, you could come up in any one of a hundred different exits spread over almost two thousand square miles.

Some were barely broad enough to allow a man with a backpack to squeeze out into a forested area, and a couple of others allowed their large craft options to fly out into the nighttime, hidden from civilization.

Mostly.

Occasionally someone might see something, but their technology had gotten much better in the seven-plus decades since they were formed in 1947 by the Executive Order of President

Harry S. Truman. Their job was to facilitate recovery and investigation of alien spacecraft.

Over the years, most of those who knew about the base and their operations had passed away. When age or strategic removal took out all the main players who had been part of the creation of the group, they went beyond black.

Now, they were line items in a budget that could hide the state of Wyoming.

They lived by their own rules, their own plays, their own goals. They brought in government connections when they needed them, always keeping the highest-level security since they, until recently, had held all of the technology cards.

Which, in the end, was also their Achilles heel.

Patrick sat at one end of the table, facing the head of the scientific side of the Majestic 12. His side, operations and special tasks, was more action-based. Dr. Eva Hocks was on the opposing side of the table, and she represented all research.

Since Patrick had called this meeting, he opened. "I'm sorry to say we have a potential problem. Knowledge of this project is now outside our control."

The other eleven individuals waited to hear what else Patrick had to say. Some were only counting the moments until they would be released to go back down to level six and seven. Their need for understanding and the dopamine it released in their system was the only high they could count on to drive their daily existence.

Others, having lived down here for so many years, had gone through these problems before and never had it become a serious threat, so they weren't worried.

"I have called a full lockdown for everyone to stay here in the base until such a time as we feel comfortable we have the situation under control, except for Tanya, who is still seeking her target. We have confirmed that the three questionable members are no longer here on Earth, or at least not in any area our markers can be located," Patrick amended.

"How is that possible?" Dr. Hocks spoke for the first time. "We have tested those to be locatable over ninety-nine percent of the face of the Earth, and even up to a quarter-mile underground."

"My suspicion," Patrick countered, "is that it's because all of our equipment is pointing down from our satellites, not up into outer space."

"Well, we didn't take them there, so... Oh." She stopped talking.

"Yes, 'oh,'" Patrick agreed. "We have pretty strong proof that they are presently being held by TQB off-planet."

"Why do they want them?" Dr. Abesemmins asked from down the table to Patrick's left.

Patrick turned to answer the doctor's question. "We believe we have someone trying to acquire some of our technology. Somehow, they located one of our employees who was easily suborned due to family and was blackmailing them. TQB figured this out, how we don't know, and carried out an operation to successfully extricate them. Fortunately, none of our data was lost."

"Told you we should have shut down the Family Project back in '06," Dr. Abesemmins commented.

Patrick put up his hand. "Well, you can be assured the project is dead. As in, we have no members with family in our group at this time."

"Good," was the doctor's reply.

"Unfortunately, we don't have those employees anymore, either. None of them had access to the lower levels or the higher clearance levels," Patrick nodded at Dr. Abesemmins, "due to concerns over their mixed allegiance."

"Okay," Dr. Hocks interrupted. "Other than a lockdown, how does this affect us?"

Patrick controlled the rolling of his eyes. As but one member of the twelve, he had power but not the ultimate authority to call for a strike using the advanced technology. "Tanya has reported our intelligence has confirmation the US Navy is underway for a second Operation Highjump."

Eva snorted. "Do they want another ass-kicking like they got the last time? Hell, we don't mess with the Thule ourselves, and I'm pretty sure we have overtaken them in technology."

"The government doesn't believe the previous ass-kicking happened, Eva. Remember, we've changed the history so much, no one believes what was printed in the past anymore," Patrick reminded them.

"There is an interesting change, however," Patrick continued. "The government has figured out the Thule haven't been answering with their 'go away' signal for a few years. No one is sure if the Thule are still alive or not," he finished.

This time, everyone watched Patrick as Dr. Hocks leaned forward, putting her hands on the table. "Is that so?"

Patrick smiled back. "Yes, it is."

The ride back to the *ArchAngel* was quiet. Hirotoshi and Ryu let Tabitha go through all the emotions of an unsuccessful operation.

When the Pod arrived, she unbuckled and turned to her team. "Thank you all. I have to apologize since I failed to realize they would erase their data and I didn't think to take any precautions. I won't make that mistake a second time."

She inhaled deeply and sighed. "Hirotoshi, I'll get with you and Ryu in a little while. I'm going to walk the halls. Guys, I won't fuck up like this again."

As she spoke, the larger Pod doors were opened by those in the Pod bay, and she turned and walked out, nodding to the two men as she strode toward the exit.

A half-hour later, Tabitha heard some coarse language coming from ahead of her, and she looked up to see where she was.

She was in R&D. The voice was female, so probably Jean Dukes. For a moment or two, she allowed herself to just float along, listening to the tirade Jean was going through, then she realized something.

She wasn't allowing herself to vent.

She put her hand to her mouth and tried to hold in her snicker. Jean was apparently really riled up. It was common knowledge that Jean loved her team and they loved her back, but she sure had a way of talking to them.

She stopped outside the door, which was closed, but Tabitha could easily hear the latest rant since Jean's voice was clear as day. "Listen, you goat-fucking morons, better unfuck this rat-fuck of a situation right fucking now before I go back in time and make the best part of you dribble out your mom's ass instead!"

Tabitha quickly walked away, making it twenty feet before she busted out laughing. It took her a few turns to realize that she had accepted Jean's comment as if it were directed to her as well.

A huge smile lighting up her face, she started walking toward her quarters. "Oh, my God," she whispered. "Go back in time and make the best part..." She didn't finish the quote out loud because she started laughing again. She tried uselessly to stifle her snorting by putting her hand over her mouth, but all she did was muffle the sounds as tears streamed down her face.

CHAPTER EIGHTEEN

QBS _ArchAngel_

There was a sharp rap on Bethany Anne's door. "Come in, John," she called. She continued petting Ashur's head as the massive guard walked in.

"Are you planning on going to the Yollin meeting in your sweats?"

Bethany Anne glanced at the top of her tablet. "Dammit!" She bolted out of bed, tossing the tablet to John as she sped around him and entered her closet. John heard the rattle of hangers and some extremely fast cussing coming from inside. Moments later, she walked out wearing blue jeans and a black shirt.

"Not exactly well-dressed today, hmmm?" John smiled as she waved him off and he followed her out of her suite.

As Bethany Anne walked into the meeting, she saw that Bobcat, William, Marcus, and Jeffrey were sitting down. Also the Yollins Captain Kael-ven, Kiel, and Royleen were there. Dan, Peter, Nathan, Patricia, and her dad were in attendance as well. She had already passed Eric and Scott in the hall outside of the doors, and John kept five feet behind her when she sat down at the head of the table.

Bethany Anne opened the conversation. "I apologize, everyone, I got captivated reading about the status of our new ships in Admiral Thomas's reports. For those who want to know, the new ships are going well, and he reports we should have the first two within the next six months."

Dan asked, "Admiral Thomas is doing pretty well, then?"

Bethany Anne nodded. "He certainly seems to be happy with the results. If we can continue to get some of the parts manufactured on Earth and transferred to him, they can keep up this pace. But should we suffer continued harassment of our manufacturing partners, the production tools we are getting from Japan increase in importance."

William offered, "Yuko is doing a good job there, and we've been able to purchase an additional twenty percent over our original agreements. I also know there are many smaller machine shops that probably have tooling and machines they'd get rid of in a heartbeat if they could find a cash buyer."

Bethany Anne nodded. "That's a good point. Why don't you and Patricia jump on that? I suspect from the noise we're hearing from the United Nations, this might get pretty nasty. I would prefer we have as much manufacturing capacity as we possibly can."

Bobcat smirked at William, who rolled his eyes. "No rest for the wicked," Bobcat told him. "If you have a good idea, make sure you're willing to see it through to fruition." He winked as William nodded at him in agreement.

"How are you feeling?" she asked William.

"Right as rain now. Since the Pod-doc finished with me, I'm as good as new. Plus, I've lost ten pounds, so the babes better be careful when the new William starts strutting his stuff!" he gloated.

Patricia offered, "I'll inform the newspapers."

William smiled. "See that you do. Also, can you get a few good pictures from my right side? It shows me off better." He struck a pose and got a snort from Patricia.

"I'll see about using some grainy old footage. Maybe we can hide a few wrinkles behind pixilation," she replied.

Bobcat laughed and William smiled, rubbing his nose with his middle finger.

"Okay, since we have the preliminaries out of the way, I'd like to discuss a few things, and I want everyone's input as I ask about Yollin culture." She nodded to the three aliens in attendance. "Understanding that so far, the only aliens we've had in our solar system recently that we're aware of are the Yollins. I don't intend to allow them to be behind us, ready to go back and attack the Earth. According to my conversations with Captain Kael-ven, we can expect hostilities as we make our way through Yollin space."

Lance opened the conversation. "Kael-ven, do the Yollins always attack other species in their territory? And is it only your home system, or your secondary or tertiary locations as well?"

Kael-ven adjusted his forelegs on the couch and turned to the general. "The only time ships from Yoll would not attack is if those crossing our territory have an obvious military advantage. In that case, we would have to presume the other species is superior to us. Therefore, our caste system would require all of us, even our king, to be subservient."

Dan asked, "So, there's no such thing as an equal to your king? I'm asking whether or not you have interactions with other species where you consider them friends, or at least allies?"

It took a moment for Kael-ven to answer this question. "There is a clarification I must make. While we do have allies, we recognize their military strength is presently beyond our ability to overcome. Internally, however, our caste system is patiently waiting for a day when we can subjugate them. Should the allies stay ahead of us, we will never attack. But should there come a day when our efforts to expand our empire provides the opportunity, that is the day they will become subservient to us."

"Kael-ven," Bethany Anne asked, "can you better explain the caste system of the Yollins?"

"Certainly." He turned to Bethany Anne. "There are four major castes on Yoll. These have been in existence for well over a hundred generations. Some historians suspect the caste system is derived from ancient religious beliefs."

Royleen chittered for a second to Kael-ven, and his translation software was unable to keep up.

Kael-ven turned back to the humans. "Royleen has clarified that among scientists, it is well understood that the caste system was religious at one time, so please excuse my ignorance. Right now, the four core castes are: first level, Kolin. This is the prime ruler, the king, and those reporting to him on Yoll. Further, any of those who operate large political areas outside of the primary Yollin system must be in this caste. The second caste is called Chloret. These are the secondary rulers and high-level leadership positions throughout the worlds, including what you call the military brass.

"The third caste is called Mont. These are the lower-level leadership positions, all high-level skilled labor positions, and management for guilds and all middle military positions. For example, Kiel here is in Mont. The fourth cast is called Shuk. It is the unskilled labor and lowest of the skilled labor. For the military, these would be the privates. Finally, there is an un-caste group called Kiene. These are the undesirables. On your world, you might call them criminals or malcontents, those who have lost their way. Often, they are transferred to land masses which have little to no civilization."

"I thought Yoll was overpopulated?" Marcus asked.

Royleen spoke up. "Yes and no. There are certain areas of the planet that are tough to live on. The landmass is not very usable to build upon, and the indigenous population, the animals, can be quite vicious. Therefore, they are considered a step up from prisons."

"Yes, we have a country that did something similar in our history. More than one, come to think of it," Marcus amended. "It all depended on how important the malcontent was."

Bethany Anne asked, "So each of these caste levels has more to do with roles and responsibility than anything to do with birth?"

Kiel clarified, "You are born into a caste, but you have the opportunity to make something of yourself and get enough acclaim to move up."

"Chloret is the highest caste level an individual can attain without the king recognizing you personally. That rarely happens," added Kael-ven.

"Because people rarely accomplish feats worth recognizing, or does the king fear competition?" asked Bobcat.

Both Kiel and Royleen looked at Captain Kael-ven, who replied, "As the highest-caste individual here and therefore the one who can answer this without others being penalized, please recognize that this is an answer which could cause an individual to be stricken of their place and become a member of the Kiene caste."

Bethany Anne nodded in acknowledgment of his concern. "We understand."

He chittered a moment before continuing. "My personal judgment is that the caste system is a method for keeping Yollin society organized, structured, and a way whereby those at the highest levels maintain their positions. Further, those of us in the first and second castes are usually recognizable by our additional set of legs," he explained.

Bethany Anne heard William murmur to Bobcat, "I was wondering how that extra pair came about."

Kael-ven continued, "It is by no means a definitive way to tell if somebody is in the Kolin or Chloret castes. I am the son of a family who has been at my level for three generations."

"Interesting," Marcus murmured.

MICHAEL ANDERLE

Dan turned to Bethany Anne. "Do you think there's a way to use the caste system to change Yollin society?"

While Bethany Anne looked at the ceiling, thinking, she did not fail to see the many heads at the table look at each other, wondering if Dan had some insights. Finally, she glanced at everyone and gave him a small smile. "Yes, Dan has it right."

She waved at the three Yollins. "I've spoken with each of them before. Well, let me amend that to say I have talked to Captain Kael-ven and Scientist Royleen before. I was yelling at and punching Kiel most of the time."

Kiel rubbed his chest absentmindedly.

"One thing that strikes me about Yollin society is that they are very structured because of the many generations of being within this system. From what I understand, the king comes from the prime family and the rules state that only those at the top level may challenge the king, yet few do so, since if they fail, they lose their lives, and their whole family is tossed into Kiene. It tends to put a damper on upsetting the political structure. Those who are in lower castes are not considered smart enough and of good enough genetics to rule. The way I understand it," she nodded to the Yollins, "and please correct me if I'm wrong, the general understanding is that each caste is just a little slower mentally and a little bit less physically fit than the one above?"

The Yollins agreed.

"Now," she smiled at the team, "the Achilles heel of the Yollin society is that anyone who can beat the king is, therefore, suitable to rule."

Lance muttered, "Uh-oh." Bethany Anne grinned at him.

"Soooo," Dan drawled. "You plan on challenging the king?"

"It's the least I can do after he attacked my people." She smiled devilishly. "What else is a queen supposed to do when offended by another monarch?"

Dan turned to Captain Kael-ven, pointing at Bethany Anne. "Is what she is proposing permissible in your society?"

Kael-ven chittered before replying, "Yes. There have been two occasions in our history when other species have challenged Kolin to Kolin."

"Why do I feel like the other shoe hasn't dropped yet?" Lance asked the table at large.

"Probably because it's about ten feet long and dropping from a thousand feet above us right now," Bobcat responded.

"What does this phrase mean, 'the other shoe hasn't dropped yet?'" Captain Kael-ven asked.

Jeffrey responded, "It means that we haven't heard the worst part yet."

"There isn't much more to add," Captain Kael-ven stated. "Except that the challenge is to the death, and you are not allowed to bring anything to the fight."

"So, no weapons, no armor, no protection?" Lance asked.

Captain Kael-ven's head turned sideways and then back upright. "No, nothing as not *anything*. The way you came into existence."

John asked from behind Bethany Anne, "The Queen gets to fight in her birthday suit?"

Bethany Anne tried to ignore the smirks around the table. "For the record, there will be no video taken of this fight," she declared.

Captain Kael-ven added one more item. "Do any of you realize that our king is approximately twice as large as I am?"

"And the other shoe has finally landed," William announced to a suddenly quiet table.

Bobcat piped up, "Well, you know what they say about the bigger they are."

"Yeah, they kick your ass twice as hard," Lance finished.

"Wow, let's not all think Bethany Anne has a shot at winning this fight or anything just because my opponent will stand twelve feet tall, have bony exoskeleton armor surrounding him, be hellishly fast fighting, and have multiple appendages. Well, hell. Yeah, he might make me sweat."

Dan asked the question. "Captain Kael-ven, I understand you and a significant portion of your crew are now vassals of Bethany Anne. What would happen if our people bested yours in challenges at this point in time? Those that are equivalent caste or higher?"

This time, most of those at the table recognized that Kiel and Royleen looked at Captain Kael-ven with curiosity. Apparently, this wasn't something pondered much in Yollin society.

Captain Kael-ven opened his mouth and closed it multiple times before finally answering, "The tests would have to be appropriate for the challenges to matter. For example," he waved in Scientist Royleen's direction, "it would be inappropriate to require Scientist Royleen to accept a challenge related to martial arts. Nor," he waved toward Kiel, "would it be appropriate to have Kiel answer scientific questions for his challenge."

Captain Kael-ven turned to his fellow aliens and chittered for a moment, then turned back. "I have confirmed with both Kiel and Scientist Royleen that they would feel that those who beat them were either in the same caste or higher. If it was apparent they were far superior, they would feel like the individuals were accredited a caste higher than themselves."

"Where are you going with this, Dan?" Bethany Anne asked across the table.

"I think that we need to consider a long-term strategy for Yollin society. I suspect we'll be implementing this plan to beat the Kurtherians for many, many decades, right?" Everyone around the table nodded agreement. "So, I'm wondering what we need to do to make sure the Yollin society attributes humans as being superior across the castes. We can't hope to modify the caste system within the Yollin society without first qualifying how we stand in the caste system."

"Don't just try to tear it down without first showing we are better than it?" Jeffrey asked.

"Precisely. Since we're going to stage the battle station in Yollin space, I would prefer to know we're working toward creating a better society for the Yollins, rather than only keeping them as a beaten opponent under our thumbs."

"You're thinking about the Japanese after World War II?" Lance asked.

"Not exactly," Dan countered. "But they are as good an example as any."

Bethany Anne shrugged. "I understand your logic, but how would we work this out?"

"Question, Captain Kael-ven," Dan interjected. He waited until he had the Yollin's attention. "Is it safe to say that the highest-level person in any role on your ship is the best individual for that position?"

Captain Kael-ven answered, "If you mean are they the highest ranking within the caste system, the answer is yes. On my ship, I believe it to be true that they are also the best individual for the role. However, I would not suggest you take that qualification and think it applies to every ship we have."

"So, would your people accept one of our people beating one of yours as being superior to them?"

Kiel interjected, "So, would Bo'cha'tien accept someone who beat me as being superior to her?"

"Yes, that's what he is asking," Kael-vcn agreed.

Kiel turned to Dan. "If not, I would beat her myself. By suggesting she was better than someone who beat me, she is saying she is better than me, and for me to keep my position, it can only be construed as a challenge."

"Well, that's right up a Wechselbalg's alley." Peter spoke for the first time in the meeting. "If you can't beat the one ahead of you in the pack, you don't have the right to fight anyone above them until you do."

Kiel turned to look at the human. "That would seem like there is much fighting then if it is always required."

Peter shrugged. "It isn't always necessary. For example, those of us who are feistier will ask someone if they want to challenge to keep their spot. Typically, you've seen someone fight before they get to you. If you're in the middle of the pecking order, you know if you are going to accept the challenge or allow them to move past you and accept they are better already. If there's any doubt, or you're just stubborn, then you accept all challenges as fights."

"Where do you rank?" Kiel asked.

"Probably equivalent to you, Kiel," Peter replied. "I answer to Dan, here, who is the brass, so to speak. I'm the muscle."

"So, if you challenge me, then we are equal, correct?" Kiel asked.

"Yes, I'll challenge you," Peter agreed before anyone could get a word in edgewise. "What are the conditions?"

"What are they normally for your people?"

"My people?" Peter asked. "The same as for your king—only what you came into the world with."

Captain Kael-ven turned to his other side. "Royleen?"

"What?" The scientist turned. "You want me to accept a challenge?"

"Yes, if the humans would consider it. You are our top scientist. If one of them can best you, then we are in agreement."

"What about you?" Dan asked.

"Me?" Kael-ven asked. "I thought it was painfully obvious that I have already been beaten by you. For me, it is leading my ship. I had the element of surprise and a tactically superior position, and I accepted my defeat. I am not at the level of Queen Bethany Anne here." He nodded at her. "So that isn't a question for me."

"I'll accept the challenge," Marcus stated.

"You?" William and Bill both blurted.

"Way to support your teammate, you two," Bethany Anne remarked.

"It's not that, boss." Bobcat pointed his thumb back at his friend. "Marcus here hates to play Monopoly or checkers, or…"

"*Bet*," added William.

"So yeah, we're a little surprised," Bobcat finished.

"Perhaps," Marcus admitted. "But you guys have never been around scientists when we get confrontational."

"Uh, yeah, that's true," William agreed.

"Word. And two scoops of hell-yeah to go on top of that. You start drawing in squiggles…" Bobcat began.

"That's scientific notation, you Neanderthals," Marcus retorted.

"I've got that shirt," Bobcat mused. "It's just dirty at the moment."

"Oh, sorry about that," William interjected. "I think I used it last week to clean up an oil spill."

Bobcat turned to William. "Shit, really?"

"Pretty sure. The grayish-green one?" Bobcat nodded. "It's gone."

"Well, damn." Bobcat turned back to Marcus. "Sorry, no t-shirt, but I'll agree with you."

Bethany Anne put up a hand to stop the trio and looked at Kael-ven. "What would the challenge look like for the scientists?"

"They would each pick a subject, and the final question would be agreed upon by the two teams."

"Teams?" Bethany Anne asked.

"Well, yes, of course," Royleen explained. "The scientist always has a second who is subject to the direction of the scientist. It allows the scientist to drive the direction of the research and then move forward with other projects. Is this not how you do it?"

"Well," Marcus answered, "in some cases. In others, we are our own mini-group of one person. Is there any limitation to who the support person is?" He looked pointedly at Bobcat and William, who both leaned away from him.

Royleen chittered as he watched the byplay between the three humans. "No. It cannot be mechanical, it must be organic and be able to confirm who it is, but they are allowed to support their lead in any way," he pointedly looked at the two men leaning away from Marcus, "they possibly can."

"Oh, good, then." Marcus smiled.

Bobcat and William looked at each other, confused.

CHAPTER NINETEEN

QBS _ArchAngel_

It took two days for them to get together. They already had half the crew of the Yollin ship with them on the _ArchAngel_, and for the challenges, most of the rest of the _G'laxix Sphaea_ wanted to be there as well. Since the other half of the _G'laxix Sphaea_ crew had been housed in fourteen containers on the moon, those on the ship took a few hours to move the _ArchAngel_ in position and transit the aliens up to it for the event.

Not that the aliens weren't watched surreptitiously by the Guardians to make sure no one decided to go on a walkabout by themselves.

Fortunately, they did not.

The largest open area available besides the Pod bay was cleared out, and Peter and Kiel were in the middle of the room. It was twenty feet high, seventy-five feet wide, and a hundred long. There were a few spots William had to clean up since he had been using it for ripping apart something mechanical.

Bethany Anne sat between John and Darryl, with Kael-ven on the other side of John and Scott and Eric behind them. "Where is Royleen?" she asked, leaning around John.

"He is not much into the martial arts," Kael-ven told her. "He is busy learning what he can about the gravitic drives Marcus has selected as his area of expertise."

He put a raw potato into his mouth and bit a chunk off. After a couple of crunches, he swallowed. "He was surprised to find that Marcus was the one responsible for some of the latest changes to the gravitic drives for humans."

"He was pretty sure he was going to beat Marcus easily, I take it?" she asked.

"Yes. Scientists, I think, are always sure of their superiority."

"What is his subject?"

"Old alien languages." Kael-ven chittered in laughter. "He is sure no human has knowledge of either aliens or what they say to be able to answer his questions."

"I see, and the final subject?"

"General mathematics. I don't suppose it will help Marcus at the moment, but gravity is but a small and very precise aspect of math. Royleen must have at least three to four different kinds of mathematics that Yollin scientists have been working with for at least four of our centuries. We have yet to encounter any human activity in those disciplines. So, if he can't figure out the gravitic answers, he plans on stumping him with those."

"I...see," she mused.

Kiel had rested for the last two days. While he had worked hard to learn from his many, many fights with the humans, he had refrained from using some of the double-jointed moves his kind was capable of during martial trials.

Now, he was going to surprise the human with styles they had not seen from him.

As he stood in the middle of the room, he could hear the chittering and exultation of his people, encouraging him and supporting him.

It felt good.

He had nothing against this human in front of him. In fact, he had not even sparred with this human yet. For his age, which seemed young to Kiel, he held a high position, so he expected this to be challenging.

But he had personal armor, where a human had nothing but soft skin. He had hard claws that cut and stabbed, and the human had soft fingers.

While he needed to worry about blunt trauma from kicks and punches, at least he didn't have to worry about knives or swords.

"Did you hear?" Tabitha asked as she sat down next to Gabrielle, offering her some popcorn as the two watched Kiel and Peter walk to the middle of the room.

"What, little one?" Gabrielle asked, reaching into the bag and grabbing a handful.

"We're going to get an eyeful of Peter candy."

"Huh?" Gabrielle asked around her popcorn.

Tabitha tossed a couple of popped kernels into her mouth. "He has to strip before he fights the alien."

"Oh, six-pack solicitousness time?" Gabrielle asked after swallowing. "I'm good with that."

"No kidding! His stomach could be used to teach Braille," Tabitha agreed.

"Wonder what it would say?"

Tabitha snorted. "Who cares? Probably 'You think this is hard?' or 'Go lower.' No, I mean strip."

"Ooh," Gabrielle replied, putting out her hand to push Tabitha back in her seat. "Move back, you're blocking my view.

"Hey!" Tabitha responded, slapping Gabrielle's hand. "You've got a boyfriend!"

"Yeah, a boyfriend who's going to be with Bethany Anne if she ever has to fight the king of Yoll, and she will be butt-ass naked."

"Oh." Tabitha paused, then leaned back. "Good point."

Kiel nodded at the human, who took off his clothes and handed them to a person next to him, who folded them and then walked off the floor.

Kiel stretched up, raised his legs to their full height, and roared a challenge. His people roared back their response, shaking the walls.

Kiel smiled at the human, who was patiently waiting for Kiel to finish.

"My turn."

Peter waited for the noise to die down.

The sounds coming from his people impressed Kael-ven. They had come out to support Kiel and Royleen, even those who had chosen to stay locked up on the human's moon. He checked with them from time to time. Other than the lack of space, which wasn't too bad considering they had been on the *G'laxix Sphaea* anyway, they were bored but were not being mistreated.

He turned to look around John at Bethany Anne. "I think you might want to close your eyes. It could get a little ugly."

"I'll bet you that this is over and Peter wins within twenty human minutes of the start." She didn't take her eyes off the two on the floor.

"What do we have to bet?" Kael-ven asked.

She turned to him. "If Kiel wins, I'll drop your time of service to two solar years." She elbowed John when he snorted. "If Peter wins, you have to be willing to listen with an open mind and help me with an idea I have for after I take out your king."

Kael-ven shrugged. "Done." He leaned back. This was going to be an honorable way to reduce the sentence for him and his people. He wasn't sure if she realized that when his time was up, so was theirs.

The Yollins finally quieted down as Peter spoke.

"In my life, there have been many times I have been called upon to fight. Sometimes, it had the potential to kill me. In one instance, one time, I saw someone I loved killed. Or," he turned to find Ecaterina and Nathan in the audience, "she would have been if someone hadn't intervened."

Peter turned back to Kiel. "Since that time, in rare cases, I am called to pull from my people's abilities, my kind. It takes something to trigger this, and I always," Kiel saw Peter's eyes start to change color, "always," his voice went deeper, grittier, "think about what I felt when she was hurt."

Kiel took an involuntary step back when the human in front of him changed. No longer was he smaller and soft. Now, he was easily as tall as Kiel, covered with fur, and had knives for nails on the ends of his hands. Then he howled, and the humans' side roared their support.

The fight was on!

Kiel leaped toward the human, who ducked under him. But his foot was caught, and Kiel had to push his arms under him to stop his face from slamming into the metal floor.

Then he was yanked backward, and he twisted twice in the air before landing halfway to the far wall with a painful crunch.

The screaming was loud, reverberating off the walls from both sides of the room.

Kiel grimaced. This wasn't going to be easy, after all.

The human walked toward him.

Oh, and teeth, Kiel thought. Stay away from the teeth, too.

Kiel jerked forward, feinting to his left before launching, and this time, using his legs to scissor-kick, he scored a hit on the human's body. When he landed, he saw blood on his toes.

Good!

He turned back to see the human, who didn't look like he was much bothered by the cut.

The cut that was healing in front of Kiel's eyes.

This was bad.

"Question," Kael-ven asked as he saw Kiel's successful slash across the changed human's body start to heal. "Can all of you do that?"

"You might call it a caste thing," Bethany Anne answered.

Kael-ven didn't fail to recognize she didn't answer fully, but he wondered, if this man followed his Queen…

What could the Queen do?

"You know," Tabitha was eating popcorn as the two guys fought, "that was some serious eye candy, but you're fucked."

"Yeah, well, I'll just make sure I screw him blind the night before her fight with the king," Gabrielle replied.

Tabitha nodded her approval. "Good plan."

Kiel loped to his left in a counter-circle. He had suffered two hard cuts through his soft sections, and he had found out that the human's bite could break his arm.

He was in a world of hurt, and the worst damage that the human showed was some blood on the floor and some panting breaths.

So glad he was giving him a workout.

"Dooooo yoouuuu exxxppeeeecccctt too wwiinnn?" the human asked him.

"I expect to try until I can do no more, human," he answered, to a roar of approval from his people.

The human shrugged. "So be it." He looked up at the ceiling and back at the Yollins for a second before turning to Kiel. "I doonnn't sssuppose yoooou cannn fllyyyy?"

"Oh, God, this is going to hurt," Bethany Anne moaned.

"What?" Kael-ven asked.

"I think Kiel is about to go for a longer, higher flight," she told him.

"He has already gone," Kael-ven pointed, "from there to there! How much farther can he be thrown?"

"Try, up there," John answered as Peter roared and charged Kiel, grabbing the alien and twisting around, flinging him from under his shoulders up toward the ceiling. Kiel's body only stopped when he slammed into the top, then crashed back down to land among his supporters, some of whom had tried to dodge, and a few more of whom had tried to help catch him.

"Ohhhh, I think we need someone to go help a few of them," Bethany Anne suggested as aliens scattered among the chairs, Kiel's comatose body pinning three of them to the floor.

Peter roared his challenge as Nathan walked out to the middle of the floor. Bethany Anne watched as Nathan snapped his fingers to gets Peter's attention and then calm him down, helping him focus enough to change back.

"I'll give that ass an eleven, though." Tabitha turned to hide her blush. She moaned, "Oh, my God!" when Peter winked at her.

Gabrielle busted out laughing, then started coughing out the popcorn kernels that were still in her mouth.

It took an hour to clean up from the first challenge, and some medical attention was needed for both Kiel and one of those he had squashed at the end. Fortunately, the medical team had been studying Kiel since he had been hurt so frequently and knew he would be good again in a couple of days, not including his broken arm.

The friend that had tried to help soften Kiel's fall was still out cold.

For the second challenge, Royleen and Marcus had a table brought to the middle of the room, and both set down electronic devices. Marcus pulled his from a brown backpack.

Royleen had another Yollin standing behind him as Marcus pulled out another large device and sat it on the table.

"I don't suppose you want to go for double or nothing, Kael-ven?" Bethany Anne asked as everyone resumed their seats.

"What is the double part? How can I listen to your information twice?"

"No, sorry. Here's the deal. I'll still give you guys only two solar years, but on my side, if I ask you something that is not against your ethics, you promise to do it for me. Or, you explain why you wouldn't or couldn't do it if you say no." She nodded to the two out in the middle. "If Royleen wins, you don't have to listen to anything, and only have two solar years."

Kael-ven looked back out to the middle of the room. He

resisted the urge to see if there was any skin he could chew on. He had been informed it made the humans sick to watch, and he didn't want to offend those around him.

"Have you talked to Marcus about what he plans?" Kael-ven finally asked.

"No, I haven't asked him," Bethany Anne replied.

"You haven't talked to Bobcat or William either?" Kael-ven asked.

"No. In fact, I have not spoken to any human to ask what Marcus might be planning," Bethany Anne assured him.

"They're about to start," John told Kael-ven. "So your answer is…" he prompted.

Kael-ven stared at the two on the floor, wondering where Marcus' backup was. Finally, rushing before the two hit their flags in the middle of the table, he said, "Deal!"

"Good luck," Marcus told Royleen.

"Where is your second?" Royleen asked him as he sat on his seat. "Not having a second will not require me to release T'llek here."

"Oh, sorry." Marcus grabbed the second box as he sat. "My second is right here. He can't be here physically, so he's speaking through this."

Royleen looked at the box. "What is that?"

"That," said a voice from the speaker, "is a sound amplification box to allow me to speak to everyone so they can all hear me."

Royleen grimaced. "Who are you?"

"TOM," the voice replied.

"Who is Tom?" Royleen asked, looking from the speaker to Marcus. "There are so many human names, and some of you carry the same one."

"I'm also known as Thales of Miletus," the voice told him, humor coloring his tone.

"This name, this 'Thales of Miletus,' is familiar to me," Kael-ven mused aloud. He turned to Bethany Anne. "Why do I know this name?"

"Oh, just wait," Bethany Anne replied. "It will get better."

Kael-ven turned back, dreading the next surprise the aliens were going to bring to the testing.

Royleen pointed to the speaker. "I thought you were going to have either of your two research friends back you up?"

"Bobcat and William?" Marcus asked, surprised. "They're two of my best friends, and I would bust down the doors of hell with them. But I would just as soon have one of them back me up on science as I would trust Bobcat with beer," he finished.

"Ouch," Bobcat was sitting next to William and Barnabas. The crowd on the human side of the room laughed.

"He was wrong to say that?" Barnabas asked him.

"Oh, hell, no. *I* wouldn't trust me with beer, but damn, he could have said it a little nicer," Bobcat replied.

"Word," William agreed. "And no, I wouldn't trust Bobcat with beer, either," William told Barnabas.

"I hate you too," Bobcat shot back.

"I've got a fresh twelve-pack of Shiner Bock," William offered conversationally.

"I love you again," Bobcat replied automatically.

Barnabas smiled.

"Then who is this?" Royleen pointed to the speaker. "How do I know he exists and is not a computer program of yours?"

TOM's voice answered. "Scientist Royleen of the Chloret caste of the fourth planet revolving around the D-122.221 star system found by the Kurtherians in Solar Year…"

"No!" Royleen shouted, jumping up from his seat, surprising those listening. "This is not possible!"

Marcus smiled and spread his arms. "Why not?" he asked. "You said I could have anyone be my backup."

Royleen looked down at the speaker, at Marcus, and at his captain, who was confused, and then back at the speaker and asked, "What is your real name?"

"Why is Royleen so agitated?" Kael-ven asked.

"Because he didn't do his research," John answered. "He didn't find out what kind of friends Marcus has to call upon as his backup."

"What friend could bother him so much?" Kael-ven asked.

"The unbelievable kind," Bethany Anne answered.

A string of numbers started spewing from the speaker, and Royleen put up a hand after the first fifty. "I cannot keep them all in my head!"

TOM stopped.

Royleen's shoulders slumped. "How many languages?"

"Dead or still in existence?" TOM asked.

"Never mind." Royleen looked at Marcus while pointing at the speaker. "How is it you have a Kurtherian as a friend?"

"TOM is a Kurtherian!" Kael-ven exclaimed, astonished.

"Well, yes. Didn't Royleen just say so?" Bethany Anne asked.

"But you said…you said," Kael-ven went silent, then turned to look at Bethany Anne, who returned his attention. "You told me you had not spoken to any human about his plans. It was a Kurtherian who told you what was intended."

"Perhaps I was informed that the Kurtherian was asked to participate. But you know Kurtherians. They decide for themselves what they want to do," she stated enigmatically.

Nice. Are you going to admit this Kurtherian is dependent on you for his life?

Hey, I didn't start that situation. I woke up, and your alien ass was already along for the ride. You might remember that I never told you what to do with Marcus. That was you two cooking this up totally, so don't tag me with it.

Would you look back at Royleen? I want to enjoy his shocked expression again.

Bethany Anne looked at the scientist, who was still appeared bumfuzzled.

Don't worry. I have ArchAngel keeping video records of all of this. We'll watch it again.

In slow motion, TOM agreed.

CHAPTER TWENTY

Charles walked into the reading room, noticing the chessboard. He stopped, realized that Fred was going to win his match with David in three moves, then turned toward his chair to sit down. He pulled out his laptop and worked for a couple of minutes before he heard Fred and David coming down the hallway.

"I'm telling you," David insisted, "it was a TQB operation that attacked TarHunt in Kentucky." David looked at the chessboard and moved a pawn, then continued toward his chair. He heard Fred stop at the chessboard.

"TarHunt got hit?" Charles asked, looking up from his laptop. "When did this happen?"

"We got word yesterday morning after they did a complete review," David answered, pulling some folders out of his briefcase. "They lost a couple of hours of video that wasn't backed up and some people got knocked around, and one went to the hospital, but no one got into the data."

"Your move," Fred called as he continued into the room. "I've got you in two moves," he added as he took a seat and turned on the lamp next to his chair.

David looked over. "You always tell me you have me in this many moves, but you rarely do."

"You move your bishop to queen's four?" Charles asked Fred, who nodded he had. Charles turned to David. "Yes, you're done in two."

"Well, shit." David scoffed. "I'll double-check, but I'll move the thousand into your column."

"What does that put me up to?" Fred asked.

"Not up to anything. You're still down fifty-three thousand from the presidential race," Charles interrupted.

"Well, who the hell thought *that* would happen?" Fred grouched. "It was a sure thing."

David shrugged as he opened the tiny betting book. "Sure or not, you still owe the pot." He wrote in the win.

"You think TQB was behind the TarHunt attack?" Charles asked before turning back to Fred. "And you said the attack in South America was a bust?"

Fred grabbed a blue folder and set it on his lap. "Not only was it a bust, but it was also a complete and utter failure that defies imagination. That is," he amended as he looked up at Charles, "if you believe a bunch of South American yahoos who are probably coked up gutter slime."

Charles thought about it for a minute. "I believe we're going to need to double up on our efforts in the United Nations." He turned to David. "Don't we have Timothy James working on that?"

"Yes. He's asked if we wanted to hop on with any of the countries that are making waves. At the moment, most of them are smaller, and can't get into the race to upgrade the technology. He feels the small ones are looking to leapfrog and catch up if everyone gets the technology at the same time from the United Nations."

"Why they think TQB is going to listen to them," Fred muttered, "I'll never know."

"TQB's stocks are down ten percent across the board," David told him.

"Lots of selling in damn near every one of their companies," Charles added, peering at his laptop.

"Who's buying?" Fred asked.

Charles spent a few minutes looking, long enough for Fred and David to go back to reading their own stuff before he answered, "Research says everyone from governments to large corporations."

"Something is weird," David mused. "It doesn't make sense. Those companies have been tightly held for years. Decades, even."

"Well, is the UN stuff causing a loss of faith in some of the holders?" Fred asked.

"If it is, then there are some big players sweeping in on the change in ownership," Charles murmured. "My vote is to tell Timothy James to find alliances and see who needs funding. We want to be in as many of these as possible."

"For the least amount of money," David added.

Charles looked at David with a smile on his face. "You even had to add that?"

Near Dulce Lake, NM, USA

Patrick Brown headed down to the main spaceship bay, Bruce walking with him.

"I want four ships for this," Patrick called over his shoulder. "Make sure they head up to space, and then come down and try to either make it look like they're from outer space or coming up from the ice. If we get TQB blamed, that's good, or if we continue with the idea that it's the Nazi society, we're good there, too."

"You want us to deep-six the Navy?" Bruce asked, no judgment in his voice.

"No. We aren't against them here. Hell, we're on the same side. They just shouldn't be messing with this technology, so they need to back the hell off." Patrick punched a sequence into the lock, put his finger on a pad, and spoke into a microphone. A second later, there was a buzz, and Patrick opened the door, waving Bruce ahead of him and closing it behind them.

"What we want to do is find out where they're going. We don't have their direct coordinates so far, which is rather surprising."

"How can that be?" Bruce asked as the two men continued down the rough-hewn hallway, heading deeper underground.

"Honestly, I don't know," Patrick admitted. "I think the ships are being given coordinates to approximate locations, and as they get near, they get new coordinates. Someone is holding this information very close to the vest, and none of our normal data acquisition has been successful, or we would have already dropped down to check it out."

The two men walked to the end of the hall that opened into a natural cavern of significant size that held twelve ships. Ten of them looked like round UFOs, sitting on four legs each. Two were bell-shaped and taller than the rest, and one still had a Nazi swastika on the side and machine guns sticking out the bottom.

"You should take old ring-a-ding there," Bruce joked. "That would cause all sorts of confusion for the Navy."

Patrick laughed. "If I wasn't trying to get TQB blamed for this shit, I probably would. That would be effective in throwing them off the scent, and the military would get their underwear all bunched up thinking we have a bunch of Nazis still around."

"Don't we?" Bruce asked. "Down in Antarctica?"

"Well, maybe," Patrick allowed as they approached four men, all in dark-gray flight suits with helmets in their arms.

"Okay, guys." Patrick and Bruce joined the four airmen. "The

Navy ships will be approaching Schwabenland tomorrow morning. You guys are going to go up and hang out over the South Pole. When we pinpoint where the Navy is going to land exactly, you guys need to get them to leave."

"If we're shot at, sir?" Primary Flight Leader Antony Rikert asked.

Patrick shrugged. "We shoot back. The originals did, so they should expect nothing less. See if they're going to pack up and leave, and if not, then keep ratcheting up the response until they decide it's a losing proposition." He thought about it for a moment. "If you have to, sink one."

"Understood, sir."

A few more minutes of talking, and the four men headed toward the latest ships Majestic 12 had been able to build with their advanced technology.

They were unleashing the latest of truly human technology, not that hybrid bullshit of TQB.

Patrick and Bruce turned back around as the ships, silent in their flight, navigated out of the large caverns. They took the route that would have them rise silently to the sky thirty miles to the north.

QBS *ArchAngel*

Kael-ven's feet clicking on the floor alerted Kiel to his arrival before his door slid open and his captain entered.

"How are you feeling?" Kael-ven asked, looking at the cast covering Kiel's arm.

"Like I was tossed around by a koron-dak." Kiel grunted. "But the koron-dak," he lifted his arm," was nice enough to fix what it broke."

"These humans are difficult to understand," Kael-ven stated. "Now we see what must be Kurtherian modifications, but they do not have Kurtherian overlords."

"Perhaps the humans kicked them out?" Kiel chittered his laughter. "I know humans can be a bit of a pain in the ass and sneaky when they want to be."

"Yes, I found that out." Kael-ven walked to the small chair and lowered himself down, locking his legs underneath. "Their Queen beat me in two different wagers. Now I have to listen to her questions, and I have to consider her offer."

"If they didn't keep beating us," Kiel offered, "I would think they were just lucky."

"No, they are more than lucky. They have a history." Kael-ven looked around the room and assumed anything he might say would be recorded. "I have spoken to the one named Frank Kurns." Kiel groaned at Kael-ven's comment. "You have met him?"

"Royleen calls him 'the human with a thousand questions.' You can pick him out because he is always writing in his books."

"Yes, that is the one," Kael-ven agreed. "But he will answer questions as readily as he will ask."

"I hadn't thought to ask him questions," Kiel admitted, trying to scratch his arm in the cast.

"I was top of my class in strategy, and I wanted to save my voice," Kael-ven explained. "So I needed to come up with an idea quickly. As it worked out, he did not mind answering questions that helped explain to me why humans are so hard to pin down."

"Okay, I have nothing better to do than stay in this bed and listen, sir."

"Oh, I'm here to talk, Kiel, both to you and Royleen. He is next."

"Does Royleen know you are coming to speak to him?"

"I doubt it," Kael-ven replied. "Because I have not informed him of it at this point. I figure if he knows, he will try to hide from me."

"Is he still upset about losing to their scientist?"

"Yes, but in an area I was not expecting. Once he understood he was going to be challenged by a Kurtherian, he lost his courage. I think he is more bothered by the fact that TOM is the friend of a human, and he doesn't expect to ever be able to overcome that advantage. I can't understand scientists, Kiel," Kael-ven complained.

"He should try bragging to his fellows about how easy it will be to crush the tiny human under his feet, only to have the human change into a koron-dak in front of his eyes. Between you and me, Captain, it was all I could do not to pee in the middle of the floor," Kiel offered.

"I couldn't tell. You seemed to be fighting very admirably to me," Kael-ven replied. He had quit trying to get his people to stop calling him captain. "Well, until he threw you up to the ceiling and you landed on J'llock."

"Yes, I remember his eyes growing larger as I came down. He didn't listen when I yelled for him to get out of the way." Kiel snorted.

"Once he gets out of bed, he would do well to work out with the martial team to enhance his reaction speed," Kael-ven suggested.

"That is almost adding insult to his pain, but I will tell him, Captain. So, now that you have the pleasantries out of the way, what can I answer for you?"

"Your pain medicine must be wearing off." Kael-ven chittered his laughter. "You are more forthright than usual."

"My apologies. It is being around these humans. When we are in meetings, they seek to find the solution and do not allow caste or role to get in the way."

"True. Let me explain what I learned from Frank Kurns, and why I believe we are most fortunate that the humans are focused on the Kurtherians."

"It would be nice if someone could get rid of those galactic assholes, sir," Kiel remarked.

"Yes, but you are thinking as a Yollin again. You are thinking

207

what we might overtake if we didn't have to worry about a Kurtherian clan showing up and causing us trouble." Kael-ven grabbed a flaking piece of skin, popped it in his mouth, and started chewing on it. "I've had enough hints from the Queen's people. They are building an enormous space station."

"Please tell me it will not be a larger version of the hideous one at the moon?" Kiel asked, his voice almost pleading.

Kael-ven chittered. "No. I did find out that the hideous station at their moon was a temporary base. It is their first space station, I understand, and eventually would have been abandoned or enhanced at some level. They are a 'practical before pretty' type of species. Or, I understand this group is at least." Kael-ven sighed. "They are going to make sure Yoll cannot attack their homeworld."

"How can they possibly achieve that?" Kiel asked. "We are in four solar systems. We will rally around the king."

"No, we will rally around the monarch. It is what we have done for generation upon generation, and now I understand how Bethany Anne intends to protect her world from Yoll." Kael-ven looked at the floor and then back at Kiel. "How dangerous do you believe this human Peter would be if there were many of them?"

"Very dangerous, Captain. He heals, he is unbelievably quick, and he has natural offensive weaponry. He does not have an exoskeleton, so he does not have as much armor perhaps." Kiel shrugged. "Not that it mattered in my case."

"What if you had to fight him wearing a suit of armor?" Kael-ven asked.

"It would be a much more even fight. The advanced speed of the armor would offset a lot of the speed advantage he displayed. The armor would take a lot of the beating. I assume he wouldn't fight me that way. I certainly wouldn't."

"No. I've been introduced to another person, a female. Jean Dukes is her name."

"Another?" Kiel laughed. "Females were pretty rare on the

space station, and now you can't fling an arm out without hitting one. Where were they, then?"

"Apparently, there were orders to protect them. Unlike Royleen's first assumptions, they aren't stupid, although they may be lucky."

"Is there a world of these beings down there?" Kiel asked. "Because if so, it is a world of demons, and perhaps our failure to notify the king…" His voice ground to a halt.

"Do you play Kabesh, Kiel?" Kael-ven asked him.

"The bones, sir?" Kiel asked, to Kael-ven's nod. "I have at times, yes."

"Every time Yoll has subjugated another race, we threw the bones. This time, we came up all white. It was bound to happen sometime. One way or another, this will change Yoll forever."

"Our names will end up slaughtered in the history books." Kiel remembered how he had thought that by now, he would be rich back on Yoll.

Kael-ven unhooked his legs and stood up. "I'm not so sure of that yet. I think Yoll has been subjugated already for many, many generations."

Kiel turned his head. "By who?"

Kael-ven stopped at the door. "By the Kolin, Kiel. By the Prime Rulers of the First Caste. Remember, we are here by the king's decree to subjugate other species. This time, a species refused our offer."

Kael-ven took a couple of steps and stopped, looking back. "Kiel, think about this. If the human Peter turned into a koron-dak, what does his Queen turn into?"

The door closed behind Kael-ven, leaving Kiel to consider his question. At first, Kiel laughed off the thought that the little human female did anything of the sort. Then he remembered her punch and rubbed his chest.

Did she change shape? *Could* she change shape?

CHAPTER TWENTY-ONE

German Ship *Adler*

"This is butt-fucking cold," Craig muttered as he turned around to find Melissa behind him. "Oh, sorry, ma'am!"

"Apology accepted." Melissa walked around him. "I needed to feel what cold really was so inside it feels warm by comparison."

"That's...logic of a sort," Craig agreed. "But I'm pretty sure I would just grab more clothes, ma'am."

Melissa stomped her feet on the deck. "How do they get so cold so fast?"

"The blood," Craig started, then stopped. "Sorry, rhetorical question, right?"

Melissa glanced at the soldier.

Craig turned around and then back to Melissa. "Something wrong?"

"No. Yes... Maybe?" Melissa asked. "I'm not trying to be a bitch, but you're using words I don't expect to hear from people in the service."

"What, rhetorical?" Craig asked and laughed. "Ma'am, it can be pretty damned boring on a lot of our tours. Plus, we have to do more than just pushups and swim forever."

"Sure, shoot guns and kill things, right?" Melissa asked.

"Sure, that too," Craig allowed, not taking offense to what was the truth. "But we also usually speak multiple languages, sometimes with different dialects. We have to understand the religious and societal rules where we are stationed, as well as all the different skills both physically and mentally to move up and advance."

"How many languages can you speak, Craig?" she asked him.

"Not including English, I speak Spanish, Pashtun, and some German," he answered.

"I've never asked Terry how many he can speak," she mused.

"Terry? Shit...oh, sorry ma'am." Craig got a little red in the cheeks. "He can speak at least six that I'm aware of."

"Six? Wow, I didn't know that." She looked at the sea, so cold and so deadly as their ship passed, occasionally seeing ice in the distance bobbing up and down. "I hope we don't become another *Titanic.*"

"Fat chance of that. We have the equipment to stop that from happening," Craig replied.

"Good." She turned back to him. "Why did you say six you are aware of?"

"Terry?" Melissa nodded. "Because he can be a tricky SOB." Craig's eyes swept the water. "The guys and I figure out something new about Terry all the time."

"Why?"

"Well." Craig put an arm out and moved Melissa closer to the wall. "Hold on, I can feel the ship turning a little. The wind is about to get pretty biting if you don't move next to the wall here."

"Thank you."

"No worries." Craig looked out over the water. "You know that Robert, our lead, and Terry go way back, right?"

"Yes. He says they were good friends when they were younger?"

"Yes, they did a lot before they enlisted together, and then when they got on the teams, they stayed together. Those two have twin senses. Every time they got into a bad firefight, Robert had a sixth sense about it. And damned if every time that happened, Terry had somehow procured extra weapons that helped them get out of the...ah..." Craig stammered.

"Just say it, Craig. Believe it or not, Ph.Ds can cuss quite well."

"Okay, so Terry always seemed to have special weapons he shouldn't have had whenever they got dropped into the shit and it all went to hell. In this business, you find out who has the luck, you know?" Melissa nodded but didn't have a clue. "So, all the guys learn quickly to ask Robert if he has that itch."

"Anytime Robert has the itch, Terry has the answer?" Melissa asked.

"No, not all the time. Sometimes we saw some action when Robert had an itch but Terry didn't have anything special, but it was never too bad. Anytime Robert had the itch and Terry had an answer for it?" Craig chuckled. "Well, we knew it was going to suck tar babies then, ma'am."

"That's what happened over in the Pit?" Melissa asked.

"The Sandpit? Yeah. It was the first time those two had been together in a lot of years, and it's like it never stopped, this connection they have."

"So, Terry had the box brought on the trip," Melissa stated.

"Yeah, but then the President asks a favor from TQB and we get a group of rainmakers dropped on the pricks jumping our asses, and problem solved."

Melissa looked around. "Terry didn't bring a wooden case this time. I checked."

Craig crooked his finger in a "come here" gesture and pointed at the bow of the ship.

Melissa's eyes crinkled, and she took a step into the wind. "Oh, my! This is cold." She looked toward the front of the ship, the bow lifting high in the air and slamming down. There was a man up front.

"What the hell is he doing up there?" she asked, her voice rising. "He's going to freeze if he doesn't fall into the water!" She turned around and stepped quickly back to the wall. "Sorry, my momma didn't raise a fool." She looked back at Craig. "What's he doing? He's going to freeze or fall off or something equally bad."

"No, he isn't," Craig replied. "His name is Samuel, and he's been there with that medium-weight jacket for the last four hours." Craig looked back at the man. "Terry didn't have a box join us this time. Samuel is one of the two men Terry pulled in to help."

Craig turned back to Melissa. "Ma'am, I'm not trying to scare you, but I know a little about what Samuel and his friend can do. The boys and I are sure..." Craig looked back out over the water and spoke to her, as well as to the wind.

"This mission is *screwed*."

Terry went up to the bridge. "You wanted me, Captain?"

"*Ja*, Terry," the captain affirmed. "We are getting updates that the Americans are about ten hours behind us. If you guys want to get in ahead of them, you will need to get going as soon as we can get you in close." He nodded to the stern. "You can take the smaller craft, and we can run farther west. Maybe draw some other attention if you want?"

Terry chewed on his lip. "We have five kilometers to go to the first entrance. If we...yeah, we can do this. I've got to go make plans. Thanks, Captain."

"No problem, *ja*?"

Terry waved and turned around. He headed toward the stern, his thoughts whirling.

There were two sharp raps on her door, and Melissa heard Terry's voice. "You decent?"

"Yes." Before she turned from her work toward the door, he had it open. "What is it?" she asked.

"We have the US Navy a few hours behind us. We're going to have to take the smaller vessel and the snowmobiles."

"Weather?" she asked.

He shrugged. "Looks fine. Well, fine for Antarctica."

"Who?"

"You, Dr. Tooch, Mr. Jameson, Robert, Richard, Samuel, and Craig, plus some supplies. If we don't find anything, we'll try to jump back on the ship in thirty-six hours and head out. The information the German government provided will be considered bad at that point."

"No storms heading this way?" she pressed.

"Huh? No. Well, you can't ever be sure with either of the poles, but no. Why?" he asked.

"Just checking. Wondering what can go wrong out there," she explained.

He scratched his chin in thought. "Well, plenty. I can tell you about the problems during..."

"Stop!" Melissa had her hand up. "You don't need to recite the facts from a dozen different Wikipedia articles, thank you. Will the US Navy kick us out?"

"We have the right to be here, and maybe they won't find our cave entrance. If they do, and we tell them we've contacted Germany, they still might stay out. Possession is nine-tenths of ownership. They might choose to eject us, but I don't think so. And like I said, they still have to find us. The captain is going to take the ship in another direction to work on throwing them off the scent if he can, to give us a few more hours."

"Okay, when do we leave?" she asked.

Terry's voice got soft. "Melissa, you still want to do this?" he asked. "It's going to be miserable out there, and there's always a chance of dying. In the Antarctic, there's an even better chance of dying."

"Terry, I've taken the money, and frankly, I would be pissed with myself if I missed the opportunity to find an old Nazi base and see it firsthand," she replied.

He shrugged. "Okay." He stepped to the door before turning back to her. "Pack as many spare socks as you can, and make sure you have spares of *everything.*"

"Hey, we can snuggle for warmth, can't we?" She smiled.

He grinned and winked at her. "I don't see why not. I'm good with the other guys spooning for warmth if they need to." He stepped out and closed the door on her laughter.

USS *Cowpens*

Captain Forstal turned to answer the question. "Yes?"

"Sir, we have unidentified ships coming over the horizon," Radar Operator Andrews stated crisply.

"Distance?" he asked.

"Seventy-five miles, close to the ground, and sir?" The radar man paused. "They're coming in faster than anything we have."

"Speed?"

"Mach 12, sir."

The captain's lips pursed. "Communications, see if we have any reason TQB could be out here."

"Aye aye, sir," Tinbert replied.

"Bring the Phalanx online, and inform the *Ford* and the *Wasp* of our intentions," the captain commanded.

Another voice spoke up. "This is the *Cowpens…*"

"Squad leader, Navy ships are pinging us at this time," Dorsal called over their comm. "The LHD *Wasp* is damned impressive."

"Agreed, Number Two," Antony replied. "Remember, try to scare them, not sink them."

"We have radar lock," Evert reported. "They've seen us."

"Split up and do some damned impressive maneuvers," Antony instructed.

Tyler quipped over the open line, "You know, everyone, fly like an alien."

"Holy fuuuuddgge," a voice called out on the bridge. The radar pings became solid aircraft, flew past the three ships, and went in four different directions so fast if you blinked, you missed it.

Doing ninety-degree turns.

"We have UFOs."

"Four bogeys, random directions. Speeds all over the map."

"No fire, no fire," the captain called. "Where the hell did those bogeys go?"

"Two straight up, one east, one west. All are turning back and heading in our direction."

"Do we have Mark One Eyeballs on any of these?"

"We got saucers. Okay, we had saucers," another called as two of the flying objects went past the three ships.

"Anybody get my call out about TQB?" the captain asked.

"Sir, those don't look like TQB ships."

"Who the hell knows what they have?" Captain Forstal asked.

"Well, sir, we saw them on radar," Andrews replied.

There was a slight pause. "Good point. Well, then, who the hell are they?"

"Think there's some truth to this being an alien Nazi base?" a voice asked.

"Quiet on the bridge. Let's not jump to conclusions, and break a leg here, people," the captain reminded them.

CHAPTER TWENTY-TWO

Schwabenland, Antarctica

"No wonder no one came back here." Melissa's teeth chattered as the six snowmobiles cruised to a stop fifty feet inside the large cave. "My butt is frozen to the seat."

Terry got up off of the snowmobile and gave Melissa a hand to help her off. "Need me to rub it to increase the blood flow?" he asked. She looked pointedly at the others and rolled her eyes in exasperation.

Terry smiled and looked around. There were no marks in the pushed-up snow. He clapped his hands, hoping to increase the blood circulation.

Robert and Samuel came over. "We're going to check out the cave system. Be right back."

Terry nodded. He didn't command these guys, and he knew their prime objective was to protect them, so giving them an order against that directive was just stupid.

That was when Intelligent-but-Brain-Dead accosted him. "Where are those two going?" Dr. Tooch demanded, pointing at Terry. "They could find something and blow this whole trip!"

Terry raised his arm and pushed Dr. Tooch's hand away from him. "They're checking the cave."

"I can see that!" Dr. Tooch shrieked. "That's what I'm worried about. They could mess up our first opportunity to speak to someone here."

"Or," Terry replied, speaking slowly so his annoyance didn't color the conversation, "they could trip any traps and perhaps make sure none of us gets hurt in the process."

"Traps?" The good professor looked in the direction the two men had gone. "Why would there be any traps here?"

"Why would any humans be here?" Terry asked.

Dr. Tooch turned back to him. "Well, we have the notes that the base was built, and we don't have any confirmation the people ever came back."

"So, do you think, considering the timeframe they came from, that maybe they wanted to make sure no one was coming here to kill them? You know, war and all?"

"Well," Dr. Tooch looked down toward the darker back of the cave where the two men had disappeared, "I suppose we could wait a few minutes."

In all, they waited thirty minutes for the two men to come back out of the darkness.

The team had moved an additional twenty-five yards into the cave and set up a small camp behind a snowdrift. The drift helped block the remaining wind coming through the cave entrance.

Terry turned when the lookout called out. The people came together as the two men in their light jackets joined them. "We found fourteen traps and disabled them," Richard told them.

"Then, we found the door that enters their base. We stopped there and came back," Samuel added. "We can't promise all of the traps are cleared, but we think we found them all." He shrugged. "Anyone good with first aid?"

Robert, Terry, and Craig all raised their hands "In the service, it's kinda required."

Richard nodded. "That is acceptable. We left the door we found untouched."

"No contact with people?" Dr. Tooch asked.

"No, not so far," Samuel answered.

Inside, beyond the door Richard and Samuel had not opened was a small room with four black and white monitors and eight lights.

Seven of them were blinking red.

One was blinking green.

Five people followed Richard and Samuel back through the cavern, which darkened as they went farther in. Soon, the people turned on their hardhat lights, and the beams cut through the darkness. Twice, Richard called for the team to tread carefully, and only to step where they could see the men's footprints on the floor.

For a change, none of the scientists and professors asked any questions.

Soon, they came up to a copper door, still in miraculous shape. It had a green patina in a couple of places, most notably around the handle. The door was larger than normal, four feet wide and approximately nine feet tall. Mr. Jameson and Dr. Tooch both took multiple pictures before Dr. Tooch argued he should be allowed the opportunity to knock and then open the door.

He knocked, but no one came to answer. In five minutes, he agreed he would work to pull the door open. He turned to smile for a picture and realized everyone had taken the opportunity to step away from him. "Guess you think this could be booby-trapped too?" he asked.

"Absolutely not!" Richard called from twenty feet away, hiding behind a large jut in the wall. "But I've been known to be wrong, so I'm following the herd mentality."

Dr. Tooch snickered and shrugged his shoulders. "Well, I suppose if I die," he turned around, "there are worse ways to go."

Dr. Tooch pulled, and nothing happened. He yanked harder. "It seems stuck."

"A likely story," Mr. Jameson called, laughter following his comment.

"Very funny," Dr. Tooch snapped. "No, really." He put one gloved hand against the wall next to the door and pulled harder. "I feel a slight give, but I can't open it. Perhaps it's frozen closed?" he asked no one in particular.

Richard left his place by the wall and headed toward Dr. Tooch. "Tell Gabrielle I'm truly sorry about making this the decade of rash decisions," he told Samuel. "And well, about you know what, too."

"Dr. Tooch?" Samuel called, and the man turned around. "You might want to come over here. If Richard goes up in flames or something, we don't want his sacrifice to be in vain, right?"

"Oh!" Dr. Tooch patted Richard on the shoulder as he hurried past him. "Quite right."

Richard came up to the door and started looking at all the corners, then studied the ground in front of it.

Robert got Terry's attention and raised an eyebrow. Terry shrugged.

Richard stood up. "Here goes nothing." He put his gloved right hand against the frozen rock, and with his left, he grabbed the handle.

"Should we count down for you, Richard?" Samuel asked.

"Bite me," Richard replied.

"No, I'm good. Thank you for the offer, though," he replied to his friend. "Do hurry up. I'm really poor at…"

Richard grunted, then shouted, and with a crack, the door opened. Richard twisted out of the way as the door slammed against the wall.

Everyone's breath was slowly released. Richard put an arm in the doorway and waved it, finally putting his head around the corner. "Seems clear. Ten-foot hallway and two doors."

Samuel broke from his position. "Well, tally-ho and all that. Let's see what those Nazi fuckers were up to down here, shall we?"

"It's green," Terry announced.

"Admirable choice of stating the obvious," Richard remarked. "I want to know what the seven red lights mean."

"Well…" Terry replied, reaching forward.

"DON'T!" Richard and Samuel both yelled, causing Terry, Robert, and Melissa to jerk back. The rest of the people were in the short hallway watching them.

"What the hell!" Terry shouted. "You aren't going to have to save me. I'm going to die of fright here!"

"Well," Richard replied, "we were trying to save their lives." He pointed to the hallway. "What if some of those buttons are 'kill the goons in the hall' switches?"

"Well, then only Craig is in trouble," Terry replied. "Mr. Jameson and Dr. Tooch are not goons."

"That's pretty funny, asshole," came from the hallway.

"Hey!" Robert objected.

"Oh, my apologies. That's very funny, asshole, sir!" Craig added.

"Yeah, yeah," Terry replied. "However, Richard has a point." He rubbed his hands together. "We can't all get in here, so…"

"Everyone but Samuel, back outside the door," Richard finished.

"What, me?" Samuel exclaimed, surprised. "Who voted me?"

"Why I did, of course." Richard patted him on the shoulder. "I took the first chance, so it's your turn to pull the trigger."

"Can we get off the gun metaphor?" Melissa asked.

"Sorry, macabre humor helps," Samuel responded. "It's been that way since 1710."

"What?" Melissa asked, caught off-guard.

"What happened in 1710?" Terry asked, trying to remember anything about 1710.

"Don't let Samuel stop us from moving outside," Richard replied. "Let's go. The answer is the Reverend Jonathan Swift."

"*Gulliver's Travels?*" Terry asked as he ushered Melissa out ahead of him.

"The very same," Richard agreed and winked at Samuel, who rolled his eyes. Richard closed the door behind him and moved everyone back out into the cavern. "Jon had a pretty deadpan sense of humor."

"Jon?" Melissa asked, trying to follow the conversation.

"Yes, loved a woman in Ireland. She said no, so he left and went to England. Biting tongue, that man," Richard answered absentmindedly.

Richard shoved the door closed, and Melissa whispered to Terry, "He talks like he knew Jonathan Swift personally!"

Terry nodded. For all he knew, Richard had.

Moments later, there was a loud *SCREEECH*. Everyone in the cavern jumped, except for Richard, who knocked a couple of times on the door after a moment, then nodded.

"What are you nodding at?" Melissa asked.

Richard turned and smiled. "Making sure Samuel is still alive."

"Could you hear…" A sharp *BANG* startled her, and she stopped talking.

A second later, Richard knocked twice. Waited and knocked twice again, then nodded.

A few moments later, the door started opening.

"I said, *GOTT VERDAMMT*, that was loud!" Samuel screamed as he used his fingers and acted like he was trying to clear out his ears.

"What happened, drama queen?" Richard asked.

"Why no, I don't want any cream right now. Funny time to be asking me that," Samuel replied.

"I didn't say 'Did you want cream?' I called you a drama queen. You know what? Never mind. What happened, you twit?" Richard asked.

Samuel smiled and stopped playing with his ears. "Well, the first time, we got some old metal stuff that came out of the floor. Tell you what, that would have opened everyone a new asshole for sure. The second one was more of a sound defense. Probably break everyone's eardrums, and when you're incapacitated, they come in and beat the shit out of you."

"So, did you figure it out?" Richard asked.

"Yes. When I turned my head after the second button, I realized there was another switch that had been hidden by the door and went over and pushed it. The other door is open now."

"Huh, five more red switches," Terry muttered before Melissa slugged him. He put up his hands. "Just curious."

The team followed Samuel back into the base. Richard closed the door once everyone had passed him.

"Oh, my God!" Melissa exclaimed into the quiet of the large room. There were over two hundred metal caskets connected to power in the room.

Richard and Samuel had gone farther into the base and were coming back. "It's the mother lode back there." Richard jerked a thumb behind them. "Lots of stuff to go through, and not a soul to be found. Plus, there is some sort of a… I'd call it a séance room."

Craig asked Richard to show him, and the two of them left.

"Well, now what?" Terry asked the group.

Mr. Jameson turned to Terry. "Excuse me?"

"I said, 'Now what?'" He pointed at the caskets. "Looks like you have some people on ice," he jerked a thumb behind him, "and the US Navy behind us." Terry shrugged. "Seems to me you need to make some quick decisions here, buddy."

"Wait, why?" Mr. Jameson asked.

"Terry?" Robert called. "Stepping out for a moment." Terry nodded his head, not paying much attention to his friend as he tried to get the businessman to focus.

"Because, Mr. Jameson," Terry explained. "If you don't get some adequate political cover here, the US Navy is going to sweep in, and I guarantee you they won't be bothered by," he pointed at the metal coffin-looking devices, "anybody who's in those things right there."

CHAPTER TWENTY-THREE

Inside Base, Antarctica

Terry was getting frustrated. "Mr. Jameson. I'm not here to fight the US Navy and a bunch of Marines. One, that's my country, no matter how much I'm paid, and second, are you *nucking futs*?" Terry almost screamed the last phrase. "Which part of US *Marines* didn't you understand?"

"Terry!" Robert called as he reentered the room.

"What?" Terry turned, exasperated.

"We got problems."

"I know that!" Terry bitched. "Mr. Jameson needs to make a call and get the German government to call off the US Navy, or we're going to have visitors of the 'pissed off and carrying guns variety!'"

"Bigger problems, Terry," Robert's voice was even as he came up to the group.

"Oh, shit!" Craig exclaimed from the doorway as he and Richard came back. "Did you say we have bigger problems?"

"Yeah," Robert agreed.

"Itchy-bitchy ones?" Craig asked, and saw Robert's sharp nod of agreement.

Terry stared at his friend. "Oooh, *shit*."

"Wait, what 'oh shit?'" Melissa demanded. "We have your aces in the hole right there and there!" She practically screeched, pointing at Samuel and Richard, who looked at each other and shrugged.

"We can take out some Marines, but I'm not giving us good odds on more than fifty," Samuel replied.

"We have the door. Maybe we block the room and switch on the other five red buttons?" Richard asked.

"No!" Terry turned around. "I don't want to fight the US Marines."

"Good, 'cause bullets sting like a bitch," Samuel stated.

Robert, Terry, and Craig turned to look at Samuel with their mouths open, then all shook their heads and got back to their own conversation.

"Okay, out with it, Robert," Terry urged.

"The Navy is under attack," Robert told him.

"What? Who?" Terry asked, confusion wrinkling his brow.

"Aliens, Nazis, UFOs, TQB?" Robert finished.

"It's not Nazis. They're all popsicles." Craig pointed at the metal boxes behind him.

"It's not TQB," Terry countered.

"How do you know that?" Mr. Jameson asked.

"Let me get back with you on that one," Terry replied.

"That leaves aliens and UFOs," Robert offered.

"None of your people knew about this?" Terry asked, and Robert shook his head. "Nothing anyone has shared with me."

Terry followed up his question. "Are they shooting at the Navy?"

"Not yet, not that I know," Robert answered.

"Dammit!" Terry turned around. "Well, shit. Mr. Jameson, new question."

"What now?" the man asked, trying to understand the new parameters.

"We have a foreign group, unknown whether it is domestic or alien, and I mean alien-alien, not foreigners, harassing the Navy. They aren't from here, because we have a bunch of Nazi popsicles at best. I didn't want to believe it, but these are probably not true Nazis. These people are the Thule society, I'd guess. They were used by the Nazis, and I'd guess they struck a deal. They gave technology guidance to those in power in exchange for this base is my shot in the dark, but at the moment, it's a likely one. We have another group of flying saucers out there that are pushing away the Navy because *they* want what's in here," he finished, pointing a finger at the floor.

"Why are we concerned about the second group?" Mr. Jameson asked.

"Because," Robert interrupted, "they aren't worried about three warships right now. That means their stuff is pretty damned advanced, and we aren't going to have shit we can do against them."

"Options?" Mr. Jameson asked.

"First, call the German government, but they aren't anywhere close, so I'm saying that's a no-go. Next, get our supplies, close the door, hunker down, and hope there's a back door and a ride out of here," Terry offered.

"That seems like a good way to need to get into one of these ourselves," Mr. Jameson answered as he nodded at the metal boxes.

"Agreed. So, next choice is we close the door, get on our snowmobiles, and drive like a banshee back to the *Adler* if possible. Basically, run like crazy and hope no one sees us," Terry added. "And pray we don't freeze."

"What about these people?" Melissa broke in. "If we run, what happens to them?"

"They stay popsicles until whoever wins outside comes in. If it is the US, they'll probably figure out a way to thaw them," Terry answered, and noticed Robert's very slight head shake. "I guess.

Then again, they might leave them in the boxes and take everything out of here."

"What?" Mr. Jameson asked, surprised. "They would leave them?"

"I have no idea, Mr. Jameson. I would hope they wouldn't. I bet no one except you guys in Germany truly expected to find anything here. I didn't, and I'm in this group."

"Do we have any other options?" Mr. Jameson asked.

"Yes, but you aren't going to like it," Terry replied.

"Here we go." Craig got Melissa's attention and told her, "It's 'Terry pulls something out of his ass' time."

Melissa smirked and nodded her understanding.

"Are you telling me," Mr. Jameson asked, his speech slow as he thought about what Terry just told him. "That you can call TQB and get their help here?"

So far, revealing that he could get TQB's help had gone over better than he had expected.

"Are you a plant for TQB?" Dr. Tooch asked.

Well, until now, Terry thought.

"No, but they do help me from time to time," Terry admitted.

"Why?" Melissa asked.

He turned to her. "Because the stuff everyone is looking for can be dangerous, and those looking for it need to be watched." He nodded at the caskets. "Because some will look at all this and see technology, not people."

"And what will TQB do?" she asked.

"The Queen," Richard interrupted, "will protect the people here first, waking them and finding out what needs to happen."

"How is she going to do that?" Mr. Jameson asked. "The US Navy or the flying UFOs out there are going to be knocking on the damn door pretty fast here."

"If the Queen tells Richard and me to hold this door for her until she comes, we will hold this damn door for her until she comes," Samuel told him, finality in his voice.

Robert and Craig shivered, thinking back to the El Diablo incident.

Mr. Jameson turned. "We aren't going to get access to this technology, Dr. Tooch."

Samuel asked, "Don't think she wouldn't allow a few people the chance to be here and observe. Ask her permission, she would likely do it for you as the ones who found it."

"What about the technology?" Mr. Jameson asked.

Samuel spread his arms out. "I'm sorry, but I don't have an answer for that. I can tell you she's fair, but if she determines the technology should not be shared, it will not be shared, except for what you learn while you observe."

"How come when you say 'observe,' I hear 'watch and keep my mouth shut?'" Dr. Tooch asked.

"Because you are a wise man," Samuel replied, "and have learned that there is a season for everything."

Something buzzed loudly, and Robert looked down. "I set out signal extenders on my way back." He pulled up his small table. "Oh, crap. The Navy apparently felt threatened, and they've opened up with R2-D2s."

"With *what?*" Melissa looked confused.

"Sorry," Robert replied. "The Phalanx close-in weapon system. It's a 20mm radar-guided Gatling gun with a dome on the top that looks like—" Robert stopped when Melissa interrupted.

"R2-D2, got it," she finished, and he nodded.

Robert's tablet buzzed again. "The UFOs are firing back."

"We don't have anything that can challenge something that can fight the US Navy. Call your contact and see if they can do anything," Mr. Jameson ordered.

Terry nodded and started jogging out of the room. "Where are you going?" Mr. Jameson called out.

"One bar on his repeaters!" Terry answered over his shoulder. "Got to get a little farther outside."

Once he got out of the room, he grabbed a second tablet, one that didn't need a signal because it didn't use normal cell technology.

Dan was sitting at his desk, reviewing the plans for the new battle station, when his tablet pinged. He looked at the screen and then grabbed it. "Dan here."

"It's me, sensei." Terry's voice came in loud and clear.

"What's going on?"

"Would you believe we found an old base full of frozen Nazi popsicles, or maybe people who were in contact with aliens back in the forties who have advanced technology? At the same time, we have three US Navy ships being fired upon by four UFOs outside right now that probably want this shit, too."

"Did you say Nazi popsicles?" Dan asked.

"Yes."

"Are they alive?" he pressed.

"No idea. None of the lights look like they're burned out, and frankly, we aren't sure if they are Nazis or simply Germans from that era."

"And UFOs fighting the US Navy outside?"

"Yes."

"How the hell do you get into this shit, Terry?" Dan asked as he typed commands into the tablet.

"You know me, Dan. I'm just trying to survive in a cruel world."

"Right, like the time we pulled your ass out of the whorehouse in Africa with the Forsaken," Dan responded, answering the questions coming up in his text.

"Where do you think I learned it was a cruel world?" Terry

replied. "Surrounded by all that flesh and figuring out that 'bite me' wasn't what I thought it was."

Dan chuckled.

The lights in Dan's office started strobing red, and he heard the orders being issued in the halls outside his office. ArchAngel kept the noise from flooding his space. She was smart that way.

"Okay, looks like ETA in seven minutes."

"You guys are close?"

"Who, us? No, we aren't close. We're already heading that direction, but it will be hours before we get back to Earth's orbit. The Queen is going to be there with something...else."

"Seven minutes?"

"That's right," Dan confirmed.

"I hope the Navy *has* seven minutes," Terry mused.

"Me too," Dan agreed.

"We have Phalanx attacks, we have Phalanx attacks," Antony told his three crew. "Next time, Tyler, don't put a high-velocity round so close to a Navy ship. They don't like that shit."

"Wow, I figured they would realize it was a warning shot," Tyler justified.

Evert asked over the comm, "And how are we supposed to tell them that? We can't do video, or the whole alien gig is up."

"What about pretending we're TQB?" Spencer added.

"Let's let them assume that," Antony replied. "Do you know what TQB clothes look like?"

"Nothing like what we have on, I imagine," Spencer replied.

"Keep dodging, people," Antony ordered.

Kavala, Greece

Alexi Ouzo was tired.

He had been playing soccer back at the new field where the old warehouse had been. It had been torn down so the land would be worth more for someone else to purchase and build a new building on top of it.

Unfortunately for the developer, Greece was going through tough times, and here in Kavala, not much was going on.

So far, it had worked out well for him and his friends. Now, on weekends and after school, he and another ten or fifteen guys all made it over there to play. A couple of welders had helped them put together a few of the pipes lying about, and they now played with makeshift goals.

Day done, his team had won two to one. He was walking back home, taking a shortcut through the warehouse.

That was when his life changed.

He was daydreaming, kicking the ball as he was walking down the dirt path, when a screaming siren started up behind him. He grabbed his ball and turned around as one of the super-large warehouse doors began to open. He could see that there were some sort of flashing red lights inside the building. The red lights strobed the inside walls and occasionally flashed out.

There wasn't anything close to the warehouses, which was strange. Usually, these types of buildings were packed together.

Then he dropped the ball, forgotten, his mouth open.

"MOVE IT!" Marcus yelled. "We have a rush exit, rush exit!" Marcus was waving his tablet. "Get on the ship or disappear, and for God's sake, make sure the Queen's receiving room is fucking clear!"

"I'm on that!" Marcus heard from someone running up the gangplank.

Marcus watched as people pulled cords off of the *G'laxix*

Sphaea. Those they needed later were being put on board, and others were being tossed to the side.

They had talked about what would happen if they needed to exit the hangar fast, but now it was really happening. He hoped they had it right.

Marcus was tapping his foot and looking at his watch. They had two more cables connected, and both dropped from the back of the two wings at the same time. "Leave them!" Marcus shouted. "They aren't special. Get your asses on the ship!"

Marcus turned around, trying to see if they were missing someone, when he heard a bark and turned back to see Ashur staring at him, and then *her* voice cut through the bedlam. "Marcus, get your rocket-science ass on my ship!"

"Oh, shit!" Marcus started trotting to the ship and then up the gangway. His red face greeted Bethany Anne. "Sorry!"

She looked outside, then slapped the control to close up the ship. "You did good, but like any absent-minded professor, you forgot about yourself."

Bethany Anne jogged to the bridge and slid into the pilot's seat. "C'mon, boys and girls, we have a battle to stop."

"No...way," Alexi muttered as a huge spaceship started sliding out of the large warehouse. It came out, and out and...out.

By the time it was out all the way, Alexi noticed another ten people on the street with him. At least he would have witnesses.

It silently lifted into the air, turning to the south as it went up a couple hundred meters. Then, the rear engines came to life. They were much quieter than Alexi would have thought and the spaceship...just disappeared with a loud *BOOM*.

"What the hell was that?" asked a tall guy with a red shirt.

No one answered him.

C'mon, TOM, time to earn your piloting keep.

Stay at vampire speed. I got your back, BA.

Good. Let's not look like idiots in front of the help.

John Grimes leaned over to Paul Jameson. "Aren't you the pilot?" he asked in a soft voice.

Paul answered, his voice a little above a whisper, "Yeah, but right now I'm learning. I've never flown this ship before."

John nodded toward Bethany Anne. "How is she doing it?" he asked as they watched Bethany Anne's hands blitzing over the controls.

Paul shrugged. "She's Bethany Anne?"

John sat back up. "As good an answer as any other, I suppose."

"ETA to South Pole forty-two seconds," Bethany Anne called. "Make sure my turrets are manned!"

Marcus looked around. "Oh, I forgot about that, too."

"Not a problem," one of the Wechselbalg replied. "It looked like we might get to shoot something, so we have them all manned." He added, "Not sure we need them to be manned. They're hooked up to EI targeting at the moment."

"Just so long as a human is starting and stopping the firing, that will work for now," Bethany Anne responded. "Target's in range. Ten seconds."

"Oh, holy fuckazoid!"

Captain Forstal ignored the outburst. Right now, they couldn't hit the four UFOs, and four times now, the return fire had hit their ships. The *Wasp* had lost three helicopters and the *Ford* a front turret.

"Sir!" Radar called. "We have a new inbound bogey."

"What now?" the captain wondered.

"I'm telling you, if those asswipes hit my ship one more time, I'm going to do more than just drop their helicopters into the water," Spencer snarled.

"The Phalanx can't rotate fast enough. It was some lucky shooting," Antony responded. "You need to be careful not to cross another one of their path lines and run into more bullets."

"Hey, that's easier said than done," he retorted.

"Guys? Hey, *GUYS*!" Evert called. "Are you seeing this new ship coming from one one four?"

There was a pause. "Who the fuck is that?"

"TQB?"

"Their ships are all out at the belt. They can't get here for hours, even if they wanted to get involved."

"Then who the hell has a… Oh, fuck, that is a monster!"

"New plan. Head toward that ship!" Antony commanded.

"The UFOs are turning toward the new bogey."

"Well, it looks like the UFOs don't like them, sir."

"Doesn't mean we like them yet either. Enemy of my enemy isn't necessarily my friend," Captain Forstal mused. "Keep an eye on it."

"That's not going to be hard, sir. It's almost a football field long."

"We have four ships heading our direction," Marcus reported.

"Make sure the shield is on. I don't want them scratching the paint," Bethany Anne directed.

"Oh, good idea," Marcus agreed and turned to make sure the shield was live.

Bethany Anne looked to her left and slapped a blue button. "People, this is Bethany Anne. If any of those four ships shoots at us, light them up."

"Plans, sir?" Spencer called.

"Buzz them. See if our anti-electronics affect them," Antony answered.

Captain Forstal walked over to see what was happening on radar. "Damn, they are fast."

"The four ships are passing the large one. Sir, that thing is huge." Kelly looked it over.

"Heading this direction," another voice called. This time, multiple people got up and looked out.

"Oh, holy Jeezus!" Kelly exclaimed. "THAT one is TQB." The large ship passed the Navy. "I saw it on the Japanese video, but it has more stuff on it."

"Okay, that means the other four are definitely *not* TQB, right?" Jenkins asked.

"No, they could be playing us," Captain Forstal replied. "I don't think they are; just want to make sure everyone keeps their minds clear of assumptions."

"There go the four UFOs." The heads all turned as the four round ships sped after the TQB ship.

"They don't seem to be as fast," Kelly commented.

"Well, ain't that a bitch? They are playing catch-up," Bethany Anne stated. "Sure hope this thing has a good turning radius, Marcus."

"What?" Marcus was doing his best to keep up. "Yes, we applied full grav plate technology to the Yollin specs. You can stop on a dime," he finished. "Although, I wouldn't want to do that, actually, you could."

TOM, where is the system to... Oh, here it is.

"All right, everyone, stay frosty. I'm sure they're going to turn soon. When they do, cut across the turn and we'll... *WHERE THE FUCK DID IT GO?*" Antony yelled. "Anybody got a lock?"

A bunch of negatives came back to him. "This is bullshit!" He looked around. "Back to the Navy ships. We know they'll end up there."

Evert called over the comm, "Sir, that's TQB. The base says the ship matches the one at the Japanese event." There was a pause. "Except for a few differences, sir."

The four ships turned and headed back toward the Navy ships. "And what are those, Evert?"

"Big-ass guns, sir," came the reply.

"Sir, we've lost the TQB ship, and the four UFOs are coming back in this direction."

"Prepare the missiles," Captain Forstal ordered. "No firing without permission."

Antony gritted his teeth but made the hard call. "We need to get the Navy out of here before TQB gets back. Permission to attack the ships? We'll sink the USS *Cowpens* if the Navy shoots at us again. We tried to be nice, but that didn't work."

Captain Forstal thought about his options.

"Bogey's back in ten seconds, sir. Command on missiles?" Two seconds later. "Sir?"

Captain Forstal nodded to himself. "Denied. Lock them down."

Bethany Anne hit the blue button again. "You guys ready back there?" Almost immediately, she received affirmatives. "Okay, time to let our unknown and unwanted friends understand something about the new and improved *G'laxix Sphaea*..."

Bethany Anne hit the buttons to turn off the cloaking device. Appearing from thin air, the ship cast its shadow over the USS *Cowpens*. She sat on top of them as a protective hat, guns aimed toward the four UFOs.

"*My ride is a bitch,*" Bethany Anne stated, "*and she is now going to fuck you up.*"

She hit the blue button. "Light them up!"

"UFOs heading toward us, sir."

"We have a ship on top of us, sir!" The suddenly appearing shadow dimmed the light coming through the windows.

"Timmons, get me information from outside!" Captain Forstal called.

"UFOs firing. TQB is already firing back, sir."

"Get us out of here. Move it, people!" Captain Forstal ordered. "I don't want to be underneath that ship if it comes crashing down."

"USS *Cowpens* moving out from underneath us," Marcus reported.

"That's fine. They probably don't want to be underneath this fight, not that I blame them," Bethany Anne responded.

"Hit, hit, hit!" Tyler sang. "My defensive shield is down sixty-two percent."

"Fucker packs a wallop," Spencer replied. "I've fired four rods, three hit, one destroyed. No damage to them."

"SHIT SHIT SHIT! Dammit, where did it go?" Tyler asked as seconds later, the four ships passed by where the big ship had just been.

Timmons came back inside. "TQB is playing hide and seek again, sir. It was there, hanging in the air, firing something from their guns, then poof, disappeared. I could feel air movement, so I'm pretty sure they took off somewhere."

"Son of a bitch!" Captain Forstal exclaimed. "Give me *Wasp* and *Ford*. We need to vacate the area." He sat down in his chair and got comfortable. "We can't hit those four little ships, and they can't hit the TQB ship. We are so outclassed here, it's damn embarrassing."

"Navy is leaving," Evert announced as he looked at his systems. "Operational Task Number One completed."

Antony answered, "Yeah, but it's the unexpected added challenge I'm thinking we're going to come up short on this time guys."

"Fuck, we aren't supposed to be the ones with the inadequate toys," Tyler complained.

"Yeah, but if they don't find us, we can live to pay them back another day," Antony replied. "I've got confirmation from Director Brown. He leaves the decision to me, so split up. Make sure we know where the fuck that ship is and let's disappear. Don't go straight back to base, and confirm they aren't following you. Break apart alpha alpha gamma in ten, folks."

"See you guys back at base," Spencer told them.

Ten seconds later, Antony's voice came over the comm. "Go!"

"Bogey's leaving, sir," a voice called.

"We have TQB on radar," Kelly reported.

"Where are they?" Captain Forstal asked.

"They have taken up a position between us and the land, sir," Kelly answered.

"Seems like they've decided they don't want us landing," Timmons commented.

"Hail the ship. See if they'll talk," the captain commanded.

CHAPTER TWENTY-FOUR

<u>**Dulce Lake, New Mexico, USA**</u>

Director Patrick Brown was waiting for his team to arrive back in the underground hangar, his hands clasped behind his back as he chewed the inside of his cheek and thought about the situation.

Majestic 12 had a lot of resources, including some TQB probably wouldn't consider using if they had them. Now, TQB had stymied an effort to acquire information that had gone back to their beginning and stopped them from gaining the one thing Majestic 12 had been coveting for decades.

Technology to reach out and speak with the aliens in Alpha Centauri.

Whether the aliens were truly in Alpha Centauri or somewhere else, they had never been able to confirm. It didn't matter. Majestic 12 could prove that the technology Maria Orsitsch and her group of mediums speaking with the aliens had received did work.

And it had been nothing Earth had seen before in its history. At least, not anything an Earthling had devised.

Which meant the aliens were still ahead of Earth with their

technology, and Majestic 12's focus was to acquire that superior technology.

Through whatever means necessary.

Now, other humans with connections to aliens were acquiring technological assets and prohibiting Majestic 12 from doing their stated duty, one they had been accomplishing for both the United States and the United Nations (whether they understood it or not). It was time their relationships in the United Nations paid back the help they had been provided in secret for so long.

Patrick was going to call in a lot of debts.

The modified alien spaceship Dr. Eva Hocks and her team had reviewed on the video was superior to what they had, and what they had access to. Worse, it had shown that even their offensive options were limited. Majestic 12 was as limited compared to TQB as the world was compared to their own technology.

An arms race was an enjoyable competition when you happened to be laughably ahead of everyone else. Not so nice, Patrick thought, when you were behind and didn't yet have a plan to get the advantage back.

The first ship to arrive was drawing into the hangar, the lights glistening off of her sides. Patrick could see the marks the Navy's guns had made on the ship. He noted there was one hole in the bottom before Spencer set his ship down.

Soon, two more ships came into view. Patrick's eyebrows lifted when he got a good look at Tyler's ship. It was blackened on one side. That must be where TQB's gun had hit it and reduced the shield by so much. More than enough to cook the outside of the ship, as well. They would probably be down one ship and pilot if they had gotten two hits.

Patrick pulled his tablet out of his pocket and dialed a number. "Eva? It's Patrick. I need one of your teams to come down and assess Tyler's ship. It's severely burned on one side. Yes, his shield was in place. Yes, I thought you'd like to see the damage so you might be able to figure out what they're using. No, his ship won't go anywhere if you need to finish your meeting. Yes, goodbye."

Patrick hit the end button and considered the plans. Contact the United Nations, get this damage checked out, see if they could modify the shields to handle this threat in the future, and figure out if they could salvage anything from Antarctica.

Berlin, Germany

"This," Dr. Schäuble pointed to a location on the map, "is where they found the base, just like the old maps and notes from World War II said they would."

The agent from Germany's Federal Intelligence Operations sighed. "We were so close. Those damned Americans and TQB..."

"Not entirely," the doctor interrupted. "Whoever attacked the Americans caused TQB to get involved. Our team is still down there, but they are not leading the research."

"Fine, it's semantics at this point," the agent replied. "We had the information and possibly the people to explain it all to us in the same place."

"Do not think we are without hope," Dr. Schäuble encouraged. "Dr. Tooch is very, very good. He has already provided many insights in the last three weeks down there."

"Oh, I know we are not without hope, Dr. Schäuble," the agent replied. "Not only is Dr. Tooch very good, but our agent Mr. Jameson can be quite crafty as well."

Dr. Schäuble looked at Agent Weisz for a moment before nodding his head in understanding. He had been wondering which of the people on the trip were plants. While he suspected half the crew, he had not expected the occasionally brash capitalist Mr. Jameson to be one.

Dr. Schäuble thought to himself, *Keep one's eyes open and one's brain willing, and you can learn something new every day.*

The voice rang across the bridge. "Captain Forstal? Call, sir."

"I'll take it in my stateroom," Captain Forstal replied.

Jack picked up his coffee from his chair and walked to his stateroom, closing the door behind him. The call came in, and he picked it up. "Captain Jack Forstal here."

Jack listened for a moment, his eyes widening slightly at the level of the political person on the other end. He pursed his lips. "Sir, I'm not going to begin to track down how you came to be reading the early documents from the crew and me about the incident in the Antarctic. However, I reviewed everyone's, and signed off on them being the truth."

The man on the other end of the line, apparently not hearing what he wanted to hear, got heated.

Jack pulled out his chair and sat down. He had been in the profession long enough to know that for blowhards like this, it was best to let them rant and rave and then send them on.

Sure enough, after a couple of minutes, Jack was able to interject, "I understand how you could think that, but it simply isn't true. TQB did not fire on any Navy vessels. They did appear very close to our ship, but it was in a defensive position as the four UFOs came back to our location once they lost track of the TQB vessel. In my estimation and that of my crew, TQB was trying to protect our ship, and did not instigate or at any time aggravate the event with the US Navy."

Jack pulled the phone away from his ear and reached to grab his coffee, taking a sip, then another, before he set it back down and continued talking.

"Well, I'm sorry to aggravate you, sir, but those documents have all been signed appropriately, and they will not be modified. Perhaps you can discuss this situation with someone higher, sir."

Jack winced when the man, in frustration, yelled and

slammed the phone down. Jack hung up his phone and sat back, thinking.

This was the second request to change the records he had received this week.

QBS *ArchAngel*

Bethany Anne sat in the captain's chair, reviewing some notes from Yuko in Japan and an update from Barnabas on Tabitha's ongoing investigation.

The click-click-click of Kael-ven's four legs sounded in the corridor, and soon he arrived at the bridge, asking for permission to enter.

"Permission granted." Bethany Anne turned in her chair to watch the alien approach her.

"You wanted to ask me something, Captain?" When she sat in this chair, Kael-ven refused to call her anything else. In a way, she understood and agreed with him.

"Yes, I do. This has to do with the support promised for your ship. As always, if I go beyond your personal ethics, please explain them to me." She recognized his chittering as agreement before the translation node spoke in her ear.

"Good. Down below in the ice cave, my people are about to wake up some humans who have been asleep for a while. We don't believe they know anything about the rumors and truth swirling about regarding TQB, aliens, and space." She reached over and grabbed her water. "I want to wake them up, but I want you to be there with me."

"Me?" Kael-ven asked, surprised. "Why would an alien down there help the humans wake more easily?"

"Because everything we have been able to deduce says they contacted or received contact from aliens a long time back. The theory we have going is if those we wake see an alien with us, they might be more receptive to us, not less." She put the water back down. "Probably the only group this will ever work with, by the way. Damned happy you're around."

"Standing with you somewhere is wholly within the contract, Captain."

"Yes, it is," she agreed. "But here's the second part, Kael-ven." She paused for a moment, then asked, "What do Yollins know about acting?"

CHAPTER TWENTY-FIVE

Tokyo, Japan

Akio took point as he and the team supported Yuko's trip to the building housing the National Diet, the upper and lower houses of the legislature.

This time, like before, Yuko had argued, and Akio had agreed to no swords. He had, however, added a significant number of hidden weapons.

Some in plain sight. Yuko understood her role and allowed him to provide the hairpins she would wear in case he had need of them.

Furthermore, many materials did not set off the metal detectors she expected they would.

Once inside the building, they were directed to a smaller room. Two guards outside the room confirmed their identities. Yuko and Akio were the only two to enter.

Two minutes later, three additional men joined. They bowed respectfully, and the first started the discussion.

"I appreciate you doing this, Vicereine. We have difficult news for Queen Bethany Anne coming from our contacts in the United Nations." None of those in the room sat down.

"We appreciate your support," Yuko began. "What can you tell us?"

The Prime Minister nodded. "Many members of the UN have made allegations about TQB, some of them outrageous. However, the outrageous make the highly unlikely seem plausible. It is not just one faction, either. There are many countries, smaller ones and larger, who are working to suborn and implement rules and regulations against TQB. Due to our acceptance of Queen Bethany Anne's legitimacy, we have been targeted on multiple fronts. It is unlikely that we can continue to provide the same level of support outwardly as we have been doing so far without Japan suffering significantly."

"What kind of timeframe do we have, Prime Minister?" Yuko asked.

He blew out a breath. "I doubt we have more than three months, Vicereine."

Boston, MA, USA

Fred walked into the room, stopping at the chess table. He looked at the pieces and grimaced. He was playing Charles now, and so far, he hadn't figured out a way to get out of checkmate in three moves.

He continued into the empty room and raised an eyebrow.

There was a manila envelope in his chair labeled National Intelligence Estimate - TQB Antarctica.

Fred picked up the document and set his papers down before turning around and dropping into the seat. The older he got, the more the body gave way. It was a shame, really. His mind was in tip-top shape, and he was more powerful, with his brother David and their friend and partner Charles, than many small countries, and the cold-hearted bitch Time was stealing it all away.

Death came for everyone, it seemed, except for the people in TQB.

He started unwinding the string that kept the envelope closed and slid his hand inside to pull out the report. Fred had worked hard to get the three ship captains to change their reports.

But the bastards wouldn't do it.

As Fred read, a small smile began to play across his features and a twinkle appeared in his eye.

Oh, yes, yes, yes! Fred heard the other two men coming in, and he turned around to see David first, with Charles behind him.

"Was this you, Charles?" he asked as he held up the National Intelligence Estimate.

"It was," he replied as he looked down at the chessboard. Noting nothing had changed, he continued into the room.

"Well played. How did you get it changed?" Fred asked.

"Senior Military needed the NIE quickly," Charles answered, sitting down. "So, Opportunity Number One." He pulled out his laptop and opened it. "The National Intelligence Office has a grudge against TQB, and I was able to have a couple of IC analysts word their responses in such a way that the NIO could choose, and show he had cause, to tweak the response. He did so, such that TQB was now the aggressor in the dust-up down south. When that," he nodded to the document in Fred's hand, "gets circulated, everyone with a grudge against TQB is going to pile on."

Fred looked down at the report and started reading from the top. He murmured, "Checkmate."

Schwabenland, Antarctica

It had taken Barb and Frank two weeks to find the appropriate person to help the team. Dr. April Keelson knew the history, she was German, and she was both a medical officer and understood engineering.

Finding her had had the same chance as finding a purple-spotted unicorn. Actually, it had been a little less likely than the unicorn, but Barb and Frank had done it. Dan had decided to take her interview himself, and it had been pretty eye-opening.

Dr. April Keelson had been abrupt, in his face, and very hard to impress.

Until he took her on the Pod ride Barb had suggested. Then she became putty in his hands. It was, Barb had said, a take on something Jean Dukes had mentioned one time. Find the right lever, and you could get a female to change her attitude in a second.

Cold. She was so cold.

She heard the same gurgling noises of liquid moving through pipes she remembered when she laid down to wait for the aliens to arrive, but in reverse, leaving the stasis chamber.

She and her people had lost hope after so many decades, so much time waiting for them to come and pull them out of this frozen wasteland, and allow her people to join them in space. Away from the hell of war or the subjugation of her people to the cruelty of those who didn't understand they had been forced to work with Hitler.

Maria felt the slow introduction of warmth to the stasis chamber. It was a design given to them by her benefactor.

She had offered her full belief and support to the engineering team that what they built would save them all for the time when they could go to the stars. Now, she would find out if it was true.

Had they been saved?

The chamber's top hissed as fresh air came into the system. She had two humans dressed as doctors appear over her. One, a female, asked, "Maria Orsitsch?"

Maria nodded.

"Lie still while we figure this out. I've only done this five times, and so far, I'm good five out of five, so don't ruin anything for me," the abrupt woman with a German accent told her.

Maria's mind was racing. Why was a German woman helping her? What had happened to the plan?

The doctor released the mask from around her face and gently pulled it away from her hair. "Sorry, but you're going to be in there a few more minutes. The aliens didn't do anything for hair growth, and we need to cut some away."

Maria nodded weakly.

"Doctor?" Maria heard a voice from behind the abrupt woman. She turned and nodded to someone, and the two medical people stepped aside, and two new faces appeared.

This time one was an alien.

"Don't worry, Maria. My name is Bethany Anne. This," she nodded at the alien on the other side, "is Kael-ven. Rest and gather your strength."

The alien chittered something, and then it was translated. He spoke in the language of the Aldebarans. "Welcome back, Maria Orsitsch. We look forward to talking to you soon."

The doctor spoke up. "You two go now. We have a lot to do." He pulled the lady back out of the way.

The doctor didn't fail to see the tear making its way down Maria's face.

Conference Room, QBS *ArchAngel*

The room was full. Bethany Anne had requested that all of her top people attend, and many of their second-level people as well. For example, not only was Jean Dukes there, but her second was as well. The first row included her father, Patricia, Dan, Frank, Barb, Stephen, Barnabas, Admiral Thomas, Captains Wagner and Jakowski, Nathan, Ecaterina, and there was a roomful of others as Bethany Anne stood up front.

The Yollins had not been invited to sit in.

She stared out at the room, and in moments, the talk stopped. Bethany Anne smiled. "We've had an interesting time for the last few months." She started pacing. "First, we've gotten everything we could ask for from our Japanese connections regarding manufacturing tools. I understand that the build of the Yollin mining equipment is ahead of schedule?"

William nodded from the second row.

"Good. We have food, we have shelter, and we have water, thanks to Dr. Brown-Williams and Marcus. We have a plan for our first battle station."

"What's the name?" Bobcat asked, and Bethany Anne stared at him. "Sorry!" He looked around and slid a few inches down in his chair.

"I'll get to the name in a moment, Bobcat," she replied and continued, "We have our first alien acquisition up and running with better armament. It worked very well, I might add. The teams went for a joyride in an area with plenty of rocks, and I understand they defeated the rocks soundly."

She smiled as a few up in the top rows started whistling and clapping.

"Just remember, you murdered defenseless rocks," she cautioned, "that weren't shooting back." She paused. "But that brings us to our challenges of the moment."

She stopped pacing and looked at her people. "We still need to be here while we get the battle station built, and it would behoove us to see if we have any additional people who would, or could, help us when we go through the Annex Gate. We have a lot of intelligence coming up from Earth, and I daresay they are really, really unhappy with us. In fact, our companies are taking a serious pounding in the stock markets."

She smiled. "If we actually still had an ownership percentage in the companies, I might be worried." There was some laughter when a few realized that she had sold her portions of the companies when they were worth the most. "Now, we've moved into precious metals and other tangibles that can be traded without traces. Unfortunately, I'm afraid our name is going to be mud."

Bethany Anne stood a little straighter. "The reason is, I refuse to provide the technology and alien access the world is demanding. Further, they really don't like that such a small group is thumbing their collective noses at them. Finally, they scream bloody murder when we allow people, of their own free will, to leave their countries and join us. The problem, as they see it, is we are grabbing the cream of the crop."

She shrugged. "The way I see it, slackers and malcontents who are allergic to hard work and those missing a backbone don't want to take up the call."

"*AD AETERNITATEM!*" someone yelled, and soon everyone took it up. "Ad Aeternitatem! Ad Aeternitatem! Ad Aeternitatem!" Bethany Anne smiled and put up her hands, and the crowd quieted down.

Bethany Anne surreptitiously wiped a tear from her right eye. "Damn, ArchAngel, are you getting the dust out of here?"

"Yes," the EI answered, her face showing up on the large screen behind Bethany Anne. "I am. Don't blame my air purification system on your inability to handle your overload of emotions!"

Okay, who the fuck is giving me away to ArchAngel?

>>Uh, that might have been me.<<

Seriously, ADAM? Damn, a pretty female EI comes along, and you go and stab me in the metaphorical back?

>>She asked a question, I answered.<<

She's getting sneaky. Good job.

>>Good...job?<< ADAM asked, confusion coloring his question.

I'll explain why some other time.

"I'm sure it was random, ArchAngel," Bethany Anne answered, to a few chuckles in the audience.

"As I was saying, we're getting hit pretty hard, so I've decided that we're going to lay low for the time it takes us to build our new home, the QBBS *Meredith Reynolds*. I want to get it as far along as possible. Perhaps, if we don't show ourselves, the noise and the pissed-off people will go away." She got a "woot woot" from the few in the audience who caught the name. She glanced at her father, who had a small smile on his face, nodding his agreement with her choice.

There was some murmuring in the audience that had to do with hiding out. "That doesn't mean we won't visit Earth, but we'll need to be more circumspect about it," she clarified.

"What happens," Dan asked, "if they try to draw us out?"

Bethany Anne shrugged. "Depends on what they're doing. If it's something we can let go, I'll let it go. My ego isn't so large I have to give it a pillow at night. But if they do something egregious? Well," she turned to point to John, Eric, Akio, Darryl, Gabrielle, and Scott, "them," and then she pointed at Barnabas, Stephen, and Tabitha, "and them." Next, she pointed at Admiral Thomas and Captains Wagner and Natalia Jakowski. "And them, and whoever Admiral Thomas has coming up for the new ships." Last, she pointed at Peter, Todd, and the Wechselbalg Guardians and Guardian Marines. "And they will reply for me."

"What if they keep pushing?" Dan asked.

Bethany Anne's face went dark and angry, and lines of red energy suffused her face as her eyes blazed. "They had better not cross my pissed-off line, or they will receive the reply from me personally. And if I have to answer?"

Bethany Anne never finished the question since the room erupted in shouts when Bobcat yelled, "They'll *learn not to fuck* with the Queen Bitch!"

FINIS

DON'T CROSS THIS LINE

The Story Continues with book 14, *Don't Cross This Line.*

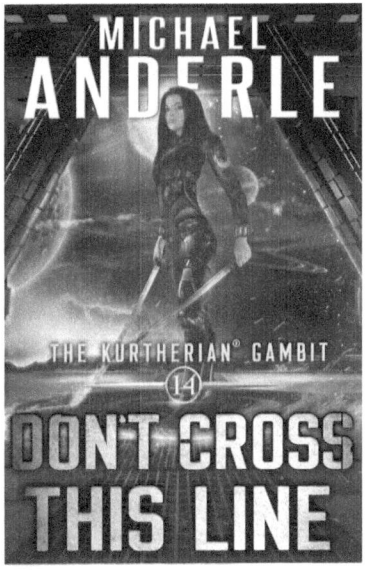

Available now at Amazon and on Kindle Unlimited

AUTHOR NOTES

First, THANK YOU FOR READING THIS BOOK (and these *Author Notes*).

It has been thirty-four days since the last release (*We Have Contact*), and it feels easily like three times that long. More for personal challenges than anything related to book writing (although that, too).

One small but funny story. My wife is tired of 'bitch' in my stories (well, to be fair, in the titles). I tried to explain that bitch is a derogatory term that has been turned around in *The Kurtherian Gambit* and is a badge of honor now.

However, since she doesn't read the books, my explanation only goes so far. Wives, it seems, can be pretty annoyed by the term bitch, and you, by God, are guilty until proven innocent, and you WILL go through multiple trials to be declared innocent.

I'm not through all of those trials, just so you know. Lord, not even close. Tack on she's Hispanic, and the evil eye is done with a foreign accent that makes you concerned and confused at the same time.

I promised her I would not use the term bitch in any more

book titles for the Kurtherian Gambit. I *didn't* tell her I already had all of the future book titles, and I knew I was not using it for any future book. So, no harm, no foul, right?

I promised not to use it, she is happy.

So, let's get off that story because one day she might read this and I want to say if my beautiful, wonderful, long-suffering wife is reading this...

I LOVE YOU, HONEY! ;-)

Now, about that little bit of German Speech...that I didn't get right!

Below is from one of my fans Mor Itz on the Facebook Forums. He and Bjorn Schmidt quickly told me that a little German I had Bethany Anne speaking was wrong. This happened because I placed a snippet (early chapters) out on http://www.kurtherianbooks.com and they noticed I said something in German that didn't work and therefore was wrong.

As in, *not even understood by Germans* wrong. That's pretty damned *wrong*. Often, here in the United States, if someone says something, we will get what the intent is. Not so much with my little effort to have Bethany Anne tell the three German Mercs they were "Gutter Swine"...No thanks to you, *Google Translate.*

Google Translate, fastest way to say something wrong in a foreign language invented to date (used by authors all over the world).

Here is Mor Itz' comments from Facebook (our conversation) explaining the new and improved German choice.

Mor: I'm fine, thx and you? Schweinehunden is a form of plural from Schweinehund that would fit there. It has multiple meanings:

1. It can be used as an affection if said with a smile between good friends, like when someone does a practical joke that doesn't hurt anyone but is really embarrassing.

2. As an insult it is a person who has no conscience and would

do depraved things (like tying a girl to a bomb) and also calls the heritage of said person into doubt (the dictionary I have here translates Schweinehund to bastard but that is not entirely accurate). It is mostly a mid-level insult. However, immigrants from Turkey take it way more personally and can get violent. Otherwise, it is used for almost anyone. From the person who just bumps into you on the way to the bus to the worst criminals one can imagine.

Bethany Anne speaking to Yuko's parents:

Now, I provide these translations below understanding that: 1) They are also from Google Translate (damn) and that I don't have any Japanese fans who can correct me like I have in Germany (double-damn!)

あなたには、美しくて知的な娘がいます。彼女は、私の個人のチームの大切なメンバーです。あなたは誇り高いはずです

is

You have a beautiful and intelligent daughter. She is a valuable member of my team. You should be proud.

Bethany Anne finishing her speech to the people in the stadium:

*ご支援に感謝します、ユウコのような強い娘が、ニール州から、私たちの世界をより安全な場所を作り、助けることができる国であるためにあなたに感謝します。貴重なお時間をいただき、ありがとうございます

is

Thank you for your time, thank you for your support, and thank you for being a country where a strong daughter like Yuko from right here in Neru Province could help us make the world a safer place.

New Shoes

Ok, wife went on a business trip for her job to China and Japan in between books 12 and 13. Not unusual, most fans know I started writing in part because my wife leaves for long business trips. She came back with extra stuff.

Again, not unusual. She will pick up things here or there, usually as small gifts to give away. Unfortunately, something new arrived in this luggage that hasn't happened before, and it concerns me.

It was a pair of shoes.

That's not a scary thing…yet.

No, what's scary is the NAME on the shoes. You see, when my wife travels for her company, they are always staying in hotels in the nicer part of the city. This makes sense because the business meetings happen there for her. BUT, it is what else is in that part of the cities that I'm starting to understand should concern me.

Shoe stores. NICE shoe stores.

When she was in China, she was in one of the nicest portions of the most prestigious city… or at least one that HAD MORE HERMES STORES THAN THE WHOLE STATE OF TEXAS.

She succumbed to temptation.

I hope she starts traveling here in the US only. In Dallas, there is only one (1) Hermes store in the whole city. I checked. Then, I checked Las Vegas. There are three Hermes stores just around the lower Strip area alone.

Son of a bitch.

I'm not saying anything. But, I see a pair of shoes and think what all men think…

Seriously? Why won't the $69.99 pair at (insert store here) work just fine? It's a few pieces of leather held together by a pretty buckle. Can't be $10.00 in materials cost, right?

I'm almost fifty. I've learned just enough to know, and I've gotten rid of enough assholious to keep my mouth shut.

Also, I will remember this story when I buy that next expensive Apple product.

Heck, I should write off the shoe cost(s) as research for Bethany Anne… BOOYAH!

Problem solved.

Snicker... Save your time, IRS people, I'm not actually going to do that. But it is funny as hell.

See you next month!

Michael Anderle
October 4th, 2016

BOOKS BY MICHAEL ANDERLE

Sign up for the LMBPN email list to be notified of new releases and special deals!

https://lmbpn.com/email/

For a complete list of books by Michael Anderle, please visit:

www.lmbpn.com/ma-books/

CONNECT WITH THE AUTHOR

Connect with Michael Anderle

Website: http://lmbpn.com

Email List: https://michael.beehiiv.com/

https://www.facebook.com/LMBPNPublishing

https://twitter.com/MichaelAnderle

https://www.instagram.com/lmbpn_publishing/

https://www.bookbub.com/authors/michael-anderle